SEVEN BULLETS

MATTHEW HATTERSLEY

VINCI
BOOKS

Vinci Books

vinci-books.com

Published by Vinci Books Ltd in 2025

1

A CIP catalogue record for this book is available from the British Library.
Paperback ISBN: 9781036700621

MIX
Paper | Supporting
responsible forestry
FSC® C018072
FSC
www.fsc.org

Printed and bound in Great Britain by Clays Ltd, Elcograf S.p.A.

Also by Matthew Hattersley

Acid Vanilla

Final Kill

Seven Bullets

The Hunt

Sister Death

Exit Wounds

Never Say Die

I am a Killer

Bad Blood

Fallen Angels

Annihilation Pest Control Series

White Heat

John Beckett Series

Darkness On The Edge Of Town

When The Kingdom Comes

A World Of Sun And Violence

A Bullet For The Past

Chapter One

A house, somewhere in North London. A rental property furnished only with basic fixtures and fittings. The furniture is the cheapest money can buy and each item is at least ten years old. There is a single couch in the front room, two single beds in the rooms upstairs. The house isn't the nicest place you could ever wish to live, but it's out of the way and unremarkable. For its current inhabitants, that's what matters.

They're not planning on staying here long.

Through the front door and straight up the stairs you can hear the faint grunts of concentration. Past the cramped bathroom and into the larger of the two bedrooms, a woman hunches over a large desk. On one side sits a battered cardboard box, half-full of ammo - 115gr FMJ 9mm rounds, made by Sellier & Bellot. Next to the box is a small stereo system - what people once called a 'ghetto blaster'. The woman leans over and twists the volume up a few notches to better hear the song – the Ramones, doing Today Your Love, Tomorrow The World *– before selecting a single round from the box of ammo. She holds it up in a beam of sunlight that slices through the gap in the threadbare curtains and smiles to herself. The cold metal is pleasing to touch. She rolls the cartridge between an expertly manicured thumb and forefinger.*

Last one.

A large industrial vice is fastened to the length of the table in front of her. She winds the handle anti-clockwise a few turns and places the 9mm round into the steel jaws of the vice. Then she tightens it and picks up the Dremel industrial engraver she bought from Amazon a month earlier. As she flicks the switch it whirrs into life, reminiscent of a dentist's drill. She goes to work on the bullet casing, scratching out letters. The metal is polished and smooth, a tough surface to work with, and the drill is not top of the line, but she has the hang of it now. Slowly, methodically, she scratches a name into the brass casing, tracing the pencil markings she made earlier and blowing off the residue of metal filings.

It doesn't take her long to finish. She loosens the vice and removes the bullet from its clutches. Done. She examines her handiwork and smiles once more. This entire process is crazy, she knows that. Yet creating these bullets – these symbols of revenge – has also quietened something inside of her. She now has a visual aid. A reminder of what she must do. But more so, with each bullet created, she exorcises some of the pent-up rage she has carried around for too long.

Acid Vanilla carries the last bullet over to the tall wardrobe in the corner of the room. The door hinges creak and groan as she opens it to reveal a space empty of clothes. There is, however, a wooden shelf half-way up. On the shelf stand six bullets, spaced out, upright in a row. Six bullets, each with a name etched down the side - Raaz Terabyte, Spitfire Creosote, Magpie Stiletto, Ethel Sinister, Doris Sinister, Davros Ratpack. *And now the last one. Bullet number seven.*

Beowulf Caesar.

Acid places the final bullet at the end of the row and steps back. Seven bullets on a shelf. Seven names. Seven people who took everything from her. And who will pay with their lives.

Her new kill list.

Chapter Two

It was Pride weekend in Manchester, and Canal Street – the sprawling strip of bars and nightclubs that catered for the city's thriving LGBTQ+ community – was a sea of exuberant partygoers. High-energy dance music reverberated from large speaker systems placed at intervals along the side of the canal, whilst exotically attired people of many different genders danced and drank and consumed illicit substances. The weather was hot, unusual for Manchester, and as the hazy day turned into evening the attendees spoke excitedly of the evening's entertainment – for many, the big draw of the weekend.

The Queeniessential Review.

Now in its twelfth year, the Review hosted top drag acts from all around the world. Big names, too. Ru Paul had appeared at one of the early events, and since then it had only gotten bigger and more exclusive. Indeed, a spot on the bill was a rare thing to come by, especially for an unknown act. Although it helped your case somewhat if you knew the promoter. It helped further if they'd recently hired you to kill someone.

"Five minutes, Davros." Stefan opened the door to the dressing room and shouted over the heads of the other queens, which was no mean feat due to the height of some of the wigs on show tonight. "Have you got everything you need, love?"

Davros Ratpack looked over and gave the okay sign before turning back to the mirror and shaking his head.

"What a bloody riot," he told his reflection.

To say he was excited to perform would be an understatement. Tonight was his first ever show as Dolly Pardon and he was determined to make it count.

He leaned forward to check his false lashes. He'd been having trouble with the left one, but it was sticking okay now. He sat back on the hard metal chair and considered the spectacular vision in the mirror in front of him. The flowing white blouse with elaborately sequined waistcoat fitted perfectly. Below that he wore a powder-blue chiffon skirt, complete with diamanté trim. It was an exact replica of the real Dolly's stage outfit she'd worn on her Blue Smoke World Tour. Although, his was a much larger size. Davros was six-seven to Ms Parton's five-foot-zero but he was proud of the look. One last touch – he picked up the large blonde wig and placed it carefully over the nude-coloured hair retainer flattening his wavy green locks. Perfect. A quick hunch-up of the ridiculously large (but anatomically correct) fake breasts, and he was ready to perform.

Despite all his work for Annihilation Pest Control over the years, despite having a kill-count well into triple figures, Davros Ratpack still felt a bristle of nerves as he headed for the stage door.

"Hey, sugar. You on next?" Betty Davis Thighs cooed, as Davros tottered past in six-inch heels.

"Yeah, my first time onstage. Any advice?"

The ageing queen considered the question. "Enjoy it. If you do, they will. Knock 'em dead."

Davros Ratpack smiled. Knocking them dead was something he was good at. He moved out of the dressing room and along the unlit corridor leading to the side of the stage. From there he could hear the cheers and laughter from the sell-out crowd. Could smell the familiar combination of booze and body odour and amyl nitrite.

The compère – a young queen calling herself Kim KardASSian – glanced into the wings and gave Davros a wink. "Anyway, I'm going to shut my big gob and introduce the next act. That okay?" It was a rhetorical question, eliciting more cheers and wolf whistles from the audience. "So here she is, all the way from the US, with a terrific pair of – ahem – lungs. The tits from Texas. The one. The only. Dolly Pardon."

Davros took a deep breath and sashayed onstage to riotous applause. The nerves dissipated as the bright lights hit him in the face, and he was off.

The next thirty minutes were a blur of laughter, lip-syncing, audience interaction and sharp put-downs. It helped to know he'd happily slay anyone in here who wound him up, who took the piss. But he didn't have to worry. The crowd loved Dolly Pardon. By the time she got to her grand finale – dragging a weak-chinned young man onstage and acting out a stellar version of Jolene – she had the whole venue eating out the palm of her hand. Once she'd ignited the fireworks in each of her fake breasts, they were on their feet.

"Thank y'all so kindly," Davros drawled, in his best

Dolly impersonation. "I hope I see y'all again soon. Much love." Cue kisses, tears, waves, one final hunch-up of the still smoking breasts, and then exit stage left.

"That were amazing," Kim KardASSian gushed, slipping from her Cali-whine to a voice that wouldn't be out of place in a Grimsby fish market. "I can't believe that were ya debut."

Davros pouted. "Been practicing for it my entire life."

He left Kim and tottered back to the changing room. It had emptied while he was onstage, with most of the acts now in the wings, warming up for a mid-show singalong of Kinky Boots. He made for the chair he'd sat in earlier and slumped down in front of the mirror. Relieved. Elated. Spent.

Only one other person was left backstage. A short, slight-framed queen Davros hadn't noticed earlier. She was sat in a make-up chair a few feet from him and wore a red sequined mini-dress with black fishnet tights. She looked the part but was too femme for Davros' taste. He liked his queens the same way he liked his men – big and gruff and hairy. He narrowed his eyes to better take her in. A spiked scarlet wig covered most of her face.

"Good show?" Red asked, not looking at him.

He smiled. "Fucking great show. The best." He leaned into the mirror and peeled off the fake lashes. Blinked a few times. "Are you doing a show yourself?"

Red didn't answer.

Davros shrugged it off. He unzipped himself and let the fabulous outfit, complete with double-D inserts, drop to the floor. Stepping out of it (dressed underneath in simple black leggings and black t-shirt) he removed his wig and kicked off his heels. The plan now was to freshen up, get changed, remove some, if not all, of this war paint, then join the swarm of fevered bodies out in the main room. Davros didn't go for intimacy too much these days. Not even casual sex. But tonight was a special night, and all this tension needed an outlet.

"What's the act?" Davros tried again, rubbing an alcohol-soaked cotton pad over his eyes and eyebrows. He squinted over between rubs. "You look familiar actually. Do you do a lot of these?"

Red didn't flinch, kept on staring into the mirror. "No. My first time."

"No shit. Mine too." Davros removed the hair retainer and rubbed at his hair. Still enough product to style it his usual way – messy with a slight Mohican lift in the centre. "It's a real blast. You'll love it."

"Well, I do love a good blast."

The words caught Davros' attention. Not what was said, but how it was said. Like it was loaded with something he couldn't pinpoint.

"Sorry," Davros said. "What did you say your name was, kid?"

The small drag queen was silent, before turning his way and slowly smiling. A familiar smile. Sultry but cruel. Along with that recognisably arched eyebrow, it made Davros sit upright.

But it was the eyes that made his heart stop.

One blue.

One brown.

"You know my name, Davros," Acid Vanilla purred, as she pulled a sharp, ruby-ended hairpin from her wig. "So wonderful to see you again."

Chapter Three

Acid gripped the steel hairpin in her fist and launched herself at Davros, who was on his feet with surprising nimbleness for a man of his height. He grabbed a pot of powder from the dressing table and flung it in her face. She dodged around it, but it was enough distraction for him to put distance between them. Now they stood facing each other in the narrow dressing room. Muscles tense, eyes alert. Ready.

"You don't have to do this, kid," Davros said.

"Don't I?"

The manic energy shooting through Acid's veins was too much to bear as she shifted her weight from foot to foot.

"Let me talk to Caesar for you. I heard what happened in Germany. Maybe now we can all move on. Fair's fair."

"Fair? You killed my mother."

Davros tilted his head to one side. "Wasn't me."

"You were there. You were party to it."

Acid moved around, positioning herself with her back to the door. She raised the steel spike, ready to drive it somewhere soft and fleshy. Through his eye socket would be her first choice. Straight into the frontal cortex.

"Let's both calm down and talk about this. We were friends. We can sort this out."

"No," she sneered. "Caesar wants me dead. Which means you want me dead. And we were associates, Davros – you know full well we don't have friends in our line of work."

She scanned the room, assessing the situation. Davros Ratpack was a big guy. Muscular too. But he wasn't the sprightly young assassin he had been when they'd met all those years ago. She might not be able to take him blow for blow, but she didn't have to.

"So, what, kiddo? You're going to wipe out the whole organisation?'

Acid reminded herself of the last time she'd seen her mum. Her cold, lifeless eyes, the deep knife wound that had severed her thin neck from ear to ear.

"That's right," she told Davros. "I'm going to kill you all. Every last one of you."

"What, even lover boy? Mr Sensational?"

Acid cricked her neck to one side. "Not funny. But yes. Him as well."

He laughed. "Well, I did always love how crazy you were. But you aren't taking me out. Not tonight."

"We'll see."

With a roar, Acid lunged at him again. But Davros was quick. He dodged the slashing arc of the hairpin and got behind her, shoving her into the dressing table. Her head hit the mirror with a loud crack and she stumbled to the floor. Before she had a chance to right herself, Davros had his hands around her neck. Two huge hands, complete with stars-and-stripes nails, squeezing at her throat. She kicked back, but it was no use. He squeezed tighter. She felt sick. Faint. Her nerves fizzed with energy. She was blacking out. If that happened, she was dead.

She dropped, quick and heavy to her knees, forcing Davros to stumble forward. It was enough that she could twist around and stab the hairpin deep into his left forearm. He cried out in pain and his grip loosened. She seized the moment, slid backwards through his legs and kicked out, sending him staggering into the wall.

"Crazy bitch."

She jumped to her feet as Davros spun around. He steadied himself and pulled the hairpin from out of his arm. Held it in his fist.

"You thought you could see me off with this pathetic fucking needle?" Davros sneered, holding it up to the light. "I'll be honest, doll. I'm insulted."

She didn't blink. "That's a deadly weapon. In the right circumstances."

"Maybe. With the element of surprise on your side. Kind of fucked that bit up though, haven't you?"

Acid breathed heavily down her nose, lamenting the lack of a firearm. She had considered concealing a SIG P938 in her garter belt, but this was a big event and they had metal detectors on every entrance. She'd never have got past security.

"So what now?" Davros asked. "You still think you've got a chance here?"

She shrugged. "You know me. I always get my mark."

"Fuck me," he scoffed. "You're actually deluded. Maybe once that was true. But not anymore. You've gone soft. Everyone knows it."

Acid picked up a chair. "Everyone but me, I guess."

She lunged forward but Davros grabbed hold of one of

the chair legs. He held on to it as they circled each other in a dance of the damned.

"You're a bloody fool," he told her. "Why didn't you disappear when you had the chance?"

Acid didn't answer. She was feeling the pressure. Unsure of her next move. She spied a large canister of hairspray on a table a few metres away. She was about to make a break for it when the door of the dressing room swung open and two large black drag queens fell through the door, laughing heartily. They saw Acid and Davros. Saw the blood. The laughter stopped.

"What the bloody hell is going on back here?" one of them shrilled.

"Help me out, will you, girls?" Davros shouted. "She's a crazed fan. Trying to kill me."

The two queens (who it was clear now were two-thirds of the headline act Destiny's Wild Child) stared, open-mouthed, as Davros shoved the chair at Acid and let go. Then he rushed past them out of the changing room.

They watched him disappear down the corridor then turned back to Acid. "Who the chuffing hell are you?"

Acid flung the chair away and picked up the hairpin. She marched up to them.

"I'm Acid Vanilla," she said. "Now get the hell out of my way."

Chapter Four

The airless heat of the venue hit Acid in the face as she slipped through the gap in the heavy curtain dividing the main space from backstage. She stopped and scanned the room, searching for her prey. Floor-to-ceiling mirrors covered each of the four walls, making the room appear bigger than it was. A semi-circular bar ran along the back wall, and in the centre of the space a sprung dancefloor bounced with the weight of lively revellers. Acid moved over to the bar and stepped up onto a raised platform that housed three booths. Even without heels Davros Ratpack had a good few inches on most of the clientele and she spotted him immediately, reflected in the mirrored-wall opposite. He saw her at the same time and halted. Then with a smirk he blew her a kiss and legged it out of the venue.

Acid stepped down and followed him, pushing through the crowded venue and moving with the flow of the dancefloor to reach the exit. She got to the double doors and stumbled out into the packed street. Finding him in this lot wouldn't be easy, she needed to be higher. Weaving through the crowd, she aimed for the railing overlooking the canal and climbed onto it. Up ahead, she saw a flash of bright green hair. He was about a hundred metres in front of her. But he was getting away. She climbed off the railing and hitched her dress up before running after him as fast as she could. Crossing the intersecting bridge, she saw Davros take a right down a side street. He was heading into China Town.

Acid got there twenty seconds later and leaned into the turn. The bats — her internal embodiment of the jittery, manic disposition she carried with her — screeched encouragement as she crossed Portland Street and powered along past a grand Chinese pagoda.

She was closing the gap. Another thirty seconds and she'd be on him. As she ran she unfastened the belt around her waist. It was elasticated and the large metal clasp was in the shape of a butterfly. It could do some damage. She wrapped the elastic around her hand and positioned the metal butterfly to form a makeshift knuckle-duster.

"Davros," she shouted. "Stop."

Up ahead, her ex-colleague glanced back at her. He was stumbling now. Fatigue and lack of footwear slowing his progress. Half-way down the next street, he doubled back on himself and ducked out of sight behind a tall building. Acid got there a few seconds later, easing her pace as she drew closer. She peered cautiously into the narrow alleyway. It was getting dark and the only light came from a pink neon sign that cascaded down the brickwork of the Legs Eleven Gentleman's Club. The muted lighting leaked into the alleyway, casting an eerie glow over the overturned bins and rickety fire escapes.

Acid hesitated a moment. Over at the far end of the

alley she could see a strip of light where it opened out onto the street beyond. But Davros was nowhere in sight.

"Shitting hell."

She stepped into the alleyway and paused, allowing her eyes to grow accustomed to the darkness. Her heightened senses tingled as her awareness spread. Davros was here. She could feel him. He was waiting for her.

She carried on, raising her butterfly fist in strike position and breathing gently through her nose, consciously slowing her heartbeat. Up ahead of her was an old recycling bank for glass bottles. The nearside was warped and buckled where it had been struck with some force, but it was large enough to hide behind. She stopped. Seeing a broken bottle a few feet from her, she knelt and fingered the bottle-neck into her grasp. She got to her feet and moved around the side of the bottle bank. Three more steps. She held her breath. Listened. The sound of a low, gasping wheeze drifted from around the corner. Davros there, waiting to pounce. She had him. In one fluid movement she charged around the side of the unit, leading with the bottle and spearing at the air with the glass shards.

But he wasn't there. No one was there. She straightened, considering her next move, when something hard and heavy smashed her in the ribs. The force of the blow knocked all the wind out of her but she stayed upright. As she spun around she was met with the unmistakable silhouette of Davros Ratpack. He held a rusty piece of railing in his hand.

"Looking for me?"

"Bastard." She held up the bottle. "I'll destroy you."

Davros shook his head. "Give it up, kid. You're done. Don't make me kill you."

"You're going to have to. I won't stop."

Davros raised the metal bar and Acid sprang at him. She had speed on her side and was able to swerve his swing. She side-stepped away, slashing the broken bottle across his shoulder as she did. Davros quickly turned around to face her and raised his weapon but she was unrelenting. Taking advantage of the momentum, she lunged forward, pummelling the jagged butterfly belt buckle into Davros' kidneys. Stepping back, she slashed the broken bottle up the length of his right triceps.

He yelled out and grabbed at his arm as blood spurted from the open wound. "You snide bitch," he told her. "After everything we've been through."

She raised her chin. "You deserve everything you get."

Blood gushed over Davros' hand. The gash was deep and it would slow him down, but he still had the fire in his eyes. He stepped towards her and raised the metal bar in a fighting stance.

"You broke the code, Acid. So tell yourself whatever you want, but we both know this is on you."

Acid wasn't having that. She let the belt unravel to make a crude whip, with the metal butterfly at the loose end. Then they were back to circling each other, only now with the swaying swagger of two heavyweight boxers six rounds in. Exhausted, broken, but still with plenty of fight in them.

Davros pitched towards her, brandishing the twisted point of the metal railing. As he closed in, Acid side-stepped away and swung the belt around the end of the spear. She got purchase and yanked it towards her. But Davros held on tight. He grabbed the metal bar with both hands and thrust it at her.

"Ugh."

Her legs buckled as the metal spike pierced deep into her abdomen. She stared down at the rusty old weapon penetrating her side. She felt no pain. But in these situations, she rarely did. That was for later. If later ever came. She stared up at Davros' sneering face as he let go of the bar and stumbled away.

The world spun.

The bats screamed.

Acid fell back and slid down under the steps of a metal fire escape. She hit the wet ground with a pathetic slap.

Davros stepped over her. "What did I fucking tell you? You should have stayed dark, Acid. After what happened in Berlin we thought you'd realised you were no match for us."

"Fuck you."

"Ah, mate." He shook his head mournfully. "I never thought we'd be here. Seriously. But you broke the code, kid. Broke Caesar's heart as well if you ask me."

She gritted her teeth. Gripped both hands around the metal bar. "That assumes he had a heart to begin with," she rasped. It hurt to breathe. "So come on then. What are you waiting for?" In the darkness, the fingers of her left hand touched something cold and hard. Some sort of brick.

"You know what? I don't know," Davros said, straightening. "I think your lame ways are rubbing off on me."

He leaned over and pulled the metal bar from her side. She screamed out in pain and felt a rib crack. But the movement exposed him. She grabbed up the heavy piece of rubble and flung it at his head. It caught him hard above the left eye and he staggered backwards. It wouldn't be enough to stop him though.

Holding her side, and driven on by pure adrenaline and chaotic energy, Acid grabbed the metal bar and scrambled to her feet. Davros was still reeling as she leapt at him, aiming the end of the metal bar at his prominent Adam's apple.

But Davros Ratpack wasn't number two at the most elite and sought-after assassin network in the world for nothing. And he wasn't going out without a fight. He saw her coming at him and grabbed hold of the bar with both hands. He held onto it. Her at the other end. More dancing. They were both injured, both weary. It was a battle of wills as well as strength. But Acid knew in situations like this it was the one who cared least whether they lived or died who won out. In that respect, she had this. The two assassins glared into each other's eyes, each gaze glinting defiantly in the moonlight. This was it.

With a surge of energy, Acid shoved forward before releasing one hand from the metal bar and throwing a punch that caught Davros with a hammer fist to the radial nerve, an inch above his elbow. The force and accuracy of the strike made him release his grip and she could reclaim the improvised weapon. She put all her weight behind it, felt the skin pop and his muscles tear as she drove the rusty metal into his twisted guts.

With the bats screaming in her ears, she jerked the spike to one side and opened up Davros' belly like the gaping mouth of a muppet. Blood and sinew hit her in the face as he gave birth to a wet bag of ruptured intestines. But she wasn't done yet. As her ex-colleague grabbed impotently at the air, she positioned herself under the metal bar and levered it upwards, slicing through more skin and muscle in an act of enforced Seppuku. Death by disembowelment.

Davros groaned and slumped forward. His body was shutting down. No fight left in him. Acid let the metal bar drop to the ground and leaned in to steady him. With the last of her own strength, she sat him down by the side of the bottle bank and knelt beside him.

She put her hand on his shoulder. "Don't fight it, Ratty."

The dying assassin looked at her and let out a guttural, humourless laugh. "I always said you'd be the death of me," he whispered. "But I never thought it'd be like this."

"No," she replied. "But there you go. You knew what you were getting into when you signed up for this life. It's all you deserve."

"That what you believe?" he asked, fading now.

"What I know," she said. "None of us are innocent. Not even me. Especially not me."

She got up, supporting herself against the bottle bank. She knew pain was on its way.

"Acid," Davros rasped. "About your mum. It wasn't cool what happened."

Acid didn't answer. She waited as his eyes slowly closed and his face was washed of all expression.

Mission complete.

Davros Ratpack was dead.

Chapter Five

Along Portland Street and up into the recently revamped Piccadilly Gardens, Manchester's city centre was already buzzing with a heady mix of its citizens. The threat of violence and imminent bad choices were in the air as packs of young, coat-less girls hunched together for safety and warmth. Alongside them, football fans and beer boys rubbed shoulders with clubbers and office workers who, after one too many after-work drinks, were now stretching the session out into the evening.

But notwithstanding the exuberance and shared inebriation of the crowd, it didn't stop them staring – or letting out quiet gasps of shock – at the woman limping, barefoot, down the side of the Britannia Hotel. Her heavily made-up face was bloody and swollen, her thick black hair wild and unkempt. A red sequined dress hung from her slim frame, revealing a body covered in cuts and bruises.

Acid Vanilla held her torn side as she staggered onwards, sticking to the shadows where she could. Her plan was to get back to her hotel as quickly as possible, get out of these ridiculous clothes and examine her injury. She'd already lost a lot of blood, and her insides tingled with pain and infection.

She pictured the fully equipped survival kit on the night-stand in her hotel room, but any patch-up job would only be a temporary fix. And whilst she no longer worked for a shadowy assassin network, hospitals were still out of the question.

By the time she got to her room, it was ten-thirty. She unzipped her dress and stepped out of it before carefully unrolling the top of her tights and examining the damage in the full-length mirror beside the door.

She pulled a face. It was bad. The wound itself wasn't massive, but it felt like a piece of metal had broken off inside of her.

A rumble came from the other end of the room. "Shit. What now?"

Her phone was vibrating noisily on the dresser opposite the grand double bed. She hobbled over and picked it up, the caller ID showing *Spook Horowitz*. Acid puffed out her cheeks. It was the last call she wanted to take right now. But if she didn't answer, the kid would only keep trying, she'd be worried about her. Acid tucked a strand of blood-matted hair behind her ear and hit connect.

"Hey, Spook. You okay?"

"I am, yes," the young American said. "Are you? I thought you were going to call me the minute it was over?"

Acid glanced at her reflection in the mirror and raised her eyebrows. "I only got back to the hotel a few minutes ago. Give me a chance."

"And? Is it done?"

She nodded solemnly. "It is done. Davros Ratpack is an ex-assassin."

Spook was silent for a few seconds before she asked, "Are you hurt?"

"A little."

"What does that mean?"

Acid walked over to the mirror and inspected her side. She got a finger either side of the wound and manipulated the skin. The adrenaline had now fully subsided and it hurt like hell. She might have cracked a rib.

"I'm injured, but I can sort it," she told Spook.

"What? Injured? How?"

In the mirror, she rolled her eyes. "Calm it, kid. I'm fine."

"I knew I should have come with you."

Acid scoffed. "I'm fine. Honest. We knew this wasn't going to be a splash about in the shallow end. But I've got it under control. I swear."

Silence again from the other end of the line. But Acid sensed there were more questions coming and didn't have to wait long to hear them.

"Do you need medical help?" Spook asked.

She squinted at the wound. It needed a good few stitches, for certain. But first she needed to get whatever was in there out. She felt around some more. The piece of metal didn't move. It was embedded in one of her ribs.

"I think so," she told Spook, looking down to see a pool of blood on the cream carpet.

"Go to hospital then. Please."

"You know I can't." Acid shoved the phone under her chin as she walked into the bathroom. She turned on the mixer taps and waited for the water to run warm. Then she leaned her body over the sink and dabbed the wound to clean it. "It's fine. Don't worry."

"What are you going to do?"

"There's someone in Manchester," Acid told her. "I've not seen him in years, but he can help me."

Spook sniffed. "Who is he? Is it safe?"

Acid reached over to the toilet and picked up a roll of toilet paper. She wrapped it around her hand a few times and ripped the wad free. Dabbed at her side.

"An old acquaintance. That's all you need to know. Don't worry, I've got it under control."

"What do you mean? Who is he, Acid? Tell me."

"I'm going now, Spook. I'll ring you tomorrow." She held the phone away from her face. "Don't worry. Bye."

She powered the phone down and went back into the bedroom before removing her tights along with her bra and pants. Naked, she unzipped her case and found the first aid bag. Out came a handful of cotton wool, surgical tape, a roll of QuikClot, and a bottle of ethanol. She returned to the bathroom and stood in the bath to pour the entire bottle of ethanol into the wound in her side. It hurt like hell and she had trouble stifling her screams, but it was needed. Once clean, she stuffed the wound with the haemostatic dressing. Then she grabbed some more for the top and stuck it down with enough surgical tape to hold it in place. It was a botched job, and already blood was seeping through, but it would hold until she got where she was going.

She rubbed herself down with a handful of baby wipes, enough to remove most of the blood from her body. Then she dressed in fresh underwear, a pair of black Dior jeans, and her original Black Sabbath 1978 tour shirt.

Another handful of baby wipes took care of the blood and stage make-up from her face. She grabbed her overnight bag and got rid of the rest with removal cream, and applied Chanel Noir Profund liquid eyeliner to her upper and lower lids, finishing with a feline flick at the corners. Lastly, she ran her trademark Chanel Rouge Coco 'Carmen' lipstick over her full lips – albeit now swollen into a grotesque trout-pout on one side. She placed the lipstick and eyeliner back in the bag and brought out a bottle of pills. Pure unadulterated codeine. None of that mixed-with-paracetamol nonsense. She screwed off the lid and shook out four white pills. Swallowed them down dry.

"Fuck it." she sneered at her reflection. "That'll do."

She walked back into the bedroom and removed a thick wad of notes and a Glock 45 from the side compartment of her suitcase. She checked the magazine and stuffed the pistol in the back of her jeans. Then she slipped on her boots, pulled on her black leather jacket, stuffed the money in the inside pocket, and returned to the mean streets of Manchester.

Chapter Six

Outside the hotel Acid jumped in the first black cab she saw. "Levenshulme, please," she told the driver. "And step on it."

The driver eyed her in the rear-view mirror. She could tell he wanted to say something, but then she hit him with her best don't-fuck-with-me look and he thought better of it. She sat back and closed her eyes, trying to ignore the existent possibility she was about to make life a lot worse for herself. She held onto her side as her pulse throbbed inside the wound. The piece of railing inside of her felt alien. The rust and dirt would already be seeping into her bloodstream.

Thankfully, the driver got the message and spared no horses in getting her there. Fifteen minutes later he brought the cab to a stop half-way along Levenshulme's high street, the sprawling road bridging Manchester's border to the neighbouring Stockport. She flung some notes at the guy and exited the cab, holding her side all the while. As the taxi drove off, she stood on the side of the road and tried to find her bearings. She hadn't visited the area in over ten years and whilst the inevitable gentrification was clear (modern wine bars and vegan cafés now stood alongside the Irish pubs and betting shops), it had the same ambience as always. The streets still bristled with an air of menace.

She walked until she got to the end of the main strip. Here she took a left and circled back on herself, following the road around the next bend. And there it was. The same as she remembered it.

The Green Devil.

The music didn't screech to a halt as Acid Vanilla entered the large public house and let the heavy doors swing shut behind her, but it might as well have done. Despite being close to last orders, the pub was heaving with people. A rag-tag bunch of coffin-dodgers, part-time gangsters and Irish travellers eyed her suspiciously as she walked to the bar.

She eased her side against the polished wood top and waited for the barman's attention. A quick glance around told her she was the only woman in the place. The only non-Irish person, to boot. The air was heady with smells of Guinness and rye. Acid thought back to the last time she'd drank here, when you couldn't see across the room for the thick cloud of tobacco smoke. Today, however, the air was clear. She could now see the peeling wallpaper, the yellowing photographs and newspaper clippings pinned to the wall, not to mention the IRA and INLA insignia hanging above the wood-panelled bar. None of which made the place any more pleasant or inviting. She clutched her side as the barman approached.

"What can I get ya, miss?"

He was a stout, middle-aged man with white sideburns and a red face.

"Do you have Chivas Regal?"

He looked pained. "I don't think we do. We got an excellent selection, mind."

Acid peered over his shoulder. "A Jameson, then. Double. Two chunks of ice."

"Coming right up."

The man placed a tumbler down in front of her and free-poured a generous measure. It had never been the sort of establishment to bother with optics and measuring cylinders, and Acid was pleased it had kept some of its appeal.

"So, what brings a nice girl like you to a place like this?"

Acid watched as he took a small silver shovel from an ice tray and scooped two cubes into the glass.

"Oh, I wouldn't say I'm a nice girl. Far from it."

The man looked her up and down. "Is that so?"

"I'm looking for someone. Perhaps you can help."

"Maybe I can."

"The Dullahan. Is he in?"

The man froze. All the blood drained from his face. "Sorry. I've never heard of that person."

Acid narrowed her eyes. He was scared of something. Or someone.

"I'm not the police or anything," she told him. "I'm a friend of The Dullahan, an old acquaintance. I need to find him. Its urgent."

The barman swallowed. "You've worked with The Dark Man?"

Acid took a sip of the Jameson. "You could say that."

"Same line of work?"

She raised her eyebrows. Nodded. Now he was getting it.

"He's not here," he said, speaking in hushed tones. "Hasn't been in for years. After his wife died, he stopped drinking. Keeps himself to himself."

"I see. Do you know where I can find him?"

The man stiffened and glanced over her shoulder. A sweetener might help. Acid reached into her jacket pocket and took out two fifties. She slid them over the bar top.

"For the drink." She kept her fingers on the notes. "And any information."

The barman eyed the cash a second, then sighed. "A oner? For the whereabouts of The Dark Man? Sorry, dear. I don't know a damn thing."

Acid sneered and pulled out another hundred, and another. She placed the notes down and her hand back on top of the pile. The barman glanced at the cash, glanced around the bar. None of the pissed-up old thugs were interested.

"Fine. I'll give you the last address I had." He got a notepad from the side of the till and scribbled down a few lines, handed it to Acid. "It's around the corner. Ten-minute walk. But don't you tell him it was me who gave you this. All right?"

Acid released the money and grinned. "Sorry, who are you? Never seen you before in my life."

She downed the Jameson and hurried out the way she came. The night was drawing in and the air cold against her skin. Holding the address up in the orange glow of the streetlights, she walked on, swaying now because of a banging headache and the severe loss of blood. At the speed she could manage, the walk was somewhat longer than the ten minutes suggested. More like thirty. But eventually she turned a corner around the side of an old mill and there it was.

"What the hell?" she murmured to herself.

Her first thought was she'd been had. In front of her, standing back from the other houses and in its own grounds, was a thatched cottage. The garden was overgrown and full of rusted metal, but still, it was the last place she'd ever expect to find the mighty Dullahan.

As Acid staggered closer, she took in the quaint red window frames, the ivy sprawled around the brickwork, the terracotta milk-bottle covers. She was fading fast and hoped to god she had the right house, but it felt like a stretch. She shuffled up the path and banged on the front door, steadying herself with an elbow against the frame. The sensation of cold, hard metal under her knuckles was both a shock and reassuring. The door had been designed to look like your typical suburban wood or PVC affair, complete with number and door-knocker and painted red like the window frames. But on closer inspection, she found it was made of reinforced steel. Maybe she had the correct place after all.

A few seconds went by before Acid heard movement. Shuffling sounds. Annoyed grunts. Instinctively, she moved her hand around her back and felt for the reassuring grip of the Glock 45. Larger than her usual 19, but the extended grip gave better control and more accuracy. She removed it from her waistband and held it to her stomach, feeling the reassuring coldness of the metal barrel through her t-shirt.

She heard more movement. A key in a lock. A bolt sliding free. The door eased open to reveal a short, thin man with a thick head of white hair. He was wearing a crimson velvet smoking jacket over a white t-shirt and electric-blue jogging pants. Around his neck hung an enormous emerald-encrusted shamrock that wouldn't have looked out of place on a rapper. He gazed at her with heavy-lidded eyes.

"Fuck me. I thought you were dead."

"Nice to see you too. Can I come in?"

The Dullahan didn't flinch. "I don't do visitors. Whatever you're after, I can't help ya." He made to shut the door but Acid got her boot inside.

"Please. I need your help." She pulled up her t-shirt to reveal the leaking wound, the dressing seeped in blood. "I've got nowhere else to go. I've brought a pot of gold. Please."

The old man looked troubled, but opened the door wider. "Fine. Get yourself inside. Quick."

"Thank you," she gasped, as she fell into the hall.

The last thing she saw was The Dullahan – her old nemesis and one-time rival – locking the door behind her.

Then she collapsed, unconscious, at the old man's feet.

Chapter Seven

She felt immense pressure in her stomach. In her head, too. The bats nibbled at her synapses, leathery wings of instinct flapping at her nervous system. She tried to speak. To call out. But all she managed was slurred mumbling. Inane words with little meaning. Danger was present here, the bats told her. She had to wake up. But she couldn't move.

Time slowed.

The world stopped.

Then, later, through a dense fog of semi-consciousness, a figure appeared. It loomed over her through the haze and she felt a cold hand on her forehead. She sensed the glint of instruments. A scalpel. The skin on her stomach was stretched and manipulated. Cold steel penetrated her flesh. The dead skin cut away. A fresh wound, dragged together with stitches. She screamed into the darkness but made no sound. She wanted to tell whoever − or whatever - this was to stop. To let her go.

She had work to do.

People to kill.

She heard laughter. Annoying tittering laughter. Then the hand rested on her forehead once more. She felt a calloused palm glide over her eyes, gently forcing the lids closed.

She succumbed.

She slept.

Chapter Eight

Acid woke with a start and glanced around. She was lying on a steel gurney in a low-ceilinged room. Most probably a basement. The only light came from a small naked bulb hanging over her head. She sat upright and felt a sharp pain in her side as the memories came flooding back.

Davros Ratpack.

She'd killed him. But not before he'd inflicted a killer blow himself.

She was topless now except for her bra, and could see the wound had a fresh dressing. She peeled away the corner of a piece of surgical tape and tentatively inspected the damage. The laceration was around two inches long, raised and bulbous under a row of twelve stitches. But it was clean and properly dressed. She prodded her fingers around the area, but could no longer locate anything inside of her. To the right of the gurney was a small table with a metal bowl sitting on top. Inside this was an inch-long piece of rusting metal covered in blood. Next to the bowl lay a syringe. A tetanus shot. Acid smiled to herself and swung her legs over the side. You could say a lot of things about The Dullahan – and she certainly had done over the years – but he provided a first-class service.

She examined the room, her heart sinking as she saw her vintage Black Sabbath shirt in the corner. It had been cut in half and was caked in blood. A total write-off. The Dullahan had left a brand new white t-shirt for her, draped over the back of a wooden chair. She slipped it on before wobbling on unsteady legs over to a set of stone stairs in the far corner.

Gripping the handrail tight and taking care with every step, she slowly made her way up to the ground floor where she could hear the faint chime of classical music and the bubbling grumble of a kettle boiling. She got to the top of the stairs and saw the kitchen area to her right. The Dullahan was standing at the sink with his back to her. Doing the dishes, of all things. Seeing him here in this mundane domestic setting, Acid wondered if she might pass out again.

The Dullahan must have heard her at the door. He turned around. "Ah, you're awake, then? At long last."

She eyeballed the clock on the cooker. "Twenty past one. That's not too bad. I did lose a lot of blood."

The Dullahan walked over to a cupboard and took down two mugs. "Aye, but you think it's the next day. It's not. You've been out thirty-six hours. I was beginning to think you'd taken a bad turn."

Acid frowned. "I was out that long?"

"Ya must have needed it. I don't think it was only the puncture wound either. You were exhausted, lassie. Ya been pushing yourself hard, have ya?"

"Don't I always." She eased herself onto one of the

chairs around the sturdy farmhouse table in the centre of the room. "Thanks, though. For patching me up."

He brought two mugs of steaming tea over and joined her at the table. "I didn't have much choice, did I? Fainting in my arms like that."

She grinned. "Terrible, aren't I? So tacky. To be honest, I'm still wondering if I'm delirious."

The Dullahan brought a pouch of tobacco and some rolling papers from out of the pocket of his robe. "How do you mean?" he asked.

Acid gestured around. At the kettle, the microwave, the matching cabinets. It was the kitchen you'd expect, judging by the cottage's exterior. But the banal homeliness jarred terribly with her conceptualised notion of the man they called The Dullahan. The Dark Man. He'd been one of the most feared and skilled freelance cleaners in the business. A hero to a lot of her contemporaries. To her too, though she'd never admit it. The Dullahan was already in his late fifties when she started out as an assassin, but was up there with the best even then. Caesar had tried recruiting him on more than one occasion, but he'd always turned him down.

"I can't believe you've ended up somewhere like this," she told him. "I mean, it's nice. But it's so homely."

"Aye, well, it's what Sheila wanted," he said, as if enough of an explanation. He nodded at her mug. "Do you want sugar?"

She gawped. "You got anything stronger?"

"I don't drink these days."

"So I heard, but I didn't believe it."

"Well, it's true, so it is. Who told ya anyway?" He scowled. "How did ya find me?"

Acid looked out the window. The back garden was more

overgrown than the front. "Does it matter?" she asked. "I'm here now."

Her leather jacket hung over the chair to her left. She reached into the pocket and pulled out the wad of cash, flung it on the table.

"There you go. A pot of gold for your troubles."

"Ah, away with ya. I don't need your fecking money." He finished rolling a cigarette and screwed it between his dry lips. "I did think you were dead, mind."

"Is that what Caesar's telling people?"

He closed one eye as he lit the cigarette. "Aye. But that makes your presence here all the more surprising. If the story is you're dead, it means he hasn't declared open season on you. So why not disappear?"

She picked up the mug and took a sip of the hot tea. "You sure you've got nothing decent to drink?"

The Dullahan blew a plume of blue smoke over the table. Then he pushed himself to his feet and ambled over to a low cabinet in the corner of the room. Acid watched as he pulled out a large bottle, half-full of viscous amber.

"This is the good stuff," he said, placing it down on the table. He went to the sink and picked up a glass. Slid it across to her. "Go for your life. I won't drink it now."

"Wow. Life really is upside down. The great Dullahan, a teetotaller."

His eyes snapped up to hers. "Don't call me that. Not anymore. That person is gone."

Acid took the top off the whisky, a cork stopper, and poured herself a decent-sized amount. "Okay. What do I call you?" She took a long sip.

"Jimmy will do."

She had to stop herself spitting whisky over the table. "Jimmy? You want me to call you Jimmy?"

35

"That's my name. Was. Is again. It's what Sheila called me."

Acid straightened herself. "Fair enough. I'm sorry to hear about your wife."

The Dullahan – Jimmy – waved the moment away. He pointed to the long scar running down her forearm. "I see you still carry the mark of The Dark Man, though."

She looked at the raised red line running down the back of her arm. From wrist to elbow.

"Still hurts in chilly weather. You bastard." She smiled. "That was some fight. You almost had me."

"You almost had me, lassie. I tell ya. It was about then when I realised it was time to hang up the old spurs. You were something else, you know that?"

"Still am."

"Is that so?"

Acid looked at him. Jimmy or not, she knew he still had an ear to the ground. What had he heard?

"I could do with some more help, if it's available. I need to find Caesar." She pushed the money back over the table at him. Ten grand in used fifties. Less the three hundred she'd given the barman. "Come on, take it."

Jimmy stared at the money, then back at her. He was faltering. She kept her mouth shut. When tough-minded people were thinking, it was best to give them space. Let them reach their own conclusions. She sipped at the whisky. It was spicy and fragrant and burned her parched throat. She sighed. The old fight-or-flight keeping her going these last few days was leaving her system.

Jimmy reached over and stubbed the roll-up out on a jam jar lid.

"Ya know, there was never any love lost between Caesar and me," he said. "I always thought he was too aggressive in the way he carried himself. I don't mean the actual work. But the way he was in the industry. All about the money for him. Always."

Acid drank, nodded her agreement. "He's got worse."

"Oh, I know. Heard all about his new Nomadic Assassins Network, or whatever it's called. NAN, is that it? Load of shite. Anyway, like I say, I never had much time for the man. You though, lassie. Good god, I remember first time I saw you out in the field. Amsterdam, I think. Remember? We were both after the price on that Lebanese doctor. Ya killed two of his bodyguards with a neck scarf and a high-heeled shoe. Bloody hell. I knew then you were going to be the best."

Acid smiled. "I remember those shoes. They were deadly."

"They sure were. So were you." His face dropped, the twinkle in his watery eyes faded. "Did ya know my Sheila had Alzheimer's?"

She shook her head.

"Terrible disease. Caused her a series of mini-strokes. I lost a little more of her every time. Until one day she was completely gone. No memory of me or us or herself whatsoever. Hung on for another three years after that, she did. Just staring into space. Incontinent too. Not a pleasant time." He looked at his hands, still calloused and rough after all these years. The hands of a fighter. "What Caesar did to your mother was not on, Acid. Not on at all. So yes, I will help ya. Whatever I can do, which isn't much these days, I'll warn ya, but there ya go. But I don't want money. I got all I need."

"Thank you," Acid told him. "Can you put out a call, get me a location on Caesar? The rest of Annihilation too?"

Jimmy raised his eyebrows. "Oh, is that all ya need? Jesus Christ. I'll try my best. What's your move?"

She shrugged. "I'm going to kill them. All of them."

"I figured. And I take it there's no persuading ya otherwise?"

"Not a chance."

"Okay. Tell ya what, why don't we go upstairs?"

Acid finished her drink. "Upstairs?"

Jimmy grinned, his eyes impish once more. "Oh aye, I've got something up there you're going to want to see."

Chapter Nine

The Dullahan creaked open the unassuming wooden door at the end of the narrow landing and stepped aside to allow Acid to enter. She arched one eyebrow his way, puzzlement at the Irishman's boyish eagerness. But the second she entered the room, she understood.

"Jesus Christ, this is amazing," she purred.

A bank of flashing hard drives ran down one wall, complete with modems, servers and three large monitors on top of a grand, leather-topped desk. But that wasn't the best part. As Acid spun around she took in the wall opposite. Covered in red baize, it displayed a veritable armoury of expensive guns. Over thirty assault rifles were mounted at intervals along two rows, with eight rifles on each row. Underneath these sat a collection of handguns, maybe forty pieces in total. Some had never been fired. Some were collector's items. Moving her gaze down the racks, she took in a decent selection of submachine guns, two sniper rifles and a missile launcher. A vast selection of swords and knives completed the collection on the next wall, along with sharpened knuckle-dusters and obscure stabbing weapons from around the world. Museum pieces, some of them. Some even Acid didn't recognise.

"You like my games room, then?"

Acid wagged her finger. "I bloody knew you hadn't retired."

"I have too," he scolded. He sat in an enormous leather chair in front of the three monitor screens and shunted the mouse, awakening the system. "What can I tell ya. When you get to my age, a man needs a hobby."

The monitors flashed into life. Each one was divided into nine smaller screens. Twenty-seven portals in total. Acid scanned them. The first monitor looked to be security cameras, trained on the outside of the cottage. The portals showed the front and back garden, the side alley, a selection of recycling bins. The other two monitors were the same but showed real-time CCTV feeds from various cities around the world. Each portal window had a marker, written in a digital font in the corner: MCR, LDN, NY, CAL, TYO, MSK. As Acid watched, the footage changed, showing a new camera feed from each city.

"I've hacked into every major city in the world," Jimmy told her. "Getting good at the old cyber stuff in my old age, don't ya know. I select the footage, like so, and it pops up." He flicked a few buttons, changing the display feed from LDN to BER to PAR. "I've still got contacts in most places. Pays to keep your hand in, so it does."

"I knew you hadn't retired," Acid said.

"I fecking well have. Like I told ya, this is a hobby."

"Whatever," she said, peering closer to the screen. "So, you still have contacts in Berlin?"

Jimmy gave her a knowing look. "Aye, the Reinigers. And yes, I heard what happened."

She stiffened. "Yes, well, it won't happen again."

"You sure? Cos like I say, the deeper you get into this, Acid, the harder it'll be to get out of."

"Come off it. I'm already in with two feet, there's no getting out of this. Not until every single one of those rotten bastards is dead. Or I am."

"All right." He turned back to the screen and gripped the mouse, making himself comfortable. "Here's what I know. Your man Beowulf Caesar was in Germany for some time. Hamburg, and then Berlin where your paths crossed. After that he went dark for a few weeks. But yesterday the fat fucker pinged up over in the US. Washington, of all places. I've seen a few emails between him and the big fella. Something's going down over there soon enough."

Acid nodded, blew her cheeks out. And was about to respond, when she spotted something on one of the screens. "Wait. What's going on?"

She was looking at the left-hand monitor. Jimmy's home security feed. Specifically, she was looking at the alley that ran down the side of the cottage. The footage was dark and grainy, but the muscular figure with the well-fitted suit and the cropped blond hair making their way towards the front of the property could only be one person.

"Spitfire," she whispered, wide-eyed, at the screen. Then to Jimmy, "You told him I was here."

He spun around in his chair. "No, I never did. I've got nothing but contempt for that whole blasted organisation. After what they did." He got up and moved towards the door. "But you weren't exactly stealth-like in the killing of Davros, were ya? Not much of a leap to guess ya came here if you were hurt. Come, we need to get ya out of here. Sharpish."

Acid paused, looking over at the wall of weapons. A

particularly inviting AK-200 with snow-camo decal would solve this problem in under a minute. She glanced over at Jimmy as he held the door.

"Not in the house, lass," he said, reading her expression. "And not outside either. I know you're itching to crucify the lot of them, but it will not happen here. I can't have the two of you going at it in my borough. I still have a reputation to think about. If ya want my help, we play this my way."

Acid understood. "So what's the plan?" she asked, trailing him out the door and along the landing.

Jimmy reached the top of the stairs and lifted a small photo of a dog away from the wall. A single switch lay underneath. He pushed it. Acid heard a low whirring sound and a hatch slid open in the ceiling. Another press of the button and a ladder descended onto the landing.

"Up into the loft space. You'll see an exit over on the far side. It's a right old state up there, but you'll be fine. Once you're outside, head up the alley to the end and take a left. That'll take you back to the main road."

"What about you?"

"Don't worry about me. I'll deal with Spitfire fecking Creosote, the big ponce."

"You'll be able to handle him?"

"Won't need to. Some of us still abide by the code." He punched her on the arm. "Now get away with ya. I'll tickle his balls, send him on his way. I'll be in touch soon enough."

She put her hands on the ladder. "You'll be able to find me?"

Jimmy frowned. Playing hurt. "Yes, I think I might be able to. You take care for now, Acid Vanilla."

"You too. And thank you."

"Don't thank me. You killing that rancid excuse for a

human being is all the thanks I'll need. Now get yaself gone. I mean it."

A loud banging rose up from the front door, Spitfire attempting to beat his way through it. He knew she was here. She glanced at Jimmy, wondering if she should stay and help the old man. But before she had a chance to say as much, The Dullahan shot her his famous look. The one that made you wither up inside. Those watery eyes of his now burned with a fierce intensity. Not so much windows of the soul, but a gateway to hell. They told Acid everything she needed to know. Whether he now went by The Dullahan or Jimmy, the old man could still handle himself. It was time to get out of here. She gave a solemn nod and climbed up the ladder.

Chapter Ten

The banging continued as The Dullahan made his way back down the stairs. "All right, keep your bleeding hair on."

He went through the same ritual as always – turning the keys in the locks, carefully sliding the bolts open, slotting the chain into its groove. He wasn't going to let the urgency of his caller, or the force they were exerting on his door, move him any faster. He cracked the door open a way.

"Who the hell is making all this racket?"

Spitfire Creosote glared at him, his chiselled face red and contorted. Like an angry fist. "Where is she?"

Jimmy raised his eyebrows. Flapped his mouth in curiosity. Doing the whole bit. "Good to see you too, Spitfire. It's been a while."

The tall blond killer barged past him into the house. "I know she's here, Dullahan. Where is she?" He held out his hands. "Acid. Fucking. Vanilla."

Jimmy shut the door and looked his visitor up and down. He was wearing a dark navy suit and a crisp white shirt, complete with silver cufflinks and a navy tie. The whole James Bond shtick. It was laughable. His gaze drifted down to Spitfire's polished brogue boots. Black. Expensive-looking. He liked the boots. He'd give him that.

"Acid Vanilla?" he mused. "Now that's a name I haven't heard in a long time. Isn't she dead?"

He was enjoying this, toying with him. But Spitfire knew as much. Next thing he was over to him, sticking a sharp finger in his face.

"Listen, Dullahan. I've got a lot of respect for you. You're one of the greats. But that bitch has gone too far. She killed Davros Ratpack yesterday. Did it while he was on downtime. That's not cricket. You know as much."

Jimmy smiled his sweetest smile. Full of Irish charm. "No, you're right there. Not cricket at all."

Spitfire raised his head. "What was that?"

"What was what?"

Jimmy was trying his best, but they'd both heard it. The sound of footsteps. Creaking floorboards.

Jimmy held his nerve. "Damn squirrels. Nothing but a fecking nuisance, so they are."

"Bullshit." Spitfire pulled out a handgun from behind his back.

"Ah, so that is a gun in your pocket, but ya aren't pleased to see me."

"Shut up, old man," Spitfire whispered. He pulled a suppresser from his jacket pocket and screwed it on the end of the threaded barrel. His eyes trailed a path across the ceiling as more noise drifted down from above. Louder. Heavier.

"Squirrels? I don't think so, friend."

Jimmy didn't flinch as Spitfire shoved the gun in his

face. He eyed it as a Kimber Custom TLE. A nice piece. He had five similar ones in his games room.

"Careful now, son," he said, staying calm. "You don't want to be doing anything stupid."

Spitfire wavered the gun a moment then turned and strode up the stairs, taking them two at a time. When he got to the landing he shouted, "How do I get up in the roof?"

"What do you mean?" Jimmy asked, joining him a second later.

"Stop messing around," he said, spotting the hatch in the ceiling and scanning the walls for the release button. "Open it up. Now."

"I don't know what y—"

Jimmy wasn't expecting the fist to the stomach. A glancing blow. It winded him and he went down awkward, over on his bad ankle.

"You'll pay for that," he grunted.

But Spitfire wasn't listening. He had both hands flat against the wall, searching for the loft release he knew to be there. Another thud from above. That did it. Spitfire raised the Kimber and squeezed a few rounds into the roof, peppering the plasterboard with smoking holes an inch wide.

"Hey! Watch my ceiling, ya fecking eejit."

Spitfire readied himself for another blast, but Jimmy grabbed his arm, messing with his aim. Despite Jimmy's advancing years, he was still wiry. Still had the good fight in him when he needed it.

"What the hell are you playing at?" Spitfire yelled. "You think protecting her will end well for you?"

Jimmy glared at him. "You know the rules, son. This is my house. My castle."

Spitfire glared back. "You've fucked up here, old man. You know that. It's not your battle. You hear me?"

Jimmy held his hands up. "Maybe not, but it doesn't change the fact you've come into my abode and started shooting the place up. Caesar know you're here?"

Spitfire sniffed. "Wouldn't want to bother the big man at this momentous moment in time. But once she's dead, he'll get the full story. The order is simple. Eradicate her. At any cost."

Jimmy stuck out his bottom lip. "I always thought you were sweet on the lass," he mused, holding the shamrock medallion up to the light. "Didn't you and her have a fling once upon a time?"

"Come on, Dullahan," Spitfire said. "Stop this. I know what you're doing. Let me up there."

As he spoke they both heard the distinct sound of a window being forced opened. A cool draught seeped through the vents in the ceiling, altering the atmosphere on the landing. The two men both felt it. Spitfire wrapped his hand around Jimmy's throat and pushed him against the wall.

"Stupid old prick." He raced down the stairs towards the front door. "You'll regret this."

"I'll regret nothing," Jimmy replied, rubbing his neck. "Ya poncey fecker."

He watched as Spitfire reached the reinforced metal door and was met with a chain, two stiff bolts, two mortice locks, top and bottom, and a Yale.

"For Christ's sake, it's like Fort-bloody-Knox." He struggled with the locks, twisting at the hexagon-shaped security keys.

"It's to keep fecking assassins out of my house," Jimmy called down. "But it slows them down plenty too."

Spitfire Creosote snarled back at him as he forced the second of the two bolts free and flicked the catch on the Yale lock. As he yanked the door open he turned and pointed the Kimber at Jimmy. The venom was palpable in his face. His finger vibrated on the trigger.

Jimmy relaxed his body and waited. But Spitfire wouldn't be so stupid. They both knew anyone dumb enough to take out The Dullahan would not have been long for this world. He might have retired, but he still knew everyone in the industry, still inspired devotion and respect from a lot of scary people. Spitfire made to say something, but no sound came out. Instead, he shook his head angrily and ran out the door.

Jimmy lingered on the landing a few moments, then slowly made his way downstairs.

"Well, Acid, I hope I gave ya enough of a lead," he mumbled to himself. "Because yer man there means business."

He put his head out the door and looked both ways. Acid and Spitfire were long gone. He paused and incanted a silent prayer to the heavens. Then he shut the door quietly behind him and shuffled into the kitchen to make a fresh pot of tea.

Chapter Eleven

The Dullahan's back garden looked a long way down from the escape hatch. No matter how many storeys, a drop always seemed a lot worse when you were just about to jump. On the flip-side, once on the ground you often found it ridiculous you'd ever been reticent.

Perhaps there was a metaphor in there somewhere, Acid thought, as she yanked open the small window and made the leap into the back garden. She dropped into a forward roll, cushioning the impact on landing, and was on her feet running before she had a chance to think any more about it. She ran as fast as she could. As fast as the throbbing wound in her side allowed. She knew Jimmy wouldn't give her away. But she also knew Spitfire Creosote. It wouldn't take him long to realise what was going on. He'd be on her tail soon enough.

She scrambled up the high wall at the end of Jimmy's garden and assessed the situation. Down to her left she could see a row of small, red-brick terrace houses, their backyards facing out into a narrow alley. To her right was a long passageway, flanked on either side by pebble-dashed garages with corrugated iron roofs.

She was considering which way to go when the first bullet whizzed past her ear.

Shit.

Opting for a quick right, she zig-zagged around the shots as more bullets ricocheted off the garages, sending tiny pieces of gravel flying into her face. She reached the end of the passageway and took a left, finding herself in a small cul-de-sac. It was a pleasant afternoon and a group of children were kicking a ball around in the street, watched on by their parents sunning themselves in their front gardens.

Acid slowed her pace and smiled adoringly at the children, mouthed 'Bless them' at the parents, held her hands to her heart. In turn, the proud parents smiled back. A textbook exchange. She hurried to the end of the cul-de-sac and turned back to see Spitfire appear at the far end of the street. He saw the children, saw the idyllic scene, the grinning suburban families, and immediately deployed the same simpering facade she had used moments earlier. It was what you did on a job when finding yourself face to face with civilians. After sixteen years in the industry it became instinctive. Caesar was proud of the fact none of his operatives were on any police database. You didn't achieve that by shooting up the place.

Spitfire looked up and saw her at the end of the street. "Hey," he shouted. "Wait. Let's talk about this."

"No thanks," she called back. "I've nothing to say to you."

She turned and sped off, disappearing down the side of another row of red-bricks and through a narrow lane that opened out onto a sizeable recreation ground. She held her side as she went, the stitches straining with the exertion. Trees lined either side of the open parkland, and up ahead Acid could see a children's playground with a brightly coloured climbing frame and set of swings. But to her dismay the park was deserted, and whilst a row of red-bricks backed onto the grassland, the border of trees provided perfect cover for anyone looking to take her out with a fatally placed bullet.

Acid glanced frantically about her. She had a head start on Spitfire but he'd be here any second. She ducked behind the border of trees and continued forward, winding through the gaps in the foliage and staying hidden as best she could. The perimeter curved around the back of another housing estate, and beyond that was a main road. Shops. Cars. Another minute and she'd be safe.

"Acid. Where are you?"

She spun around to see Spitfire a few feet away, and dropped to the ground. The area between the trees and the wall had been allowed to grow wild, and the long grass hid her well enough.

"Come out, Acid," Spitfire called. "You can't run forever. I know you're here."

She peered through the grass, watching him as he surveyed the scene. He narrowed his eyes into the under-growth a few feet away. He'd drawn his gun, complete with a suppressor. She did a quick assessment. It was unlikely she'd get to him before he got a shot in. Meaning, if he saw her she was dead.

She slowed her heartbeat. Took long, silent breaths. Continued watching.

Up close, Spitfire looked older than the last time she had seen him. That was two years ago. A job in Argentina. It was the first time they'd worked together since New York.

Acid had begged Caesar to send Magpie or Davros in her place, but they were on other jobs. Or so he'd told her.

Seeing him again sent a ripple of energy shooting through her nervous system. Because whilst he looked older, it didn't mean he looked bad. In fact, if anything, the lines on his face, the salt and pepper flecks in his stubble, it only made him more handsome. *The bastard.*

Risk of exposure, be damned. If Acid had a gun right now, she'd put a bullet through his chiselled jawline in a second. Have done with it. That'd teach the charming prick.

He was still standing there. Still squinting into the trees.

"I can wait as long as I need to, darling," he called out. "Can wait for you forever. I always told you that."

He chuckled to himself and turned away. Acid stiffened. Now, with his back to her, she might get to him before he had a chance to shoot. She looked around, careful not to disturb anything. She was searching for a weapon. A stick, a bottle, anything. She let out a silent breath, cursing herself for not asking The Dullahan for a piece, something from his extensive selection of top-grade firearms. The truth was, seeing Spitfire again after all this time (resplendent as always in his fitted suit and with his tanned good looks) had sent her head reeling. But that had to stop. Right now. This wasn't high school, and she wasn't here to play games.

Spitfire turned back around, scanning the area above her head. He took a few steps to his left. A few more and he'd be at the right angle to see her. She froze. Didn't blink. Didn't breathe. It was apt, she thought, that she was about to die here, in the dirt, at the hands of Spitfire Creosote. After everything she'd said to him. Everything he'd told her in return. It'd be funny if it wasn't so tragic.

He was nearly on her now. She tensed her muscles,

prepared herself for one last hurrah, over the top into no-man's-land. She'd launch herself at him. Stay low. She might get lucky.

But then he stopped. As Acid watched, his face dropped from keen determination into frustration, then annoyance. He pulled a mobile phone from inside of his suit jacket.

"Yes? What is it?"

She couldn't hear the voice on the line, but it was a burner phone, so no doubt it was Raaz Terabyte, Annihilation Pest Control's In-field Analyst and Communications Officer. Or whatever the hell she called herself these days. Stuck-up tech-nerd was more like it. There'd been no love lost between Acid and Raaz, even back when Acid was unquestionably the best operative on Caesar's books. She had wondered initially whether it was a territorial thing – them being the only females in the organisation – but then Magpie Stiletto came along and Raaz was all over her like herpes. The fact Acid's initial impression had been correct pleased her. She still had it. Could still read people. Raaz was simply an out-and-out bitch.

"Are you serious?" Spitfire rasped into the phone. "But I had her. She's here. Give me more time I can get to her."

He glanced about him as he spoke. An expression of incredulous anger spread across his fine features. Definitely Raaz on the other end.

"Fine. Yes. If that's what Caesar wants. I'll come in straight away." He paused, shook his head at the phone. "No. I'm in Manchester. What is it with this organisation? We've fucking lost the plot... Okay... Fine. You're right. Orders and all that. I'll get the next flight. See you in a few hours."

He hung up and stared at the phone for a second before shoving it in his pocket. He scanned the area one more time, slid his gun into the holster under his arm, and set off back the way he'd come.

Acid waited until he was out of sight, then waited a few minutes more, before she got to her feet and brushed herself down. Once certain he was gone, she hurried to the main road and ducked into the first minicab office she found. It was grotty and damp, and it stank of stale beer and cigarettes. She walked up to the small counter window and spoke through the grille at the woman on the other side.

"Can I have a cab, please? To the centre. As soon as possible."

The woman was middle-aged, with thinning, overly dyed hair and the face and demeanour of an angry sloth. She sniffed and tapped a few keys of the computer on the desk beside her.

"Be two minutes, love," she said, not looking up. "Take a seat if ya want."

Acid turned around to see two old chairs covered in cigarette burns and graffiti. Old kebab papers had been stuffed down the back of one of them.

"I'll wait outside," she told the woman.

She flipped the collar on her leather jacket and leaned against the side of the building. To kill time, she got out her phone, switched it on, and was immediately presented with a symphony of beeps and vibrations. Twenty-seven missed calls. Fifty-nine unread texts. All Spook. Acid was about to switch the damned device off, but stopped herself. With a sigh, she scrolled down to her recent call list and hit dial. Spook answered on the first ring.

"Where the hell are you? What happened? I thought you'd been hurt... or..." Her voice trailed off, quivering with emotion.

Acid raised her eyes to the sky.

"Calm it down. I'm fine." She waited for Spook to reply, but she didn't. "Are you okay? You sound worked up."

"Worked up? Worked up, Acid? I've not slept in two days. Last I hear, you've been injured, and then your phone goes dead. Jesus Christ!"

A cab pulled up and Acid peered through the window of the office, saw the woman signalling it was for her. She nodded at the driver and climbed in the back.

"Manchester centre, please," she told him. "Near the station."

The man nodded and pulled away.

"What's going on?" Spook asked. "Did you get patched up?"

Acid felt at her side. "Yeah. I met my contact. He patched me up." She glanced in the rear-view mirror. Saw the driver watching her. Listening. "Listen, Spook, we'll talk later, I need you to get me the next flight out of here. I can't stay in Manchester a moment longer. Can you check for me, now?"

The line went silent for a second, followed by the distinct clack of fingers across a keyboard. Spook was already sitting at her computer. Acid smiled to herself. A tenner said she'd been checking police reports and hospital feeds.

"I've got a plane leaving in two hours I can get you on. To Heathrow. Half three. Any good?"

"Perfect. One second, Spook." Acid covered the phone mouthpiece and leaned forward to the driver. "Hey mate, can you wait for me outside my hotel while I get my luggage, then take me to the airport?"

The driver frowned and did the whole swaying his head side-to-side act. Like it was a real problem for him. "I not sure," he told her. "This my last job. Been working twelve hours."

Acid reached into her jacket and brought out a couple of fifties meant for The Dullahan.

"This change your mind? I'll give you another hundred once we get to the airport."

The driver strained his neck to look at the notes offered. "Woah, okay, fine. I do it. No problem." Then under his breath, "Fucking hell."

Acid was back on the phone. "Spook, we're on, book me on that flight. I'll see you soon."

She hung up and sat back in her seat. The driver was still staring at her, but now with an air of curiosity. Acid gazed out the window, allowing her focus to blur and trying to imagine herself on a sandy beach somewhere in the Indian Ocean, the gentle tide licking at her heels. Hard to do when the cab smelt like someone had stuffed a two-week-old body in the boot... And she knew what that smelt like.

"You know, lady, you have a splendid face."

Acid glared at the eyes in the rear-view. "I beg your pardon?"

"What I mean is, you have splendid bone structure. If you smile more, you could be so pretty."

Great. One of those cab drivers.

"Oh yeah?" she replied. "And what if I don't feel like smiling?"

"Ah, but life is good, no? What is there not to smile about?"

A laminated taxi ID card hung on the back of the seat, complete with photo. Pieter Mazur was the driver's name. Eastern Europe from the sound of it. He continued to stare at her.

"So what you do, that you so miserable?"

"You don't want to know. Believe me."

"Try me. You know, I speak to all sorts in this cab. Politicians, gangsters. Hey, some would say they the same, right?" It was a well-rehearsed line, one he'd used many times before. He followed it up with a loud laugh.

"All right," she said, fixing him dead in the eye. "I'm a hired killer. Or at least I was. It was my job for sixteen years. I killed people for a living." She gave it a beat, let that sink in. "But don't you be telling a single person, Pieter Mazur, you hear me? Because I'd know it was you. And I'd find you." She leaned forward in her seat, lowering her voice an octave. "You see, normally I kill without a trace. But I can make it a long, drawn-out affair if I need to. Lots of blood. Lots of screaming. That is, until I cut your tongue out and stuff it down your throat."

Pieter gripped both hands on the steering wheel. "You bullshit me, right?"

She kept her eyes on his, employing the dead-eyed stare she'd perfected over the years. It said, *I don't bullshit about things like this.* It said, *Don't fuck with me.*

Pieter swallowed hard, eyes fluttering between the road and the rear-view mirror. "No problem. I swear I not say a word. To anyone."

Acid winked. "Good boy."

She watched out the window as the last of the red-brick terrace houses merged into the high-rise developments of the city centre. Her thoughts turned to Davros Ratpack, her one-time ally, her one-time friend. She had assumed — stupidly, perhaps — that she'd feel some closure right now. Satisfaction, even. She'd killed one of the bastards who'd murdered her mum, and who wanted her dead. Yet all she felt was numb.

Those thoughts left her and she closed her eyes. Her

heart was beating fast, the vein in her neck ready to burst. Under Spook's watch, she'd been taking care of herself these last few months. Trying to, at least. But she knew too well she could tip over the edge in a second. A righteous mission of vengeance had seemed so simple in her mind. But maybe that was the problem. Life rarely worked out the way you planned it, even for a highly trained assassin. It seemed the further away reality got from the expectations in her head, the harder it was to cope. Seeing Spitfire hadn't helped.

The cab turned the corner towards her hotel. Another few hours and she'd be in the air. A few more and she'd be back at the house. Home.

For now.

Chapter Twelve

Acid zipped up her jacket and huddled down against the hard wooden bench for warmth. It was a futile move, done out of instinct rather than any actual sense of logic. But wasn't that the story of her life? The streets of Dagenham were cold and wet and deserted this Tuesday morning. But that was usual. Whenever she made the pilgrimage here to her old house, a static aura of negative energy seemed to hang low in the sky. She came often. To sit. To think. To talk to her mum.

Closing her eyes, Acid settled herself in the moment. Like always when she came, she started by telling Louisa how sorry she was. How she wished she'd done more. How she missed her.

"And I'm sorry you ended up alone and nameless," she whispered, dabbing at her heavily mascaraed eyes with the curve of her index finger. "I did everything I could, but it would have been too risky."

All available records showed Louisa Vandella's only

daughter had died in 2001. Meaning Acid couldn't take ownership of her mum's remains. With no apparent next of kin her body had been buried in what was still referred to as a pauper's grave. Though with space now at a premium, Acid had discovered the reality was her beautiful mum had been dumped in a mass grave. Without even a marker to commemorate her burial. Or her life. Or the fact she'd lived at all. It felt like a final knife in Acid's heart.

"I'm doing all right though, Mum," she whispered at the house opposite. "Don't you worry about me. Doing the best I can, at least, the best I know. I got one of them for you. Gutted the evil bastard."

She looked up at what was once their front room. The window was open a touch, and on the other side of the glass, curtains swayed in the breeze, off-white with a pattern of tiny pink flowers in perpendicular rows. Pleasant enough. Homely.

Not for the first time, Acid wondered why she came here. It wasn't like they were happy in this house. They'd struggled. Not to mention the fact it was where her mum had been attacked. Where she'd killed Oscar Duke and set off the bloody chain of events that created Acid Vanilla. She had no regrets or hang-ups about what she'd done but, regardless, the place held no joyful nostalgia.

She was about to leave when she felt her phone rumble in her pocket. She pulled it out and checked Caller ID, half-expecting it to be Spook and ready to ignore the call. But it was a number she didn't recognise. She let it ring one more time, then answered.

"Acid?" a gruff Irish voice asked. "That you?"

She smiled to herself. "Sure is. How are you doing, Dullahan? Sorry – old habits. How are you doing, *Jimmy*? I still find that weird, to be honest."

"You're the one still calling herself Acid fecking Vanilla. You not think that's weird? It was his name for ya."

Acid sat upright. "No, it wasn't. I chose the name. It's who I am."

Jimmy chortled to himself. "Fair enough. I didn't ring to discuss monikers."

She was about to ask him who Monica was but thought better of it. There was a time and place. "Do you have news on Caesar?" she asked instead.

"Not exactly."

She got up from the bench and began the walk back to the Tube station. "What does that mean?"

"I've got news for ya, but not about the big man. I have Spitfire Creosote's location."

"Oh? I see."

"Aye. My source tells me he's in Hanoi. Working with some new underground organisation. From the sound of it he's going to be there a few days yet. Probably more. He's a sitting duck, so he is."

Acid didn't reply straight away. She got to the corner of Reede Road and Heathway and stopped. "I want Caesar."

"You want all of them, don't ya?"

She leaned against the wall of a newsagent and poked at an old Coke can with the toe of her boot. "Yeah, I do. But if I take him down, the rest will fall a lot easier. Kill the head and the body will die, sort of thing."

"Bullshit. You telling me you wouldn't jump at this chance if it was anyone else but him?"

She kicked the can into the road. "What the hell do you mean?"

"It's no secret to me, lassie. You and James Bland had a fling, didn't ya? A few years back?"

"A few years? Try twelve."

"Way I heard it, it was serious. Love, some might say."

"Fuck off."

Acid scoffed audibly at the suggestion, but for whose benefit she wasn't sure. Her mind drifted back over the years. Their first assignment together. Her first time in New York. It felt like a whole lifetime ago now. She was a different person back then. So was he. It was a whole other world.

"Hanoi is a long way. You sure it's him?"

The line went silent but for heavy breathing. She pictured The Dullahan, his malevolent stare stripping her of all humanity.

"It's him, all right," he said. "So I suggest you get yourself on the next flight over there and kill that poncey prick. Ya hear me?"

"Why do you care so much?"

"That fecker shot up my house. No one walks into my domain and starts his own war. I want him dead. Ya hear me? You kill Spitfire and I'll help you find the rest of them. If not, you're on your own."

Acid set off walking again, talking as she went. "Fine," she told him. "I'll do it."

"Good girl. I knew you hadn't gone soft like everyone said."

The words stung. But they were meant to. She composed herself before she replied. "Can you email me everything you've got from your source?"

"Already sent it a few seconds ago. A link to a secure site where you'll find all you need."

Acid reached Dagenham Heathway Tube station and stood under the concrete awning as rain began to fall. She looked out into the dreariness of East London. "Well I guess a few days in Hanoi won't hurt. Might be fun."

Jimmy laughed. "That's the Acid Vanilla I know. God speed and all that shite. I'll speak to ya once it's done."

Chapter Thirteen

Acid arrived back to the house an hour later and put her head around the door of the front room. It was empty. An atmosphere of dead air hung about the place. As though no souls had been here all day. She checked the kitchen. Same.

"Spook," she called out. "Are you in?"

Upstairs, she followed the landing around to Spook's room at the far end and laid her ear against the door. No sound. She eased open the door and peered around. The curtains were drawn and the last burst of afternoon sun shone through the thin orange material, casting the room in a warm glow.

Acid moved inside and perched on the edge of the unmade single bed. It was the first time she'd set foot in Spook's room since they'd taken on the lease. That was more than six months ago. The place smelt musty. Clothes and takeaway cartons littered the carpet. On the wall Spook had pinned up a selection of typical film posters. *Eternal Sunshine of the Spotless Mind*. *The Life Aquatic*. An enormous

Overwatch poster was tacked above the bed - a computer game, from what Acid could gather.

Under the window was a cheap desk, on top of which stood Spook's new Linux-running hard drive and two monitors. Acid walked over and ran her finger over the keyboard. The set-up was adequate, but they needed more. Having The Dullahan on-side would be a big help. Spook had found Davros, but it had been a fluke. The more time went by, the more chance Caesar had to strike back. He might be telling the world Acid Vanilla was dead but that didn't mean he wouldn't send his own operatives after her. You could only be a thorn in someone's side for so long. Eventually you had to take the initiative and slice the evil bastard in two.

She left Spook's room and retraced her steps back to her own bedroom. Although calling this stark space a bedroom was generous. A room with a bed was the most you'd get away with. But for Acid it was a self-imposed isolation chamber. A prison cell of contemplation and contrition. A crucible for her thoughts and plans of revenge. Most of her days and nights were spent here, sat at her leather-topped desk with the seven bullets in front of her. Set up perpendicular in a row, like tiny metal soldiers, steel totems of her rage. Seven shining tributes to her desire for retribution. She held them up to the light, ran them between her fingers. They helped sharpen her confused wrath into something more useable.

"Hey, it's me. You home?"

Spook's voice carried up the stairs and Acid moved over to the door. Her first instinct was to shut it. Bolt it. But she stopped herself. She was being unfair, she knew that. Ever since the two women had moved into the small rental property in St John's Wood, Acid had been particularly hostile and unsociable. But six months ago she'd been an assassin, a hired killer, answerable to no one but Caesar. It would take more time for her to adjust to this unfamiliar world of friendship and trust.

She heard footsteps on the stairs. A moment later Spook popped her head around the door. "So you are home?"

Sat on the edge of the bed, Acid unlaced and took off her boots. "I wouldn't call this home, would you?"

"You know what I mean."

Acid turned to see her. Spook's hair had grown long since they'd been here. Today she had it styled in two cute little plaits. She'd also gotten new glasses. They were large and blue, similar to the ones Acid had worn on the Cerberix job. She didn't mention them, but watched Spook glance around the box room and saw the place now from her perspective. It was a far cry from Acid's old place. No artwork hung from the walls. No ornaments or plants on any of the surfaces. There wasn't even a lamp. There wasn't even a light shade.

"Do you want anything to eat?" Spook asked.

Acid let out a long, deliberate sigh. The sort she'd been doing a lot recently. She couldn't help herself. It meant, *Leave me alone. Piss off.*

Spook ignored it. "Come on," she said. "It's not healthy being cooped up in here twenty-four-seven."

"Look, Spook, I'm busy," she said, moving over to the wardrobe. She swung the doors wide, revealing the seven bullets on the shelf. A reminder of her goal. A reminder of the single-minded focus she'd need to achieve it. To the detriment of all others. Her shoulders sagged. She turned to Spook. "Look, kid, I'm sorry I've been such a bitch. But you knew this was the deal. I've got a lot to work through."

"Yes. And I understand. But don't shut me out."

Spook's expression was a blend of worry and bewilderment, with more than a touch of care and concern bubbling under the surface. At least, that's what Acid assumed. Being gifted either of those emotions was a novel experience for her.

"Give me five minutes and I'll join you downstairs, okay? We'll get takeout. My treat."

Spook frowned, but slunk out the door. Acid waited until she heard footsteps on the stairs then turned her attention back to the wardrobe. Back to the shelf. To the bullets. She reached inside and picked up the bullet marked 'Spitfire'. She held it up between thumb and index finger, feeling the sharp point pressing into her flesh.

"I guess I'll see you in Hanoi," she whispered. She brought the bullet to her lips, kissed it gently and replaced it on the shelf. Finally she took hold of the bullet marked 'Davros' and laid it flat. Like one might do to a king in chess. Then she shut the wardrobe, and went downstairs.

Chapter Fourteen

Spook was watching Netflix on her laptop when Acid joined her in the front room, arriving via a brief detour of the kitchen to get herself a beer. One for Spook as well. A peace offering.

"Here you go." She shoved the beer at her. "What are you watching?"

Spook took the bottle from her, but not her eyes from the screen. "A documentary, about cults. It's pretty good."

Acid rolled her eyes. "I think I'll pass. I've had enough of cults to last a lifetime."

Spook looked at her. Closed the laptop. "Is that how you see it?"

"Maybe. Sort of. Doesn't matter, does it? I'm out. And soon they'll all be dead." She widened her eyes and grinned manically, making Spook look away.

"What do you do up there anyway, with those bullets?"

Acid picked at the label on her beer bottle. "Nothing much. I wait, mainly."

"Wait for what?"

"Not sure."

Spook didn't look any less perturbed. "Do you want to talk about Manchester?"

"Nothing to talk about. I did what I went there for. Davros is dead." She took a gulp of the beer. "Now I'm ready for the next one."

Despite the silence that followed, it was clear her house-mate had something else to say. More waiting. Acid sank back into the lumpy, uneven couch and looked around the room. At the drab furniture, the yellowing walls and curtains, the eighties fireplace. What the hell was she doing here? She swigged another mouthful of beer, letting it fizz on her tongue. The malty aroma penetrated her sinuses. She'd been taking it easy on the drink these last few months – an attempt to get her head and body fighting fit – but, boy, did it taste good. And it sure took the edge off living in this shithole.

"I was hoping you might have got it out of your system," Spook ventured at last. "The killing, I mean. This crazy revenge mission."

Acid sneered. Didn't look at Spook. She'd expected something like this from her, hence why she'd stayed up in her room for most of the last few weeks.

"Well, I haven't," she told her. "I'm only just starting. Why I came down actually. I've got something to tell you. I'm going to Hanoi tomorrow. For a week. Maybe longer."

"Hanoi? As in Vietnam?"

"No, Spook, Hanoi in South London. Do you know it?" She glared at her. "Yes. Vietnam."

"Why?"

"Why do you think? To continue my 'crazy revenge

mission.'" She eyeballed Spook until she looked away. "The guy who helped me up in Manchester, he's called The Dullahan, he rang me earlier with some intel. Spitfire Creosote is over there setting up something for Caesar."

"Spitfire," Spook repeated. "Isn't he the one who…"

"Yes."

Spook nodded.. "I see."

"Makes no difference to me."

"Is that so?" She sipped at her beer. "I wondered. After what happened in Berlin…"

"I told you, that was a stupid wobble and it won't happen again," she told her, speaking fast, the words clipped. "I thought you might have offered some support. Guess I was wrong."

Spook sat forward, her face melting into a simpering look of compassion. Acid rolled her eyes. *This kid.*

"I do support you, Sid. You know that. But I'm worried too. I still don't think you're back to your old self yet. I know I didn't know you back then, but after everything that's happened, maybe you aren't as capable as you once were." She held her hands up. "I'm not saying that's bad. You've found your heart. Your conscience, even. Don't knock it."

"Enough," Acid said. "And I don't know how many times I have to tell you. Don't call me Sid."

"Why don't you like it?" Spook asked. "I think it sounds cool."

"Cooler than Acid?"

"Well, no, but it's more accessible. What if I need to shout across a room, get your attention? Acid sounds a little weird, no?"

She leaned over. "What, weirder than Spook?"

"I could call you Alice."

"No. Don't start."

They drank in silence a few minutes. Both staring at the space in the far corner of the room where, if this was a proper home, a television might have stood.

"What about my idea?" Spook asked into the void. "I take it that's not going to happen now."

Acid puffed out her cheeks. Ah yes, Spook's idea. The Avenging Angels Agency. The kid hadn't shut up about it, ever since that night in the hotel when they'd made their little pact. A pact Acid was now regretting. Spook had agreed to help her find the seven if in return they set up... What would she call it? An underground vigilante agency? Spook's vision was to provide a service for outsiders who needed help. Those who the authorities had let down for whatever reason. Like her, when Acid found her. But this was Spook's dream, not hers. The more she thought about it, the more it sounded like the lamest idea in the world. Still, it kept Spook busy at least, and kept her off Acid's back. That was a good thing.

Acid sighed. Spook was still staring at her. The question about her idea wasn't rhetorical.

"One step at a time, kid."

Spook nodded, but in the most pointed and pathetic way anyone *could* nod.

"Oh, come off it," Acid said. "I didn't mean to be a cow. I'm still struggling with all this." She gestured around the room, at the two of them sat there in semi-domesticity. Lolling around watching documentaries, cooking, mugs of tea. It was all so alien to her. She took a long drink of the cold beer.

"You're not going to help me, are you?" Spook asked.

Acid sighed once more and closed her eyes. A little dramatic maybe, but with Spook she'd learned outward shows of emotion helped get the point across. And really, whether it was small interpersonal games like this, or life-threatening situations, extremes were just about all she knew.

"I'm not saying never, okay? But I have to get this out of my system first. It's all I can think about."

She looked across to Spook, whose head had dipped while she picked at the beer label with a worn thumb nail, her glasses slipped to halfway down her nose.

"Ask me again when the time is right. Okay?"

Spook huffed but didn't look up. "When will that be?"

"We'll know." Acid finished her beer and peeled herself off the couch to get another. It was going down well tonight.

"We'll need money," Spook said. "Eventually."

She stopped at the door. "I've got my bank account in the Caymans. No one can touch it. It'll last a good few years yet."

"Not if you're jetting around the world on this suicide mission."

Acid gripped the door frame. Focused on her breathing. "It's not a suicide mission."

Spook got up and faced her head on. "It's not going to bring your mum back, you know."

"Piss off," she said. "It's not about her."

"No? What is it about?"

She gripped the door frame tighter. Her fingernails scratched at the old paint. "Revenge. Justice. For myself as much as her."

Spook stepped towards her. "I don't think killing your ex-colleagues will help you find what you're looking for."

"Is that right? Okay then, Dr fucking Oz, what will help me?"

Spook shrugged. "You ask me, you need to make peace with the past." She spoke confidently, as if she'd rehearsed the speech. "Focus on the happy times you had with your mum. Remember her that way."

"What happy times?"

"There must have been some."

Acid hid her face around the side of the door for a second. Then she turned back to hit Spook with both barrels. "No. There wasn't. Not that I remember. Because do you know what happens when I focus on my mum? All I can think is I'm glad she's dead. Is that what you wanted me to say? The little nugget you've been trying to tease out of my psyche all these weeks? I'm glad she's dead. It makes everything so much fucking easier." She stopped herself, face an inch from Spook's. The young American swallowed but didn't look away. The kid was some kind of enigma – a lost child one minute, staring down an assassin the next. Vulnerable and strong at the same time. How was that even possible? "Look, I have to continue this mission, Spook. Because I don't want to have to deal with that yet. Do you understand what I'm saying?"

Spook nodded. "What if I come with you? To Hanoi?"

Acid placed her hand on her friend's shoulder as the energy in the room subsided. "Not this time. But thank you. I need to do this alone. Spitfire and me, we've got history." She smiled and leaned in. "Now, can you print out some information if I email it over? And I need a Visa. Can you sort it for me?"

Spook watched her a moment, eyes darting around Acid's face. Then she smiled, reluctant but genuine. "Yeah, sure. I'll do it now. Will take a few days, I expect. What's the name this time?"

Acid thought. "Let's go with Tanika Taylor. She's done well for me recently. Can you sort me a flight and hotel as well?"

Spook sighed. Long and loud. Her turn to be dramatic. "Acid Vanilla," she said. "I don't know what you'd do without me."

Chapter Fifteen

Ask any tour guide or travel operator and they'll tell you Hanoi is best visited in the springtime. Between February and April. This is the season when the air is warm but not too hot. From May onwards temperatures soar into the thirties and the dry season moves into the rainy season, making the summer months uncomfortable and moving around the city so much harder. Acid's plane touched down at Noi Bai International Airport on the first day of May. The start of rainy season. As the plane taxied along the runway, she couldn't help but think how typical that was.

This was her fourth time in Vietnam, but only her second time in Hanoi. It was curious to her that she would end up back here. She'd always thought the city to be relatively calm and peaceful, with no real criminal underbelly to speak of. Though from the information she'd received from Jimmy, it seemed that was all about to change. Spitfire Creosote was meeting with the heads of a new organisation. The Cai Moi. Not much was known about them, having only popped up on the radar six months ago. But if Caesar and Annihilation Pest Control were involved, it was a safe bet they were bad news. Jimmy's theory was they were gearing up to take over heroin and arms trafficking in the country. Probably with some people trafficking thrown in for good measure. In Acid's experience, these things came in threes.

Spook had booked a hotel on the edge of the Ba Dinh and Hoan Kiem region, one street away from Hanoi's famous 'train street'. Acid had only a light suitcase with her and had carried on, so once through passport control she headed for the taxi rank outside the airport and jumped in a Grab Cab (Hanoi's answer to Uber, but so much cheaper) and gave the driver a scrap of paper with the address written in Vietnamese.

The drive to Ba Dinh took around forty-five minutes, ample time for her to decompress after the long flight. She shut her eyes. Partly to avoid any awkward conversation with the driver, who she assumed spoke as little English as she did Vietnamese, but also it helped her think. Helped her focus her attention. She was here for one reason. To kill Spitfire Creosote. She sat with the idea. Made her peace with it. Connected with it until she felt it physically as much as mentally. She couldn't let unhelpful thoughts or emotions impede her mission. For the next few days her instincts would drive her. She let out a conscious breath – shifting into a well-worn guise, from human being to cold-blooded killer. The person she had to be to get the job done. Clinical and instinctive. An artisan of death. The way Caesar had trained her.

The Silk Path Hotel looked a decent enough place from the outside. It towered over the surrounding buildings in the area. The slabs of white stone and mock art deco styling stood majestic against the inky blue of the night sky.

"How much do I owe you?" Acid asked the driver, speaking slow and loud. As if that would make any difference.

The man twisted around and beamed a toothy grin. He nodded at Acid. "Please?"

She peeled off a 500,000 VND note and handed it over. That would more than cover it, she thought. From the look on the driver's face she was correct. She dragged her case from the back seat and climbed out of the cab. The air was close, humid. The pavements smelt of hot rain. She walked up the stone stairs leading up to the hotel and entered the air-conditioned foyer.

"Hello, how are you tonight?" a man asked, as she approached the reception desk. He stood to greet her but didn't seem to gain much height in doing so. He wore a dark grey suit with a yellow tie, and an enormous smile revealing a perfect set of ivory-white teeth.

"I'm good. Thank you," Acid replied. "A little jet-lagged, but nothing new."

The man – Sang, read his name-tag – bowed his head and chuckled politely. "And you have a reservation with us?"

"I do. I hope," she replied, scanning her eyes around the room as she spoke. "The name's Taylor. Tanika Taylor."

The reception hall was grand and festooned in the way many eastern cultures favour. Modern, but timeless. A few degrees on the wrong side of chic for most western tastes. Polished black marble covered the floor, and on the wall to the left of the reception area hung a gigantic painting. Wailing spectral females peered down from a blood-red background. In front of this, four glass chandeliers cascaded from the high ceiling.

"Here we are, Ms Taylor. For five nights," Sang said, looking up from his monitor and hitting her with another top-grade smile. "You're in room eleven. A suite. On the first floor. If you wait I shall get someone to assist you with your bags?"

She held up the small suitcase. "No, I'll manage. Thanks."

Sang looked troubled at this, but concurred. "No problem. The lift is behind you. Your room is at the end of the corridor." He slid a plastic key card over the counter. "I do hope you have a pleasant stay with us, Ms Taylor."

Acid picked up the key card and returned his smile with one of her own. "Me too. I'll be out and about, I imagine, most days. You have a late bar though, right?"

Sang closed his eyes, expression melting into an easy serenity. "But of course."

"Excellent. Thank you."

She wheeled her suitcase noisily across the marble and called the lift. The doors parted immediately, and in the short time it took to get to her floor, she adjusted her watch forward seven hours. That meant it was nearly midnight local time. She had a meeting set up with an old contact of Jimmy's, but not until lunchtime tomorrow. Still, five days - that should be time enough. The lift doors pinged open and she followed Sang's directions to the end of the short corridor. Room eleven.

The suite was unremarkable. Two spaces: bedroom and basic lounge with an open doorway linking them, and a decent-sized bathroom leading off from the bedroom. The décor was beige and brown, less flamboyant than the reception, but modern. Nice enough for what she required. Like she'd told Sang, she wasn't planning on being around much.

Once she'd taken off her boots and jacket, she walked through into the bathroom and positioned herself in front of the basin. She lifted her shirt over her head and leaned into the mirror, examining her face under the stark, unforgiving illumination offered by the halogen strip-light overhead.

"Jesus. What do you look like?"

She pulled at the skin under her eyes, at the dark shadows that had formed. She couldn't simply blame it on jet lag. Next she brought both hands to her cheeks, raising the skin and pulling it back from her face before releasing. She was worn out. More than she had been in a long time. It was nothing a week of sleep and a new diet and fitness regime wouldn't fix, but she didn't have that luxury. She was here to do a job.

Stripping naked, she stepped into the shower, enjoying the feeling of the hot water on her skin. She turned it up high. Unbearably so. Then all the way down. Ice cold. She stuck her head under the stream, forcing herself to remain there as long as possible. It gave her a headache, but she stuck it out until her entire head was numb, her body too. Then she turned the shower off and howled into the ceiling. It did the trick. For now.

Back in the bedroom she unzipped her case, selecting a new matching Gucci bra and pants set in embroidered black lace, and following these up with a crisp pair of black Levis. Finally, she removed a black t-shirt from the case and held it at arm's length, taking in the faded yellow text emblazoned over the chest:

Annihilation Pest Control. No job too big. No pest too tough.

She'd packed it by mistake, but couldn't help smiling to herself. The irony of it. The 'work shirts' had been Caesar's idea, a joke for his employees one Christmas time. She pulled it on over her head.

No pest too tough.

But now she was the pest. And she would make sure Caesar ate those words.

She finished the look with her leather jacket and picked up her key card. Her belly was empty and she needed a drink. Plus, it was pointless starting her search now. Tomorrow her mission would begin.

Chapter Sixteen

Acid took a left out of the hotel and headed down the long tree-lined boulevard, then a right into the Old Quarter. Hanoi was an old city, and the reminders of Chinese and French influence were everywhere. Especially here in the Old Quarter, with its colonial-style buildings and walkways. She passed by the famous 'train street' with its actual working train tracks running down the middle of the narrow street. Souvenir stalls and eating establishments bustled for position on both sides, encroaching onto the tracks in a way that meant anyone there when a train was due had to make a quick getaway or become bird food. Acid had never witnessed the spectacle herself, but she'd read about it. The heightened excitement and rigamarole as diners and café owners frantically dragged tables and chairs from the tracks. By all accounts it was a sight to behold, and one she hoped to experience whilst she was here. But not tonight. Tonight she required stasis, somewhere calm and quiet where she could get a late bite and some decent liquor.

Taking a left off the main strip, she walked along Tong Duy Tan, another long narrow street of cocktail bars and eating hatches, bistros and banh mi houses. She was about half-way down before the smells of spice and meat and herbaceous goods were too much for her. The next place along had a sandwich board outside that read, 'Best Grilled Chicken Banh Mi in Hanoi.' That would do.

There was no one else in the small bistro. Six small tables were spaced out around the room, with four chairs at each table. The walls were yellow and charcoal, adorned with dainty, hand-painted artworks and tasteful lighting. Along the side wall was a large shelving unit housing an extensive selection of earthenware pots and vases. A modern, wrought-iron chandelier hung above the main space.

Acid walked up to the counter and leaned over, reading the menu lying flat on the counter top. A moment later, a small woman appeared from the kitchen beyond. She was a few years older than middle-aged, with short-cropped hair that framed a round face. Her build was slight but she looked tough. She stared with large, unblinking eyes and a scornful expression that remained when she smiled.

"Hello," she said. "How are you this evening?"

The greeting shocked Acid somewhat. The woman was a local, Vietnamese at least, but her English was perfect. Even down to her accent. It was unusual for this area.

"I'm good. Thank you," Acid told her. "Hungry." She continued to peruse the menu. It was a large one-sided sheet of paper with laminate peeling away at the corners. Most of the writing was in Vietnamese, but there were pictures as well. "What do you recommend?"

The woman shrugged. "Pho is always good for western taste. You like soup?"

"The sign outside, banh mi. The best in Hanoi, you say?"

"Sure is." The woman grinned, her face relaxing some more. "The best banh mi in all of Vietnam. Grilled chicken, spices, pickles. It's very nice."

Acid looked over the woman's shoulder at the large fridge behind her. She skimmed down past the rows of bottled water. Past the Cokes and Vietnamese sodas. And there on the bottom shelf: a row of beer bottles. "I'll have a banh mi and two bottles of Saigon. Thank you."

The woman pulled a face but said nothing. Acid shoved a note over the counter and took a seat at the far end of the room, facing the counter. She took out her phone from her inside pocket and opened up her Dropbox, clicked on the files that Jimmy had sent over.

There wasn't much to go off. Spitfire was here as Caesar's envoy, that much was certain. He was meeting with these Cai Moi people to facilitate some sort of deal. But what that entailed was uncertain. Jimmy thought maybe Caesar was supplying them with guns, but it was just a theory. The only other certainty was Spitfire was in town for seven days. She ran the numbers in her head. He'd arrived three days ago. With tonight already a no-go it meant she had four days left to find him. Not long.

"Here you go, dear." The woman appeared at Acid's table, breaking her concentration. She slipped a tray in front of her comprising the banh mi and a small side salad. Moist, blackened chicken burst out from a large steaming roll. It smelt amazing. After a day of eating nothing but airline peanuts, it was everything Acid wanted.

"Thank you," she said, with a smile. "Your English is very good."

The woman shrugged, but with a certain flourish now.

Playing it up. "I lived in Australia for seven years when I was younger. It does me well."

"I bet. Well, thank you for this. It looks amazing."

The woman shuffled off behind the counter and Acid greedily tucked in, ripping a massive chunk of sandwich off and chewing it hard. The meat was salty and tasty, a subtle heat of spice, mixed with the fragrance of coriander and pickled vegetables. She swallowed it down with a mouthful of beer. It wasn't as cold as she'd have liked, but it was malty and gassy and tasted good.

Acid ate staring in front of her, in a low-level trance. She finished the tasty banh mi and slurped down the two beers, was done in under a few minutes. It was after midnight in Hanoi, but early evening in her head. Sleep was a way off, but that wasn't anything new. She sensed the manic, chaotic energy bubbling away under the surface of her consciousness. The bats. Ready to rise up and spur her on when the time was right.

She drained the last of the beers and carried the tray up to the counter. The woman appeared from out back as Acid drew close.

"All done?"

"Yes, it was lovely." She slid the tray over to her. "I'm sure I'll be back again."

"Good to hear. You on holiday?"

"Not entirely. Work."

"Oh, I see. Well, come back anytime. I always give discounts to good customers. My name is Tam. Tam Quan. This is my place."

Acid smiled. Nodded. "Nice to meet you, Tam. I'm... erm... Call me Sid."

"Sid. Okay. Well, you come back anytime, Sid."

Acid felt the door open behind her, a cool jet of air

flowing into the warm café. At the same time, the smile on Tam's cheery face wilted into a worried frown and all vigour drained out of her in one fell swoop. Acid twisted around, following Tam's gaze to the two young men letting the door swing shut behind them.

"What is it?" Acid asked, but Tam carried on staring at the two men. When she looked back and smiled, it was with eyes open as wide as they'd go.

"It's fine. Nothing." She spoke hurriedly, as though trying to get rid of her. "Please come again, and enjoy your visit to Hanoi. Now if you excuse me, I need to deal with these customers. Thank you."

Acid narrowed her eyes. She knew fear, and this woman was terrified. She remained where she was, leaning with her back to the counter and watching the two men approach. Something about the way they walked through the small café made her uneasy. Prowled would be a better way of describing it. They wore matching black hoodies, with a white 'O' motif on the front. If Acid were to guess, she'd say they were in their early twenties, at the most. To complement their matching outfits, they both had shaved heads and thin pencil moustaches sitting above hackneyed sneers. They got to the counter and fixed Tam with a chilling stare. One of them barked something at her in Vietnamese. Acid had little knowledge of the language, but she picked out the word *tien* – money. She glanced from Tam to the men. Tam shook her head solemnly, looked at the ground.

One of the men turned and leered at Acid. "Who are you?" he asked, with a thick accent.

She shrugged. "I'm no one, sweetie. Was just having a bite to eat."

The man's left eye twitched. "Well, now it's time to

leave. We are closed." He pointed at Tam. "Tell her we are closed."

Acid stepped back. Held her hands up. "Listen, pal, I don't want any trouble. You okay, Tam?"

The woman glanced at her, then back to the men. She nodded. "Yes, I'm fine. I'm afraid you need to leave, please. We have business to take care of. But it's no problem. Everything is fine."

Acid raised her chin. "Are you certain about that?"

"Yes. Please. Everything is fine."

Acid stared at Tam, then at the men. Then she slowly backed away. As she did, one of them lurched forward, snarling at her like a rabid dog. It made her jump, which pissed her off, but she put it down to the jet lag. Frayed nerves. Her reaction elicited an explosion of nasty, taunting laughter from the men.

She froze, hitting them both with her trusty thousand-yard stare. The laughing stopped, but they weren't backing down. One of them stepped towards her.

"What do you want, bitch?" he asked. "A photograph?"

She didn't reply. This wasn't her fight, she told herself. She was here to find Spitfire, that was it. She held his gaze for a few more seconds, then turned and walked away. Whatever was going on here, it would only end badly and she couldn't risk getting involved. She had limited time. Limited resources. Besides, this was probably a family dispute. Something and nothing. As she got to the door, she looked over to see Tam being led into the back room by the two men. She waited a moment, then opened the door and left.

Chapter Seventeen

A few minutes earlier and ten doors down, Vinh Gia Phan had been shutting up shop for the day. He said goodbye to the last of his students (the intermediate class tonight, they'd done well) and shut the front door. His plan now was to do some marking then head off home to bed. Vinh hadn't been sleeping well at all lately. Not since Huy disappeared. Not since their row. He gathered up a large cardboard file, full of test papers, and moved through into the small window-less office at the back of the school.

Vinh's English language school was now in its sixth year, and although the days were long and the money not so great, he enjoyed his work. Plus the school was a testament to how far he'd come. With further to go, of course, but having the school helped. It had given him purpose again, after the accident. Enough that he now got out of bed each day. Over the years, his students had grown in both number and ability. Some of those studying with him since the early days were now fluent, and many of his students had landed good jobs off the back of his teaching. That was a good feeling, knowing he'd helped people better themselves. Even if he had no one to share it with.

He lowered himself into the old wooden chair and scraped it under the desk. Next he slid open the top drawer and removed the bottle of whisky he kept there, along with a single cut-glass tumbler. Vinh was managing his drinking better recently, but this, the first drink after a busy day, had always been one of pure enjoyment (rather than those taken steadily until the early hours which were more of a crutch, a way to get to sleep), and after a long day he deserved it.

He placed the tumbler down alongside the test papers. One drink, he told himself, that was all. He pulled the stopper from the whisky, delighting a little as the cork clung to the neck of the bottle and made a satisfying *pop* on release. His eyes closed as the heady aromas filled the room. It was hot and airless in the office, the tropical heat of summer already in full effect. Not for the first time, Vinh pondered how quickly the seasons came around each year. There'd been ten summers since the accident. Ten summers and a whole lot of whisky bottles.

After pouring himself a decent measure, he replaced the stopper and returned the bottle to the drawer. He took a long drink, letting the harsh liquor play on his tongue before swallowing. His gaze drifted over the table, settling on the collection of photo frames on the far corner. They were the sort of adornments that had existed for so long they'd become invisible. One photo in particular caught his eye now. He lifted it from its home and held it to the light. The photo showed Vinh with two of his students, taken after their first English exam a few years earlier. They were all so happy that day – the boys, two of his best students, having passed their exams with top marks. Afterwards they went for food and cold beer and talked long into the night. Vinh remembered it as one of the first nights he'd enjoyed in many years.

He traced his finger down the face of the boy on the left of the photo.

"I am sorry," he whispered. "I have been slow and self-indulgent. But I promise, I will not fail you."

He turned the frame over and released the clasps before slipping out the photo and studying it again. It was true, he'd let his own fears and inadequacies get in the way. But no longer. He'd made a promise and it was time to step up. Besides, the school was now closed for a week. The summer holidays. He had the time, and no excuse.

He folded the photo and stuffed it in his pocket. The marking could wait. He finished the whisky and was about to switch off the lights when he heard the front door swing open.

"I am sorry. We are closed for the day," he called out. No answer. He stepped out into the main space. "I said we are—"

The sight of the two young men in the doorway stopped him in his tracks. They wore black hooded sweatshirts with the hoods covering their faces, but Vinh knew immediately who they were, and what they wanted.

"You can't do this." He spoke angrily in Vietnamese. "We are good people. We pay our taxes to the government. This is not right."

The two men looked at each other before sauntering over to him. "The government doesn't deserve your money," one of them told him coming, close enough that Vinh backed up into the office. "You pay us. You have a good life. Good business."

"And if I don't?"

The men sneered. "Then you have a bad life. Bad business. This is a simple choice for you. Don't make the wrong one."

Vinh edged across the room. "Who says the government doesn't deserve it?"

"The Cai Moi say so."

"And who are they? I hear a lot about them. I see your street rats. But where are your leaders? Where can I find them?"

The men looked at each other. "They are everywhere. The Cai Moi is The One."

Vinh frowned. He hated this cryptic bullshit. "Okay, and who is 'The One'?"

"We are The One," the men shouted in unison. "The One is the Cai Moi. The Cai Moi is The One. Now, pay us your dues as arranged."

"As arranged?" Vinh sighed. "I arranged nothing, you stupid punks." The men stepped closer and clenched their fists. They weren't here to play games. Or explain themselves. "All right, all right, fine. I'll pay."

He moved over to a tall cupboard at the side of the room and took his time reaching for the key lying on top.

"Hurry up, old man," one of the street rats said. "We haven't got all day."

Vinh tensed but let the *old man* comment go. "Before I pay you," he said, turning back around. "I'm looking for someone. A friend's son. My student." He pulled the photo from his pocket and shoved it at them. "Have you seen this man?"

The men fell silent as they took in the photo. Underneath the hoods, their faces drop.

"What are you talking about?" one of them yelled. "What is this?"

"Just a question," Vinh replied. His heart was playing a

fast rhythm against his ribs. "He's gone missing, and I heard rumours he upset someone. The Cai Moi, perhaps. I'm asking you if you've seen him."

"No!" the men roared, speaking as one. "We have not. We are here to collect. Not to answer questions."

Vinh turned back to the cupboard. He'd known it was useless. He clicked open the latch and eased the doors open. In front of him was a bag of money, his week's takings. Next to this on the shelf was a small marble ashtray. He glanced behind him. The street rats stood a foot away. But if he moved to one side, he could obscure their vision. He did so and reached for the ashtray, felt the cold weight of it in his hand. It was heavy. Heavy enough to do some damage. But what then? Did he want to go to war with these people? Would it help find Huy? He was wrestling with himself when he felt a tug on the back of his shirt.

"Don't be stupid, old man."

Vinh released the ashtray. "What?" he spluttered. "I was getting you the money."

As he turned around, one of the street rats slapped him across the face.

"Fool. You don't want to make an enemy of The One."

Vinh held his face. His cheek stung. The fact it was an open-handed slap and not a fist stung just as much. He backed away as the street rats hustled in front of the cupboard and grabbed the bag of money. One of them pulled out a roll of notes and counted out eight million dong.

"There we go. Not so hard is it. Six million for your levy and two million as punishment. For disrespecting us."

Vinh looked down as the two men sauntered towards the exit.

"Don't make this mistake again. Do you understand?"

He didn't answer.

"Do you understand?"

"Yes!" he yelled. "Yes, I fucking understand."

With tears welling in his eyes, he strode over to the men and grabbed hold of his door, pushing them outside as he forced it closed. It was an imprudent act. He knew that. Borne out of frustration and anger. With himself as much as the street rats. The men (more like boys, he realised now) pressed their faces against the glass and went cross-eyed at him. Vinh sighed.

Not today. Not like this.

He locked the door and watched the street rats through the glass as they waved and blew kisses. Then he shuffled back into his office and poured himself another large drink.

Chapter Eighteen

Acid Vanilla was out the door of the bistro and a hundred metres down the street when she stopped in her tracks.

Damn it.

She'd been battling herself ever since seeing Tam steered into the back room of her bistro.

"Come on, Acid. You haven't got time for this."

She closed her eyes. Her head was telling her one thing – to leave well enough alone, to walk away – yet a stronger part of her, that fluttering pressure she often felt in her chest, told a different story. Her manic, bipolar energy could easily get her into dangerous situations. Yet in her profession, harnessed the right way, it could be viewed as a superpower. It drove her. Helped her stay awake for long periods. Had her take big risks that often paid off. Inspired creative thinking. So when the bats called, she listened.

And right now they were saying, *Turn around.*

They were saying, *Help that woman.*

Acid stared at her hands already balled into fists. The sinews were taut and ready, the knuckles white. She took a deep breath and looked up at the sky. Then she turned around and marched back to the café.

The dining area was empty as Acid slipped through the door and eased it shut behind her. She padded over to the counter and strained her head to see into the back room. Long blue ribbons of material hung down over the door, blowing in a gentle breeze. Beyond them a small kitchen. A thick chopping board sat on a wooden counter top, with a bunch of spring onions scattered on top. Acid looked for the meat cleaver or kitchen knife she hoped would be there, but she couldn't see one. She moved over to the doorway and pressed herself against the wall. From there she could see further into the back rooms. The kitchen was only a few square metres, but it opened out into another room with a large chest freezer along one wall. The owner, Tam, was sitting on a spindly wooden chair in the middle of the room with the two men looming over her. They spoke fast, in Vietnamese, but their tone was clear. Their body language too.

Acid scanned the area. Under the counter by the cash register she saw a plastic tray of metal cutlery, forks, spoons, along with chopsticks and napkins. Side-stepping over, she silently picked up a fork before returning to her vantage point by the entrance to the kitchen. She pressed the end of the fork down against the doorframe, bending the handle up and over in a right angle. Once done, she held it in her hand with the handle gripped inside her fist and the sharp tines jutting out under her thumb. Not bad. It would do some damage. She pumped her fist, familiarising herself with the makeshift weapon.

Shouts came from the other room. Peering around the doorframe, Acid watched as one of the men raised his hand and brought it down hard across Tam's face. Memories flooded back. A cold, silent rage rose in her chest. But it felt good. It felt like home.

She slipped through the blue ribbon curtain and into the kitchen, sneaking around the sink unit and along the back wall. The room where the men were holding Tam was a few feet away, but they had their backs to her. She moved like a ghost, the metal fork clasped in her fist, ready to strike. She was nearly on them when Tam looked up and her eyes widened. Acid made to shush her but it was too late, she'd already let out a small yelp of surprise. The two men turned and stared at her for what felt like forever. Bodies frozen in time. Brains not yet caught up with what they were seeing.

Then they snapped back to life and pounced.

Acid blocked the first man's punch and jabbed him hard in the side, breaking fesh with the fork spears. He yelled out and clutched his side as his crony parried with a roundhouse kick. She leaned back in time, the air rushing past her face. The man came down from the kick as she stepped around him. She administered a sharp elbow to the nape of his neck and he went down. A boot to the face finished him off. The force of the kick smashed the back of his head into the wall and knocked him out.

She spun around to find the first man advancing on her. He'd found a large meat cleaver and was brandishing it over his head ready to bury it in her skull. Dropping the fork she grabbed up the chopping block, shielding herself as the man swung wildly. The speed and frenzy of the attack took her by surprise but she parried his movements with the thick wooden board and was able to land a push-kick in his stomach. It sent him flying back into a shelf of pots and she could ground herself. She glanced back over her shoulder, at Tam cowering in the corner next to the chest freezer. Their eyes met. Acid looked at the freezer. Then back at Tam. The woman nodded, she understood.

Across the other side of the kitchen, the man had steadied himself and was bracing for another onslaught. He held the cleaver over his head and rocked his weight onto his back foot. As he launched himself towards her, Acid stepped back. She held the chopping block up until the last second and then spun it away from him like a matador dummying a crazed bull. The swiftness of the action caught the man off guard. He tried to correct himself but the momentum of his strike meant he was on a trajectory he couldn't pull out of. As he stumbled forward, she grabbed hold of him from behind and ran him forward.

"Now!" she yelled.

With an alacrity belying her calm demeanour, Tam yanked up the lid of the freezer so Acid could fling the man over the side. He fell hard onto piles of frozen vegetables and cuts of meat but managed to grab the lip of the freezer to keep himself upright. He still had hold of the sharp cleaver. He flailed it at Acid but she swerved out the way and wrapped her arm tightly around his forearm. Getting below his elbow to minimise his range of motion, she brought her fist to her chest, locking his arm under her armpit and applying upward pressure on his wrist. The man gnashed his teeth and dropped the cleaver. The second it hit the ground, she spun around, smashing a sharp elbow into in his face. The cartilage in his nose crumpled on impact. Then still holding his wrists, she dropped to one knee, forcing his elbow joint against the side of the fridge and snapping his arm with a loud crack. The man screamed out in pain as she brought the freezer lid down on his skull and shoved him into the freezing depths of the cabinet.

She slammed the lid shut.

A moment passed.

Stillness.

Acid rubbed a hand across her nose. Checked her lips for blood. She looked over at Tam.

"Are you all right?"

Tam staggered over to a mis-shaped plastic chair in the far corner of the room and lowered herself onto it. She was shaking. A nasty bruise had already formed under her left eye.

Acid was about to go over to her when she heard a scrabbling sound coming from the kitchen. Still panting for air, she picked up the meat cleaver and waited. A second later, the first of the attackers put his head around the corner. His face was bloody and swollen, his shirt ripped down one side. Three deep lacerations poured with blood, where the fork had torn at his flesh.

He looked at Tam. Then at Acid. Then at the large meat cleaver. Acid kept her eyes solely on him. The bravado had left him and he was no longer a threat, but she wasn't taking any chances. She gripped the handle of the cleaver. An excuse. That's all she needed.

"In there," she said, motioning to the freezer. "Get him out and piss off."

The man shuffled over and peered through the glass lid at his fallen accomplice. "Is he dead?" he asked.

"No. But that can still change. Get a move on."

He eased the freezer top open and leaned in. His friend was regaining consciousness, and despite his broken arm managed to clamber out with help. Once on his feet, he grimaced at Acid. "Who the fuck are you, anyway?"

"You don't need to know who I am," she replied. She looked at the door. "Best thing you can do, boys, is get lost. You understand?"

The men didn't move. Acid held the meat cleaver up to them.

"Do you understand?"

At last the men nodded and shuffled out of the room. But as they were leaving, another man appeared at the door to the dining room. Acid tensed, ready for another pass. This man was older than the first two, but more angry. He shouted something in Vietnamese as the two youngsters scurried past, then watched them leave, an expression of pure hate twisting up his face. Once satisfied the men had left the premises, he rushed over and knelt at Tam's feet. He held her hand as they spoke, fast and breathless. The woman shook her head, waved her arms. She gestured at the freezer. At Acid. Then she put her face in her hands and let out a soft wail.

Chapter Nineteen

Acid lay the meat cleaver on top of the freezer as the man got to his feet and walked over to her. He was about five-six, the same height as she was in her heavy-soled boots. But older, late-forties perhaps, maybe more. He wore a crumpled linen shirt and crumpled beige chinos. A crumpled expression too. Although he wasn't bad looking. His eyes sparkled with intelligence and also suspicion. Fair enough, she thought, he *should* be suspicious.

He squinted at her, sizing her up. "Tam tells me you helped tonight. Thank you."

"Not a problem," she said. "I was passing by."

The man frowned. "Is that so? My name is Vinh. I work a few doors down. Those punks paid me a visit earlier. I saw them come this way."

He held out his hand. Acid took it. It was rough, calloused.

"Name's Sid," she told him. It still sounded stupid. She gestured to Tam, sat quivering in the chair. "Did she make me sound heroic?"

The man allowed her a half-smile. "Who are you?" he asked. "I don't think many tourists could inflict so much damage."

"Who am I? That seems to be the million-dollar question tonight. Like I said, I'm Sid. I'm no one. Just a passer-by."

Vinh raised his hand. "Fine. Have it your way."

"Who were those guys?" she asked. "What did they want?"

Vinh went to speak, then held up one finger. He spoke to Tam softly in Vietnamese. Then back to Acid, he said, "I tell you what. Let me help Tam up to her apartment, and then I'll buy you a drink. We can talk some more."

Acid frowned. "Not sure."

"Come, come," Vinh went on. "A proper drink. I know a good place. It is quiet, dark, has good whisky."

She twisted her face, now only playing the role of uncertainty. He had her at good whisky. Hell, he had her at quiet and dark.

"Fine," she said. "But only the one. I have a busy few days in front of me."

"No problem. One drink."

"Well," Acid said. "Maybe two."

———

TWENTY MINUTES later they arrived at what Vinh explained was the perfect place to talk 'away from prying ears'. Erol's Place was a short walk from Tam's bistro, across the main strip and down along a snaking side street. From the outside it was an innocuous wooden door, standing between an internet café and a mini-mart now closed for the evening. No sign above the door, no sandwich board inviting people inside. It was the type of establishment you'd never know was there unless you had prior knowledge. But those were the best types of drinking den, in Acid's opinion.

She settled her weary body down at a table a few feet from the bar whilst Vinh went up to get drinks, and scoped the place out as she waited. Vinh was correct about it being dark. The venue had no windows at all. The only light came from three dim bulbs hanging from the ceiling on long, winding cords. Tables comprised four upturned crates spaced out around the twenty-by-twenty-foot room. Small stools stood around each crate and along the far wall spanned a row of plastic chairs in all colours, the type children might sit at. It was unclear whether the décor and layout was a product of design or destitution. Maybe a little of both.

Acid turned her attention back to take in Vinh, who was now being served. As she watched, he pulled something from out of his shirt pocket and showed it to the barman. She squinted through the gloomy atmosphere. It looked to be a photo. The barman took a decent look, lingering long enough to show willing, but shook his head. With sagging shoulders, Vinh retrieved the photo and stuffed it back in his pocket. Then he gathered up the drinks.

"You like this bar?" he asked, as he joined her at their crate.

"Sure," she said. "My sort of dive."

He placed two large measures of amber liquid down in front of her. "Vietnamese whisky," he said. "An acquired taste perhaps, but one worth acquiring."

He settled himself on his stool and held a glass up to her. She did the same, giving him a wink. They drank in unison, Vinh taking a decent enough mouthful and Acid gulping back most of hers. The whisky was sharp and had a fragrant smokiness to it, which was unusual but not unpleasant.

Vinh sat back with a satisfied sigh and looked about the place. Acid followed his gaze.

"So, Sid, let me thank you again for helping out my friend. She has not been well recently and those men are most unwelcome."

"Who were they?" she asked, placing her drink down and leaning in.

"Those idiots tonight were nothing. Kids. *Chuot duong* – street rats. But who they work for, who they collect money for, that's a different matter."

The man's eyes sparked with intensity as he spoke. Acid let him go on rather than reply.

"For a long time Hanoi was a peaceful city. Sure, we had dangerous elements, like in any city. But no organised crime. Nothing like in Bangkok or Ho Chi Minh City. But then, six months ago, the visits started. Young men, kids, like those sewer rats tonight. They said they worked for a new organisation. The Cai Moi. It means 'new breed' in Vietnamese. Most people here assumed it was simply a protection racket. We pay them so they don't hurt us, or our businesses. No one liked it, but what could we do? Recently, however, it has gotten worse. People have been going missing. Local drug dealers mainly. Pimps too. No one you'd miss. But their bodies turn up mutilated in the most horrible ways imaginable. Word is the Cai Moi are clearing the way for their own operations. Preparing themselves to take over the city. It is a scary time."

Acid straightened. The Cai Moi. The people Spitfire was meeting with. "And you know nothing about them? Where they came from?"

Vinh shook his head. "They appeared one day. As if from nowhere. Infecting our city like a disease."

He took a long drink. Sniffed.

"I take it the police are no use?" she asked, already knowing the answer.

He grumbled noisily. "They're too scared or too lazy. Or they're being paid off to keep out of it. Probably all three. The police in Hanoi have never worked for the people."

She waited a moment, then asked what she'd been waiting to ask since he returned from the bar. "What's with the photo?"

Vinh sat up. "You saw that?" He pulled the picture from his shirt pocket and unfolded it before handing it to her.

"Thanks."

She held it up to the light. The photo showed Vinh with his arms around two young men aged around twenty years old. The younger men were both holding some sort of certificate and all three were beaming proudly into the camera.

Vinh reached over and pointed to the man on the left.

"This one, Huy, he is Tam's son. No one has seen him for a long time. This is why it is so hard for her. Why she does not need the extra worry."

"He's missing?" Acid asked.

"Yes. For nearly six months now. He was a good kid. And a superb student. I teach English and he studied with me. But then one day, I found him on a corner selling drugs. Marijuana, a bit of cocaine. This is not good. I told him he had to stop and I thought he'd listened. But then," Vinh looked down, embarrassed, "things turned sour. We had a row. Tam and I, and Huy. Words were said. Soon after, he disappeared."

Acid finished her whisky. "How old is he?"

Vinh sighed. "This is the problem. He has recently turned twenty-one. So, no one can help. He is a man now, so they say he is responsible. But I know something is wrong. He would not up and leave without telling his mother."

"And you think the Cai Moi have something to do with it?"

The low lighting cast deep shadows over Vinh's face as his expression shifted. "Yes. I do. I spoke with some local pedlars. They told me the Cai Moi found Huy selling drugs and took him away. As I say, a lot of drug dealers have turned up dead. I am worried the same has happened to him. But we have not found a body." He finished his own drink. "I haven't told Tam any of this."

Acid considered it. Then she picked up the glasses. "Same again?"

He looked at his watch as though fighting with himself. Then he waved his hands, as if to say, *Why not?*

At the bar she laid the glasses and some notes on the counter, pointing to an exotic-looking bottle of whisky on the shelf. The gruff barman nodded and filled up the glasses, free-pouring until a meniscus of liquid bulged out over the rims. She leaned down and slurped the top off both, then carried the drinks back to the table.

"Do you know where these Cai Moi people hang out?" she asked, sitting down.

Vinh took the drink from her. "You don't want to know. They are dangerous people."

"Okay. Granted. But what if I do want to know?"

A curious smile touched the edges of his mouth. "I thought you were just a passer-by?"

She chewed the inside of her cheek. "All right, maybe I'm not just a passer-by."

"No shit. A passer-by who can beat the hell out of two

tough-guy street rats. Who looks like some punk-rock movie-star. And those eyes. I can't stop staring at them. Who are you, Sid?"

She flicked him a look. "All right, calm it down. And my name isn't Sid, okay? It's Acid. Acid Vanilla. I'm in Hanoi looking for someone. A man called Spitfire Creosote."

Vinh stared at her through a confused frown. "Acid Vanilla? Spitfire Creosote? Come on, you're messing with me, right?"

She leaned forward, speaking softly. "No, I'm not. They're codenames. Sort of. It's a long story. So I take it you've not seen him? Tall guy, blond hair, a look of Daniel Craig. Some say. Though not me. But I suppose he is handsome." She looked away. Looked down. Then back at Vinh. "So that's a no then?"

He curled up his mouth. "I am sorry. I have seen no one fitting that description. What has he got to do with the Cai Moi?"

She took a sip of the whisky. It was going down incredibly well after the first one. "Not sure. I know he's in Hanoi setting something up for our boss – *his* boss – but what, I'm not sure. What's the Cai Moi's end goal?"

"No one knows."

"I was guessing guns. Maybe drugs, if they're taking out all their rivals. I'm meeting a contact tomorrow who might tell me more."

"Jesus." Vinh sat back on his stool. "Who the hell are you, Acid Vanilla? What's the story here?"

Acid looked him dead in the eyes and blew out her cheeks. "You actually want to know?"

He held up his glass. "I've got nowhere to be."

So, buoyed by the warmth of the whisky and the strangely soothing presence of this man she'd known for less than two hours yet sensed she could trust, she told him. About how she came to be working for Beowulf Caesar at Annihilation Pest Control, arguably the best assassin network in the world. She told him about meeting Spook, and how sparing her had put a price on her own head. To the point she'd had to go underground, killing four of her colleagues. As her story went on, Vinh engaged her with empathetic nods, upping the ante with concerned grunts as she got to the part about her mother and how Caesar had murdered her along with the entire old people's home where she'd lived. Finally, she told him about the seven bullets on the shelf back in London – her kill list – and her bloody mission to eradicate the whole of Annihilation Pest Control. Caesar included.

When she'd finished, Acid leaned back in her seat and waited for Vinh's response. She'd never told anyone that story before. Not a civilian, at least. Spook was the only person in the world who knew the whole sorry tale, and she was no longer a civilian. What she was, Acid was still unsure. Although with both dismay and surprise, she found herself smiling at the thought of her. She'd ring in the morning as soon as she woke up. Put the kid's mind at ease.

"That is a crazy-ass story, Acid Vanilla. I'm sorry about your mother." Vinh gestured at her t-shirt. "This is the organisation? Annihilation Pest Control?"

Acid looked down at the logo and twisted her mouth to one side. "Yeah, it's an old shirt. Stupid, really. I packed it by mistake."

He smiled, but he was thinking. Thinking hard, by the looks of it. He leaned forward. "It sounds to me like we might help one another out. What do you say? You help me find Tam's boy and I'll help you find this Spitfire person. I have expert local knowledge. I can be of excellent use to you."

Acid tensed. She wasn't expecting this. She looked at the table, busied herself by running her finger around the rim of her glass.

"No. Sorry. I have to do this alone," she told him. "I can't risk you getting hurt. You don't know who you're dealing with."

He scoffed. Looked at the ceiling.

"I'm serious," she went on.

"Serious about dying, it sounds like."

"Maybe. Problem is, it never seems likely in the moment." She pouted her lips, thinking. "But no, sorry, I can't. I've had too many people die around me. I can't be responsible for anyone else."

"You would not be responsible," he pleaded with her. "Please, I know the dangers but I need to do this. For myself as much as Tam. Huy and me, we are close. We were."

Acid sniffed. Was there something he wasn't saying? "Why are you so bothered?" she asked him. "I get that he was your student. But if this Cai Moi are as dangerous as you say, this could be a suicide mission. You want to risk your life for this kid?"

Vinh fell quiet. His turn to stare into his glass. When he spoke next his voice was quiet and hoarse with emotion. "I want to help because I know how it feels to lose a son," he said, without looking up. "It is ten years since my son died. Ten years and it feels like only yesterday."

Acid didn't know what to say. "Shit. That's terrible," was all she had.

"He was only a small boy," Vinh went on. "Six years old. He had so much life in him. It wasn't fair." He peered up at the ceiling. An attempt perhaps to compose himself, but it was pointless. He looked back at her with tears in his eyes. "After he died, I fell apart. As did my marriage. I'll never get over losing him. I know that. And why should I? A father shouldn't get over something like that. But every day I'm learning to cope a little better, and I suppose this is another coping strategy for me. I want to find Huy so Tam can at least put her own pain to bed. The not knowing is killing her."

Acid sipped at her drink. Truth was she could do with Vinh's help. His familiarity with the area, at least.

She smiled as he raised his eyes to meet hers. "I'm sorry," she told him. And she was. But the words felt false to her. Spook liked to inform her often of her inadequacies with outward displays of empathy and compassion, but she liked to think she was getting better.

"You've been looking for Huy all this time and not found anything?" she asked.

Vinh shook his head sadly. "I've not looked hard enough. When I found out the Cai Moi may have been involved, I panicked." He chewed at his lip. "I've been such a useless fool. I should have upped my search, but I let fear hold me back. I decided tonight, when those street rats came to my school, I would not let them make me a coward any longer. So, please, let me work with you. We can help each other. You never know, I might surprise you."

Acid sat upright and rolled back her shoulders. "Sorry, Vinh, I can't risk it. Plus, I'm only here for five days. You'll slow me down. If I find anything out about Huy, I'll let you know. But I have to do this alone."

"Fine. I understand." He narrowed his eyes, and for a second Acid saw something familiar. He had genuine pain eating away at him, she'd seen that earlier, but this was something else. It was rage. Quiet, white-hot, seething rage.

Then, as quickly as it appeared, it faded away, replaced by an expression of blank composure. "What will you do to find this man Spitfire?"

Acid yawned. "My meeting tomorrow is with a local arms dealer. Over by the Red River. I'm hoping he might give me some pointers."

Vinh nodded slowly. "The Red River. I see. Do you know Hanoi well?"

"Not that well. But I'll find it."

"Why not let me take you there?" he suggested. She opened her mouth to protest but he held a hand up to her. "I understand. You do not want my help. But this is me guiding you around my city, the local's way. I swear I will not get in the way."

"Jesus, Vinh, you don't let up, do you?" She smiled, not entirely sure it was convincing but it was the best she could manage. "Fine. I guess it'll be good to have a local with me. But you keep your head down. Understand? I'll do the talking."

Vinh nodded, the twinkle returning to his watery eyes. "I understand, thank you. You won't regret it."

"I already am, sweetie. But enough of this talk." She slid her empty glass across the table. "I think the best thing you can do now is get another round in."

Chapter Twenty

Spitfire Creosote was losing his patience. He'd already explained himself once. If he had to go through it again, one of these pathetic pricks would lose an eye.

"I have an appointment," he repeated, speaking louder and slower. "Spitfire Creosote. Your bosses are expecting me."

The two young men guarding the front of the warehouse continued to watch the tall assassin from beneath their hoods. Neither spoke. They both had on the same outfit. A uniform of sorts. Black jeans, black hooded sweatshirt with a large 'O' across the chest. Plus the same nasty sneer, same dead-eyed stare. Their pitted post-pubescent skin glowed white in the moonlight.

Spitfire adjusted his tie, working the knot up as far as the material and his windpipe allowed. He followed this up by gracefully brushing down the arms of his suit jacket and flick-kicking the hem of his perfectly pressed trousers. All affectations, of course. A way of conveying to these scrawny cretins that they didn't bother him. But it was also the way Spitfire was. Neat. Regimented. With military attention to detail. As a modern, self-made man, he had few mantras he lived by, but one had stayed the test of time.

Keep your trousers like your haircut, and your haircut like your mind.

Sharp.

Sharp as hell.

A shard of static noise crackled into the silence and broke the atmosphere. One of the guards reached behind his back and lifted a handheld transceiver from his belt. He mumbled into it, speaking in Vietnamese. Didn't take his eyes off Spitfire.

"Speetfa?" he asked him.

"For heaven's sake… Yes! Spitfire Creosote."

The guard returned to the transceiver, nodding along to what was being said. Then he pocketed it and gestured for Spitfire's attention.

"Wait here," he said, in a strong accent. "I come back for you."

Internally Spitfire rolled his eyes, but to the guard he said, "Not a problem, squire. Remember - Spitfire Creosote. From Annihilation Pest Control. I don't know how many more times I can bloody say it. Your boss is expecting me."

The man whisper-repeated the names as he backed out through the door, letting it swing shut behind him.

"Bloody henchmen," Spitfire muttered, eyeing up the remaining guard. "Not worth the skin they're made from."

The guard ignored the comment. Or didn't understand. Most likely it was both. Spitfire reached into the inside pocket of his jacket and pulled out a silver cigarette case complete with matching lighter. He clicked the small button on the side of the case and the lid flipped open. Perfect engineering. Elegant. The action still brought joy after all these years. He removed a Marlboro Red from under the flat metal arm and slid it between his lips. Like most of Spitfire's movements, the whole activity was done slowly and deliberately, carried out with an air of both charisma and menace. He flicked the lighter into life and brought the flame up to the end of his cigarette. Puffed it into action. Once lit he took a long drag and blew out a plume of smoke into the night sky. It gave the scene a noir-esque atmosphere. Spitfire liked that.

It wasn't an easy semblance to pull off, the old menace-charisma combo. But Spitfire had years of practice. He believed every action, no matter how small, should be performed as though being projected ten-foot-high on a cinema screen. And in the film of Spitfire's life, he made sure he was always the leading man.

He stepped back and looked up at the tall building, an old textile factory alongside the Red River in the north-east of the city. The windows and main doorways had long been bricked up. The place was unassuming, but that was the point. The way Caesar had sold it, the Cai Moi were like nothing Hanoi had ever seen before. They were young, fanatical and inventive. It was no real leap to believe within the next few months they'd have the entire city in their clutches. Then Vietnam. Then the whole of South-East Asia. Spitfire took another long drag of his cigarette, feeling the hot smoke deep in his lungs. It was an astute move of the boss, to throw his hat in with these young chancers early doors. The deal they were about to make would mean Annihilation Pest Control getting a much-needed foothold in the region. Something that had eluded them up to now. Spitfire had to make this deal work.

He heard movement behind the door. Shouting. He took a final drag of his cigarette and blew another large plume into the air. A second later the door opened and the goon beckoned for Spitfire to follow him.

"Come. They see you."

Spitfire nodded to the remaining guard before following his friend down a long corridor lit by pink neon tubing. It only further enhanced the film noir playing in his head. Here he was, the mean, moody (and incredibly handsome) leading man, on his way to broker a million-dollar deal with a shadowy group of underworld criminals. What could possibly go wrong?

He held his head high and kept his pace measured as the guard led him through a labyrinth of narrow corridors. Raaz hadn't been able to provide much tangible detail on the Cai Moi, but Spitfire had heard the rumours. One tale in particular had made him smile. The way he'd heard it, the Cai Moi had rounded up five local pimps in an old car yard and nailed them to the side of an articulated lorry. But not before stripping each of them, cutting off their balls, and stuffing them in their mouths. It was brutal, but you couldn't help but admire the commitment.

As the guard guided him further into the belly of the warehouse, Spitfire felt a familiar vibration in his trouser pocket. He pulled out his phone to see Raaz Terabyte calling.

Stupid girl.

Why the hell was she ringing? She knew where he was. He sent the call to answerphone as they came to a door where another young man was standing guard. He wore the same hooded uniform as his colleague. Same dumb expression. He nodded as they approached and the first guard handed Spitfire over.

"Oh, are you off then?" he called after him. "Pleasant chat, anyway." He turned back to find his new friend scowling at him with a face like a slapped tit.

The man grunted something in Vietnamese and held out his arms for Spitfire to copy. The universal sign you were about to get frisked.

"Go on then, be gentle," Spitfire told him, opening his arms wide. "Full disclosure, I am carrying a piece. A holster under my arm."

The surly goon grabbed Spitfire by the shoulders and spun him around. With large rough hands he pushed him against the wall until his face was a few centimetres from the crumbling brick. Spitfire flinched as his feet were kicked apart.

"Hey, watch it, mate. They're Italian leather."

The comment elicited a deep grunt from the guard as he carried out what was, by most people's standards, a thorough body search. He started by spreading both palms along Spitfire's left arm, then his right. But found nothing. Then he reached around the front, slipping his hand underneath Spitfire's jacket and pulling his SIG Sauer P226 with Luger Parabellum chamber from his shoulder holster.

"Told you," Spitfire said. "And I will need a receipt for that."

The frisking continued down Spitfire's torso. There the guard found a Taurus PT111 and two push daggers, one strapped to each calf. He placed each item on a small wooden table next to the door. Finally, he removed Spitfire's phone from his pocket and held it up so Spitfire could see the screen was lit up. A call coming through. Spitfire squinted. Raaz again.

"It's my mother. Let it ring out."

The man chucked the phone on the table with the

weapons and spun him back around. He made a show of dusting Spitfire down, but was shrugged briskly away.

"So? Are we good?" Spitfire asked, as he straightened his tie and checked his cufflinks.

Not breaking eye contact, the guard shuffled over to the door and creaked it open. "You go," he told him.

Chapter Twenty-One

Chin up and chest out, Spitfire strolled into the room, which opened out into a vast space at least seventy metres square and four storeys high. Clearly this was once the main factory space, but the machinery had long been cleared out and the space refurbished. It reminded Spitfire of a modern art gallery in New York or Tokyo. Shiny, white gloss laminate covered the expansive floor, and the high walls were lined with sheets of thick metal. Lead, most likely, to keep radio signals and listening devices at bay, making the space a gigantic Faraday cage. Lighting comprised of huge spotlights positioned at angles all around the perimeter of the room. Spitfire grimaced at the searing glare from the halogen bulbs. The stark brightness was discombobulating after the black winding maze he'd walked through to get here.

A low stage had been set up in the centre of the room, about ten metres across. On top of this was a sizeable white table, with two white leather chairs on one side and a matching beanbag opposite. Behind the chairs, a couple of

large spotlights were angled to face the beanbag, and alongside these a pair of six-foot yucca plants stood proudly to
attention.

Music came from four giant speakers, one in each
corner of the room facing the central platform. Though
perhaps that was the wrong word. It was unlike any music
Spitfire would choose to listen to. He loved The Jam and
The Beatles and a bit of Mozart. That was all. The noise
that now erupted into the room was brutal and industrial
and loud. The type of music you felt in your chest as much
as heard it.

He was about to speak when the guard pushed past him
and intimated for him to follow. Spitfire obliged, striding
behind a few paces and continuing to scope out the place,
looking for escape routes, something he might use as a
weapon if needed. He wasn't scared, he feared no man,
certainly not a group of jumped-up tech-nerds in hoodies.
But as always his training preceded him. You didn't stay in
this industry as long as Spitfire Creosote without being
prepared and alert at all times.

The guard stopped at the side of the stage and gestured
for Spitfire to sit. On the beanbag.

"Oh Christ, no. I have to sit on that?"

The guard didn't answer. Not so much as a grunt this
time. He pointed a stubby finger at the beanbag.

"Fine. Have it your way."

Spitfire undid the buttons of his jacket and straddled the
awkward piece of furniture as elegantly as he could muster.
Which wasn't elegantly at all. He squirmed around to find
purchase, eventually placing both feet on the ground and
resting his hands on the smooth tabletop. Once settled he
looked up to see his surly guide exiting the room through
the same door they'd entered through.

"Hey, what's going on?" Spitfire called after him. "I'm here to meet with a guy called Mot. Is that right? Mart? Murt?"

No response. A loud bang echoed around the empty space as the heavy door slammed shut. Then the noise of a bolt sliding into place.

Great.

Spitfire turned back around and steadied himself as the beanbag adjusted to his movement. This was not what he'd expected. The way Caesar and Raaz had explained it, today's meeting was to sign off on the deal already in place. And if required, to offer a little sweetener, an incentive to move it all along. It was for this reason, Spitfire suspected, Caesar had chosen him as his representative. Everyone at Annihilation knew he was the most charismatic and charming operative by a country mile.

Still, as calm and collected as Spitfire was, he didn't like to wait. In fact, he hated it. After five minutes, he began to get antsy. After ten, he wondered if they'd forgotten about him. Either that or this was some stupid game they were playing. And he hated games as much as he hated waiting. By the time fifteen minutes rolled around he was quietly seething, imagining himself strangling the life out of whoever this Mot fellow was. Then, as the twenty-minute-mark neared and his readiness to storm out became all-consuming, a loud explosion snapped him to attention. At the same time, the room was plunged into total blackness.

Spitfire was on his feet and straight into attack mode. Whatever was going on, he was ready for it.

"Who's there?" he shouted. But the music in the room grew louder, drowning him out. Then it grew louder still, the volume swelling to an uncomfortable sonic overload. So much so that the bass pummelled his entire body and he worried he might lose control of his guts. He peered about him in the gloom, searching for shapes, people. Ready to strike if anyone came near. Then, as quickly as it had started, the music stopped and the two spotlights behind the chairs surged into life.

"Shitting hell!" Spitfire cried, holding his forearm over his face. He blinked, letting his eyes ease into the stark white environment. "Oh, I see. Very good."

Sitting in the chairs opposite him were now two hooded figures. He couldn't make out their faces with the light behind them, but that was obviously the point. He moved forward and leaned over the table, holding his hand out to the two hoods.

"Spitfire Creosote," he purred, in well-worn, client-friendly tones. "I believe you've been liaising with my boss, Beowulf Caesar. Is one of you Mot?"

Neither one of the hoods moved an inch.

"We are Mot," the one on the left said.

"We are all Mot." The one on the right now. "We are all The One."

Spitfire grinned. He held out his hand a few seconds longer before he pulled it back to his side.

All right, you ignorant pricks. Have it your way.

He sat back down on the beanbag. Its positioning meant he was now a good foot lower than the two hooded figures. Though, of course, that was also the point, along with the lights, the outfits, the music. All designed to put him on the back foot, to confuse and disorientate. He had to hand it to these Cai Moi fellows, it was a tasty move. If he hadn't been on the receiving end, he'd have loved the histrionics.

"Do you have the goods?" the hood on the left asked.

Spitfire gave it a beat, reaffirming himself as much as possible. "I don't have it with me right now. But you knew that already." He paused, waiting for a response. None came. "I trust the deal is still on the table."

The hood on the right raised his head a degree. Spitfire could now make out a mouth and a chin and the bottom half of a nose. The man looked fresh-faced, young. "That is correct," he said. "Ten million US dollars for the cargo."

Spitfire tilted his head. "Ten? I believe the agreed price was fifteen?"

"Things have changed. At this point we believe ten million is more than fair for what you are offering."

Spitfire held his ground, kept his smile in place. He'd planned for this. Another reason he was here.

"But we had a deal."

"You had a deal. And we were open to that deal. But now we are negotiating."

"I see," he began. "Caesar was concerned this may happen. Which is why I'm able to up our offer. This way we ensure we all leave the deal happy."

The hoods bristled in the spotlights. Just a flicker, but Spitfire noticed it.

"Please. Explain."

He turned up his smile and opened his arms. "Namely me," he told them. "I'll work for you, pro bono, for the next six months. Think of it as a try before you buy scheme. You'll get to see what Annihilation Pest Control can do for you going forward."

The figures looked at each other. "We do not understand."

Spitfire leaned forward. "Gentlemen, The One, whatever you want to be called, it is known far and wide the Cai Moi are already a powerful organisation. Despite your relative youth, you are willing and able to do what is required for your cause. We also know one of your principal goals is for the betterment of your fine country and the people in it. But there's the rub, you see. All this." He gestured around the room, at the spotlights, the yucca plants. "Don't get me wrong, it's cool and mysterious and fucked up. I love it. But we all know there'll come a point, in the not too distant future, when you need to do away with the smoke and mirrors. Get the people on board. Become legit. Or give the appearance, at least."

The hood on the left placed his hands on the table in front of him. "And you can offer this legitimacy?"

Spitfire leaned back. "Not in so many words. But what we are offering is our services. In perpetuity. Think about it. There'll be many times over the next few years where you'll be looking to remove those standing in your way. Government officials. Judges. Rival organisations. Annihilation Pest Control will handle these issues for you, while you keep your hands clean. We're quick, sophisticated, efficient. We're the best at what we do. And you get all that for the extra five million. Plus, a retainer – another five mill a year after the first year is up and you're satisfied with the arrangement."

"And if we are not satisfied?"

Spitfire held his hands up and shrugged. His own brand of theatrics. "If that's the case, we all walk away. No hard feelings." He winked. "Come along, gentlemen, this is a great opportunity for you. What do you say?"

The two figures leaned in close, whispering to each other in Vietnamese.

"How do you see this working?" one of them asked.

Spitfire hit them with his most Clooney-esque grin. "It's simple. Once you transfer the money to Caesar's secure account, I'll deliver the shipment. Then you'll have me on call, twenty-four-seven. I'll work with you for the next six months, here in Hanoi. Whatever you want done – whoever you want gone – I'm your man. Think of me as a one-man clean-up operation."

He said his piece and shut up as the two hoods huddled together speaking in hushed tones. But they were animated now, he noticed. Their ominous cool was slipping. That was a good sign. He sat back and waited. The Cai Moi might have Hanoi gripped in fear, but behind the hoods and sinister facade they were kids. And what bunch of nerdy megalomaniac kids didn't want a deadly assassin on their books.

The hoods nodded at each other and turned back. "This is a fresh development for us. But something we can move forward with. We will accept your offer once we have received the cargo. Tell your boss the money will be in his account tomorrow. Fifteen million US dollars."

Spitfire let his shoulders drop. He hadn't realised he was so tense. "Excellent. You've made the right choice. As soon as I get the all-clear from my people, I'll bring the cargo." He eased himself up from the beanbag and stuck out his hand to them. "Great doing business with you, gentlemen. I look forward to working with you."

"And we you," the hoods intoned. But Spitfire's hand remained hovering over the table, unshaken once more. *Rude bastards.* He waited a few more seconds, then curled in the bottom three fingers and pointed to the hoods.

"Good talking with you, lads. And as I say: love all the special effects. They're incredible." He straightened himself, fastened the middle button on his suit jacket. "Don't get up," he told them, pre-empting the situation. "I'll see myself out."

He stepped off the platform and strode to the door, sensing the eyes on the back of his head. Once at the door he banged loudly with the base of his fist and it creaked open. The grim-faced guard from before stepped aside to let him through.

"Thank you, darling," Spitfire crooned.

The door swung shut behind him and he walked over to the small table to retrieve his armaments. He took his time replacing the guns and knives in their designated holsters and then adjusted his tie.

"You know, you have a tremendous air about you," he told the guard. "I expect people tell you that all the time. You come across so earnest and fascinating." The man stared back at him with a blank expression. "Well, I'm sure we'll be seeing more of each other in the weeks to come," Spitfire went on, picking up his phone and slipping it into his pocket. "Perhaps we could get a beer sometime."

With that, Spitfire turned on his expensive Italian heels and sauntered back the way he'd come, down the long zig-zagging corridors leading to the warehouse exit. Not a bad day's work, all in all, but the Cai Moi were nothing like he'd imagined them to be. Interesting characters, sure. But not brutal thugs. Not the sort to mutilate and crucify their foes. He wondered now whether the rumours were simply that. Rumours. More smoke and mirrors. Fake news. If they were using social media to spread fear and uncertainty it was impressive, but to Spitfire it was also cheating. He harked back to the old days, when men were men and killers were killers. It was so much easier back then. More fun too.

Outside he patted the guards on the backs, told them thanks for their help. Then he strutted over to where his hire car – a silver Alfa Romeo Giulia – was parked up alongside an old storage container. As he walked, he felt his phone vibrate in his pocket. This time he answered it.

"Raaz? What the bloody hell are you playing at? You knew I was meeting with the Cai Moi."

"I know. I'm sorry." Raaz's voice was muffled on the line. "How did it go?"

Spitfire looked back to see the scrawny goon eyeballing him. He gave him a quick salute. Got nothing in return.

"I'm insulted you need to ask that," he told Raaz. "Come on, babe, this is me you're talking to. I sold them the offer. Was my usual charming self. And they bit my bloody hand off. We've got the contract. We are now the covert killing solution for the Cai Moi."

"That's outstanding. Caesar will be pleased."

"I know he bloody well will be." Spitfire beeped the fob on his keyring and opened the car door, but didn't climb in straight away. He leaned against the frame and rested the elbow of his phone arm on the roof. "Never mind that. You haven't answered my question. Why the hell are you calling me when I'm in an important meeting?"

"Sorry. I had your time zone mixed up with Magpie. But I do need to speak with you."

"Yes. Six missed calls. I gathered. What's going on?" The line went silent. He looked at the screen, checking she hadn't been cut off. "Raaz?"

When she spoke, her voice was icy and clipped. "She's there. She's in Hanoi."

A bolt of energy shot up his spine. Adrenaline, he told himself.

"You sure it's her?"

"I'm sure."

"And I take it she's here for me?"

"No other reason as far as I can tell."

He nodded. Useless on a telephone conversation, but it helped him think. He narrowed his eyes, feeling his body tense.

"Do you want me to send backup?" Raaz asked. "Magpie finished her job yesterday. I can get her to—"

"No," he said. "I can handle her."

"You sure? Because—"

"I can handle her."

Shitting piss.

He hung up and threw his head back, staring at the swirling blackness above. He always knew this moment would arrive, he just hadn't counted on it being so soon. Well so bleeding what? Who she was, what they'd shared, it didn't matter to him one bit. He felt nothing but contempt for her. She was a pest. That was all.

He jumped in the car and started the engine.

If Acid Vanilla was coming, he'd be ready for her.

Chapter Twenty-Two

Vinh woke early and despite a dry mouth and a head full of sharp needles jumped straight out of bed. Straight into his new morning routine, devised yesterday as he walked home from Erol's Bar. Fifty push-ups. Two sets of twenty-five with a minute rest between each set. Then two planks of two minutes each, again with a minute rest in between. Once complete, he moved over to the small low bench he had set up at the end of the bed and sat. There he meditated for ten minutes. Using the clock in his head, the one he'd fine-tuned over many years.

After this he went downstairs and straight to the cupboard under the sink. He lifted out seven bottles of liquor, all in various stages of fullness, and poured them down the sink. It made him feel powerful, watching the poisonous orange and brown liquid drain away. This was a new start for him. A new improved version of Vinh Phan. And this Vinh would get the job done, no matter what. No more bullshit excuses. No more letting fear and shame hold him back. He picked up the last bottle. Wall Street Whisky.

Blended. He held it over the sink, but then stopped himself. No. This would be his reward. For when he found Huy. He returned it to the cupboard before throwing the rest of the bottles in the trash.

Next he made himself a modest breakfast. A bowl of congee, sprinkled with fish meal. He sat at the kitchen table to eat. In the same spot as always, facing the room with his back to the oven, at the head of the table. Although, could he say he was at the head of the table when no one else was there to give context?

As Vinh ate, his mind wandered to last night. The strange English woman had certainly made her presence known. But now, in the cold light of day, he had concerns. Not that he doubted her abilities. She was a strong woman. You could see it in her eyes. Intelligent. Mean. Determined. And she could handle herself physically, he'd seen that already. But regardless, taking on the Cai Moi, it was a dangerous game.

Vinh had never had a problem with strong women. In fact, he'd always had a soft spot for them, truth be told. His mother was a firm but kind matriarch. His wife too was a fiercely strong and independent woman. Or at least she had been before the accident. Tam as well was strong. She'd had to be. Vinh shook his head, as if to shake away those thoughts.

Once breakfast was done with, he placed his empty bowl in the sink and went upstairs. After washing and dressing, he grabbed a bottle of water from the fridge and locked up the house. He'd arranged to meet Acid at Tam's bistro, but not for a couple of hours. He decided to take a walk, clear his head. Though easier said than done when every inch of the city reminded him of his past. Of what he'd done. As he walked through the streets, each shop window reflected grim memories of pain and guilt back at him.

He'd gotten all the way to Hoan Kiem Lake before he fell out of the morbid swirling thoughts in his head and back into the moment. The day was still in its infancy, the blazing summer sun not yet high in the sky, but the area here was already a sea of eager tourists, all waiting to visit the famous Ngoc Son Temple.

Vinh hadn't visited the temple in many years. In fact, he couldn't remember the time when he was last here. Although not large, and often busy with tourists, it had always been a pleasant and peaceful place, away from the clamour and pace of the city. He had visited the temple often in his youth, mostly when he was feeling confused or troubled. Maybe that's what had brought him here today. Inside the ancient pagoda was the perfect setting for contemplation and reflection – two qualities missing from his life these last few years. He crossed over the bright scarlet Rising Sun Bridge and gazed up at the tall Pen Tower. It was an ancient symbol of literature and study, and he paused a moment to give thanks for his profession. Training to be a teacher of English had been the first new start. It had kept him alive. Allowed him something to focus on, away from the pull of the darkness and the bottle.

Vinh made his way through into the main space and sat on the steps outside the Tran Ba Pavilion. He closed his eyes, gave thanks here, too. For his health. His wisdom. He wasn't a religious man, but being in such a holy place it felt apt to follow this up with a request for clemency.

Forgive me for all I have done.

Give me strength for what I must do next.

He remained here a while, his mind empty of thought, focused on nothing but his breathing. In with the good. Out with the bad. His mind drifted to General Tran Hung Dao, the great military commander of the Tran Dynasty, to whom the temple was dedicated. Vinh had read about him in his youth. In the thirteenth century, Hung Dao's bravery and cunning meant the Vietnamese army defeated 300,000 Mongolian soldiers led by the Emperor Kublai Khan.

Vinh opened his eyes, smiled to himself. Maybe it was no accident he'd wandered here this morning. It was like a dose of strong vitamins to be this close to the memory of such a great man. A humble man too - he had eschewed the offer of a royal mausoleum on his death, preferring to have his ashes scattered underneath his favourite tree. Vinh took another deep breath and got to his feet. Something had shifted inside of him. It wasn't so much that the trepidation had left him, but he felt lighter, clearer. Ready for action.

When he arrived at Tam's bistro a while later, it was still too early to meet Acid. He was about to walk past and buy another bottle of water from a nearby shop when Tam saw him through the window and beckoned him inside. His first instinct was to wave her away, let her know he was busy. But he wasn't, not yet. He opened the door and entered.

"How are you feeling today?" he asked, noticing the dark bruise under Tam's left eye. "Those dirty street rats."

"Ah, it looks bad, but it isn't," she told him. "Would you like something to drink? To eat?"

Vinh halted and looked at the clock over the counter. 10.35 a.m. "I'm meeting the English woman from yesterday in an hour."

Tam looked down her nose. "So? You want a drink or not?"

He held his hands up. "It's not like that. I said I'd help her find someone. Provide local knowledge."

She shook her head. "I don't care. Do you want a drink?"

"Coffee, then. Thanks."

Vinh sat at a table down the far side of the room beneath the large shelving unit. Behind him Tam's ancient coffee machine whistled and rattled into life. A small wicker bowl sat in the centre of the table, full of brightly coloured sachets of sugar and sweetener. He reached over and took out one of the sachets. He was holding it in his hand and absent-mindedly shaking the contents when Tam placed a steaming mug of dark black coffee in front of him.

"Still not taking milk?"

Vinh glanced up at her. "No. Thanks." His heart sank as she sat across from him and smiled, looking like she wanted to say something. "You okay?"

"I am," she said. "It gets hard, you know. I try and stay upbeat."

He returned her smile, but it felt weird. "That was the first visit you'd had from those punks?"

Tam adjusted herself on the chair. "Yes. First and last, hopefully. I would not have given them anything. They'd have had to beat me to death first."

"Don't talk like that." Vinh ripped the corner off the sugar sachet and poured the whole lot into the dark liquid. "I asked them about Huy, if they knew anything, but I got nothing of worth."

She curled her lip. "I wanted to ask, but I clammed up. Them with their stupid threats. Pay up or else."

He selected a spoon from a small pot and slowly stirred his coffee. It was too hot to drink. "I will find him," he said resolutely, to the coffee. "I promise."

She reached over and touched his hand. "You're a good man, Vinh Phan. But that's a big promise."

"The woman from last night. I'm going to persuade her to help me. She's someone who can help. I know it."

"You talked long after you left here?"

"A few hours. Over a drink or two."

Tam frowned. "Did you tell her?"

He stared into his coffee. Shook his head. "No. I thought about telling her. But I couldn't."

"None of it? About your past? Who you are?"

He brought the hot coffee up to his mouth and took a sip. Still far too hot. Too bitter as well. He placed it back on the table and picked up a second sugar sachet.

"I will do. Maybe. If I can convince her to help me."

Tam tutted softly but said no more. They sat together in silence. Vinh stirred his coffee. Attempted another drink. Still too hot.

Tam placed both hands flat on the table and got to her feet. "You'd best be going to meet her," she said. "I've got some preparation to do in the back. I'll see you later."

"Tam," Vinh called after her. "Wait."

At the counter she turned to look at him.

"I swear to you. I will find him."

She bowed her head and did something with her mouth that was close to a smile but not fully. "Be careful," she told him. Then she went into the kitchen, leaving him alone with his coffee and his thoughts.

Chapter Twenty-Three

A few blocks away, Acid Vanilla woke up in her hotel room and sat bolt upright. Memories of the previous evening swam into her consciousness. Along with a blinding headache that had her reaching for her overnight bag. She dry-swallowed two painkillers. Not easy with a mouth like a bar-room floor.

"Bloody Vietnamese whisky."

They'd had six more rounds in total in Erol's. Maybe more, she'd lost count. She did remember, however, arranging to meet Vinh at Tam's bistro at 11.30 a.m. From there he'd take her to the Red River. She found her phone on the nightstand and peered, bleary-eyed, at the display: 11.07 a.m.

Shit

Her phone display also informed her she had four texts. All from Spook. Each one asking her to call back in increasing levels of eagerness and despair. Acid rolled her eyes, then rolled off the bed, straight into the bathroom. She slipped off her pants and stepped into the shower unit.

Today she went for cold water and stuck her head under. Her skin bristled with shock as the icy shards numbed her to the soul. But as before, it helped. Woke her up in both body and mind.

Once clean and revitalised, she wrapped a towel around herself and strolled back into the bedroom, then through to the lounge area where she found an electric coffee machine. A selection of coloured pods sat on a wire frame attached to the side. She picked what looked to be the strongest one and stuffed it in the machine, before placing a cup under the nozzle and switching it on. Whilst the machine hummed and popped, she went back into the bedroom and dried herself off.

Dry, she opened her case and pulled out a zip-lock bag containing two thick wads of Vietnamese currency. She counted out a gigantic pile of ridiculously zeroed notes onto the bed. A hundred and eighty million dong, to be exact, around five and a half grand in GBP. She dressed in fresh underwear and yesterday's jeans, but a new top. Today she opted for a dark-charcoal ribbed-cotton vest. Then she stuffed the money and her phone into a small leather money bag and swung it over her shoulder.

The oppressive sticky heat of the season was already apparent as Acid stepped out onto the main street. She was pleased she'd mistrusted her air-conditioned room enough to leave her jacket behind. Once away from the hotel she carried on around the building to join Tran Phu – train street – from the north side. The bars and shops here were already bustling with bodies and noise. Pungent aromatic smells and excited chatter filled the air, while locals and tourists alike perused stalls and the wares offered by the street vendors, exchanging money for tasty-looking morsels and exotic trinkets. Acid took her time walking down the narrow strip, nodding politely at shopkeepers, picking up the odd knick-knack here and there to examine. She was hoping a train might appear, but by the time she got to the point where the street intersected with Tong Duy Tan, the track was still quiet. No sign of any trains. Maybe later. She waited another few minutes, then took a right towards Tam's bistro.

She saw Vinh before he saw her. He was wearing a similar outfit as yesterday, crumpled shirt and chinos, but today's shirt was a coppery-mustard colour. He looked older in the daylight. Smaller too. Acid glanced at herself in a shop window as she walked past. The hangover was still nibbling at the edges of her sanity, but her large sunglasses and the fact she'd tied her hair up hid a multitude of sins. She cricked her neck and turned her attention back to Vinh. He spotted her, held his hand up and waved.

"Good morning," she chimed as she got closer. "How are you?"

Vinh shrugged. "I felt terrible when I woke up. But now I'm not so bad. How about you?"

"I'm great," she lied. "So, you ready to go?"

"Remind me again where we are going."

She peered at him over her sunglasses. "To meet my contact. So I can arm myself. I'm hoping he might have some leads too. He's been working this area for a few years so will no doubt have an ear to the ground. Can hopefully tell me where these Cai Moi people hang out."

Vinh looked at his feet. "We shall see. Thank you again for allowing me to accompany you."

"Yeah, well, I'm not sure why I agreed to it." She sniffed. "But here we are. He might have seen your friend."

"Thank you. His name is Huy."

"Huy. Right. But you have to keep your mouth shut

when we get there. I've never met this guy before so we have to step careful. Don't want to piss him off."

"I understand."

"Good."

An awkward silence fell between them as they looked at each other. Acid pushed her sunglasses up her nose. "You ever wonder if you have a death wish, Vinh?" she asked.

"I've spent too long getting caught up in my own wonderings. It did me no good. Now is the time for action." He narrowed his eyes at her, as if seeing her afresh. "Do you? Wonder?"

"I don't wonder. I know." She raised her head and looked down the road. "But it keeps life interesting, doesn't it? Shall we go?"

Chapter Twenty-Four

Acid was to meet The Dullahan's contact – a gun-runner named Sonny Botha – at 1 p.m. underneath a bridge in Yen Phu along an anabranch of the Red River. It would take them an hour by foot, but they had time. Besides, the walk would do wonders for both their heads. Blow the cobwebs.

It had started off so well. They'd chatted some more, about life, about Vinh's English school. About Huy. But as they passed by Long Bien Railway Station, the entire heavens opened and torrential, stinging rain drove them up the steps and under the station's concrete awning for shelter.

"What now?" Vinh asked. "You want to wait until it stops?"

A large clock a few feet above them showed they had half an hour to get to the meeting point. If they waited for the rain, they would be cutting it fine.

"How long do these tropical storms usually last?" Acid yelled over the thumping beat of the rain on the station roof.

"Could be five minutes, could be fifty." He shrugged.

"We could wait ten minutes then get a taxi there if we need to?"

She looked out at the enormous pools of rain already forming on the parched ground. It was coming down thick and fast. Now she wished she had her jacket.

"Fine. We can wait," she told him.

And so it was that fifteen minutes later they were drying off in the back of a warm Grab Cab as it trundled at a snail's pace through the back streets towards their destination.

Acid glanced across at Vinh with narrow eyes. "I thought you were taking me on the local's route. Being my guide. I think I could have found a cab on my own."

He beamed at her. "Yes, but you have to be careful. With a local man on your team, you won't get ripped off."

She snorted heavily down both nostrils. "Team? Jesus, is that what you think we are? Well, we're here now, I guess. How much further, do you think?" She peered around the driver's seat to check the digital clock on the dashboard.

"A few more miles. Will take us fifteen minutes. Maybe less."

Acid leaned back and watched out the window. Hanoi was a beautiful city. But unlike similarly spread-out metropolises – such as LA or Tokyo – there didn't seem to be much going on in between the main areas of activity. As they left the Old Quarter, the trappings of tourism dwindled to make way for vast expanses of low-rate housing projects and concrete wastelands. They passed the odd convenience store here and there, but that was about it.

"Have you visited Hanoi before?" Vinh asked.

"A long time ago,' she replied. "Only for a few days. I was on a job, so didn't have time to do much sightseeing."

He laughed softly. "I see. A job. Shit, I can't believe I'm

sitting here with a goddamn hit man. Sorry – hit person, is it?"

"It's neither," she drawled. "Assassin is better. Hired killer is my go-to." She swallowed, turned back to the window. "*Was* my go-to."

"You don't seem like... one of those... if I may say."

She smirked out the window. "And what do those seem like?"

"I don't know. Cold. Robotic. Indifferent to life."

"I think you might be getting confused with The Terminator."

"Perhaps. You know what I mean."

Acid removed her sunglasses and looked at him. "Yes. I do. What you mean is how did I kill so many people and still maintain a degree of – what – humanity? Compassion? I don't, Vinh, to be honest with you. A lot of my colleagues, my contemporaries, are as you describe. I guess a lot of them got into their line of work because they simply wanted to kill people. They're psychopaths. But for me it was different. I sort of fell into it. Or was pushed. But I found I was good at it. Exceptionally good, in fact. And it paid well. Helped me have a life I wouldn't have had any other way." She leaned back. She'd been speaking twenty to the dozen, barking into Vinh's wide-eyed face. "But it takes its toll. It has done. As I explained last night. For a long time, I justified it to myself, told myself the people I eradicated deserved what they got. And you know what? Most of them did. But who am I to make that judgement?"

She shoved her sunglasses back on and turned back to the window. Vinh was quiet, but she could feel his eyes burning into the side of her face.

"How many people have you—"

"Nope." She held her hand up to him before he could

finish. "Never ask a girl her age, or how many people she's killed."

Another laugh from Vinh. "I understand. Sounds to me like maybe you're on the right side of this now. Doing the right thing. It's good to face up to your past. Good to make amends."

"Jesus Christ," she whispered. "You sound like a friend of mine."

Shit.

She hadn't returned Spook's calls. Not so much as a text to say she was safe. She imagined the poor kid climbing the walls. First thing she'd do when she got back to the hotel was call her. But for now she turned her attention back to Vinh.

"That's not true, though. What you said about making amends. It's not what I'm doing. Not why I'm here."

"So why are you here?" he asked.

"To find the man I'm looking for."

Vinh pulled a face. Not convinced. "What about Tam? You came back to help her last night. You didn't have to."

"Yeah. I wobbled." Acid sneered out the window. "And look where it's got me. You in tow, slowing me down. Someone else to worry about."

"It must feel good though, to know you can help people?"

"I have too much to think about in my own life," she said. "I can't save everyone."

Her words echoed both around the cab and in her head, only halted by Vinh a few seconds later saying, "Tell me about this man Spitfire. He is an ex-colleague? You were close?"

Acid raised her head to glare at him. "He's no one. All right? Another name on my kill list."

She felt a quiver of something in her chest as she spoke. Heard the bats stirring in her psyche.

Another name.

Is that all he was?

She pushed the thought aside. Couldn't deal with the perplexity of the question. Not now. She had one purpose. Bloody retribution. Spitfire Creosote was going to die because of his involvement in her mother's death. That was the end of it.

"Well, whatever it is you need, Acid Vanilla," Vinh said. "I hope you find it."

She didn't reply.

A few minutes later, the cab pulled up on a side street opposite the river. Acid paid the driver and they departed the vehicle. The rain had stopped by this point and the hot midday sun was already drying out the wet concrete. As the cab drove away, Acid waited on the side of the road and stretched her weary muscles. Over to the east flowed the vast Red River, and a few hundred metres down the road spanned the Huong Duong Bridge connecting the centre of the Hoan Kiem District with Long Bien.

"We're meeting over there, under the bridge," she told Vinh. She held her hand over her eyes to shield off the bright sun. "I think he's already waiting. Come on."

They set off at a pace, marching down the busy main road and then cutting through the back streets leading to the riverbank. A black VW Transporter was parked up under the bridge. No one else around.

Stepping carefully, Acid approached the van from the side, circling around the back until she could see herself in the wing mirror on the driver's side. She locked eyes with the man in the driver's seat. He stiffened. Frowned. She raised her hands and gave a curt nod that said, 'It's me.'

The man reached over to the passenger seat to get something and then opened the door. As he stepped out onto the gravel bank, he pointed a small pistol at her. A Springfield Compact from the looks of it.

"You have the code?' His voice was gravelly, no doubt the result of many late nights in smoky bars.

"Mr Botha?" Acid ventured. "I'm here to make a purchase."

"The code!" he said, screwing up his nose. "I need the code or I'm gone." His accent was strange. Afrikaans, mixed with cockney, mixed with Jamaican. A mid-Atlantic twang curled his vowels.

"Blue Lagoon," she said firmly. "The Dullahan sends his regards, by the way."

The man paused a second, before his face cracked into a wide smile. Age-wise, he was hard to place. Late sixties possibly. But he had a certain energy to him that, coupled with decades of sun exposure, meant he could have been younger. With his wild grey hair and masses of silver jewellery, he reminded Acid of late-period Keith Richards. A bundle of dirty shammy leather held together by bracelets and pirate-charm.

"The Dullahan. Fuck me." He whistled. "Hearing from that old fucker again sure took me back. I couldn't believe it when he called me up. Thought the old bastard had retired."

Acid grinned. "He says he has. But we both know, people like him don't ever really retire." She stepped closer and held out her hand. "My name's Acid Vanilla."

He took her hand in his rough palm. "Charmed," he drawled. "But don't worry, love, I know who you are. The great Acid Vanilla. I've heard all the tales."

"Is that so?"

"Oh yeah, your reputation doth proceed you, and all that shit. How's your boss doing? I've sold to him occasionally over the years. Big Ceez."

"He's not my boss any longer" she said. "But I am looking for him. Do you have a location at all?"

"Sorry. What do you need him for?"

"I'm going to kill him."

"Oh?"

"Will that be a problem?"

Sonny looked away and chewed on his bottom lip. Acid glanced behind her, at Vinh standing pensively around the back of the van. She widened her eyes at him. *Stay cool.*

"Will that be a problem? No, course it won't be a fucking problem!" Sonny held out his arms as the tension dissipated. "Jesus Christ, if I had any bleeding allegiances in this game I'd be broke within a week. Nah, you go for it, love. And call me Sonny, by the way. 'Cos that's me name." He let out a long wheezing laugh and stepped forward. He was about to open the van's side panel when his face dropped and he pointed his gun over her shoulder. "Who the fuck are you?"

She spun around to see Vinh had appeared from behind the vehicle.

"Woah, woah," she yelled, holding her hands in the air and stepping between the two men. "He's with me. I can vouch for him."

Sonny kept the gun raised, his sinewy arm stiff with vigilance. "Who the hell is he?"

"My name is Vinh Phan. I am a friend of Acid's," he said, speaking softly. "I am a local man. A teacher. I am not a threat to you."

"It's true," she added. "He's helping me get around the city. He's golden. I swear to you."

Sonny held his poise a few seconds longer, then lowered his gun. "All right. I trust ya." He stuffed the gun back into his belt and closed one eye at Acid. "You got the payment?"

She patted her shoulder bag. "Right here. You got some toys for me?"

"Sure have." He ran his hand under his nose. "Take a look at these bad boys."

He slid back the side panel of the van to reveal a large black holdall, the only item in the cavernous space. He grabbed one of the handles and dragged it towards him. Acid watched eagerly as he unzipped the bag and spread it wide.

"May I?" she asked.

"Be my guest."

The bag was full of weapons. Handguns mainly, along with two SIG Sauer Copperheads and a Scorpion VZ61. Small for subs, and powerful, but still cumbersome for the covert mission she had planned. A black shiny Glock 45 lay on top of the pile. She lifted it out and felt the grip. Checked the sight, checked the clip release.

"One of my best sellers," Sonny told her. "Comes with the standard seventeen mag. But I can do you a twenty-four, if you'd prefer."

"Sounds perfect."

Next Acid pulled out two Beretta FSs. Brand new. Reassuringly weighty in her hands. They were fast becoming a firm favourite of hers. Accurate and reliable with impressive firepower.

"Berettas. Now we're talking," Vinh exclaimed behind her.

Sonny turned and looked him up and down. "Teacher, huh?"

Vinh shrugged.

"I'll take all three," she said, aiming the two Berettas out at arm's length. "What else have you got in there?"

They returned to the bag and she selected two Cold Steel Recon 1 tactical knives and a Safe Maker push dagger.

"Can you throw these in too?" she asked, lifting out a double shoulder holster in oxblood leather and a couple of Octane 9K silencers.

"Sure can, love."

"What about ammo?"

Sonny chuckled to himself. He leaned around the side of the inner compartment and came back with a box of Speer Gold Dot 9mm.

"Hollow points. Core bonded for zero separation and maximum damage," Sonny told her. "Ten cases. Each with twenty rounds. Should do you all right, no?"

"Sure will. Thank you. You got something I can put all this in?"

Sonny grumbled, but began lifting the remaining weapons out of the holdall. "It's a good job I like you, girly. Here, take this." He slid the bag over and helped Acid pack her weapons. Once done they faced each other.

She squinted into the bright sun. "What's the damage?"

"A hundred and fifty-eight million dong." Sonny grinned, as if relishing the ridiculously large number.

From her bag, she took two rolls of notes and handed them over. "It's all there. Count it if you want."

"Oh, can I? That's very kind of you." Acid went to reply but Sonny erupted into more chesty laughter. "Don't worry about it. I trust you. And if it's not all there, I'll come looking for you and cut your bloody hands off. Simple as that."

She stuck out her bottom lip. "Fair's fair."

"Indeed."

Next to her, Vinh bristled. She could feel the energy coming off him. "One more thing, Sonny." She stepped closer, dropping her voice. "There's a reason Vinh is with me. We both have a vested interest in the Cai Moi. I take it you've heard of them?"

"Heard of them?" Sonny told her. "Everyone in Hanoi has heard of them, though few have seen them. Although I have. Bunch of bloody weirdos, if you ask me."

"One of Caesar's men is over here setting up some deal. But I'm not sure of the details. My first theory was drugs. But now I'm leaning more towards guns."

Sonny was silent, but you could see the cogs turning. He was working out her angle, how much he should say. He coughed up a ball of phlegm and spat it on the ground.

"Nah," he told her. "Not guns. I sold to those guys a few months ago. Like I say, weirdos. I won't bore you with the details, but suffice to say they like drama. Theatrics. I thought I was meeting with Siegfried and fucking Roy at one point. Thing is, though, they bought enough firepower to take down most of the Vietnamese army. A shit ton of subs, pistols, assault rifles. They don't need any more damn guns."

"I'm worried they've taken my friend, or worse," Vinh cut in. "I wondered if you might have seen him."

Acid turned to him and muttered under her breath. "Don't screw this up, Vinh."

But he wasn't listening. He pulled the photo from his pocket and offered it. "Please, have a look. He has been missing now for some time."

Sonny let out a deep sigh but held out his hand. "Go on, let's have a look."

Acid chewed the inside of her cheek as Vinh handed over the photo. "The man on the left. Huy."

Sonny held it out in front of him. "You know, it's funny. He does look familiar."

"You know him?" Vinh asked, his face lighting up.

But Sonny twisted his mouth to one side. "I'm sorry, I can't think. Maybe I've seen him somewhere, maybe nowhere. I wouldn't want to give you false hope, mate. The old thinking box isn't what it used to be, you know how it is." He handed back the photograph.

"Thank you anyway." Vinh bowed his head and turned to Acid. "Apologies. I had to ask."

She gave him a thin-lipped smile. Then back to Sonny, she said, "So you met with the Cai Moi? Can you provide some more intel? I'll pay, of course. Where they're based. Names. Whatever you know."

Sonny laughed. Shook his head. "Not a chance, love."

"I've got plenty more dong where that came from."

"It's not worth it. But truth is, I met them in a location similar to this. I didn't get a good look at them. It was dark and they wear hoods. They all do. Like I say, a bunch of weirdos."

Acid thought of the street rats from Tam's place. "Nothing else you can tell me?"

"Sorry, love. Even if I wanted to get involved, which I don't, I've got nothing."

"Well, thanks for everything." She heaved the holdall strap over her shoulder and nodded to Vinh that they were leaving. "I guess I'll see you around, Sonny."

"Sure," he replied, sliding the door shut. "One thing, though. They might be weirdos but they're bad news those Cai Moi buggers. If you're going after them you'll need a hell of a lot more firepower than what you've bought. And if you ask me, you're going to need backup."

She turned, walking backwards as she spoke. "Don't have backup. But thanks for the heads up."

Sonny shrugged. "You have no idea what you're getting yourself into. A girl and a teacher against those crazy bastards..." He tilted his head back. "No offence, but I don't fancy your chances much. I mean, I hope you prove me wrong. But from what I've heard, you're as good as dead."

Chapter Twenty-Five

"A girl and a teacher? Cheeky bastard." Acid sat back, dropping her head to the headrest. After flagging down another Grab Cab they were now on their way to her hotel.

"But he might be correct about needing backup," Vinh told her. His eyebrows knotted above his small nose. "Why don't I stick around a while longer?"

"We've been through this."

"But one person against the Cai Moi? It's a stupid idea."

Acid peeled her shoulder away from the hot, sticky leather of the seat-back and looked him in the eye. "I'm all about stupid ideas, sweetie. The stupider they are, the more unexpected. The more unexpected they are... well, you got the element of surprise on your side."

She opened her eyes wide, a manic grin spreading across her face. She'd felt the bats awakening the last few hours and now they were on a feeding frenzy, nibbling at her nerve endings and filling her soul with an unenviable drive to put herself in harm's way as soon as possible. Vinh, though, was watching her with an expression she couldn't entirely read.

"Seriously, don't worry," she told him. "My plans don't involve taking on the Cai Moi. I'm here for Spitfire. I'll find him, get him alone, and do what I need to. I'll leave the Cai Moi to do what they want."

He sighed. "I see. And if that means killing innocent people? Taking sons from mothers?"

She rubbed her hands over her face. "Ah, Vinh," she said on a sigh. "Give it a rest, will you? I don't know what you want me to say."

"I want you to say you'll help me."

A surge of annoyance and chattering tension clouded her thoughts. The only thing keeping her from pushing Vinh out the taxi door was the dawning realisation that most of this frustration was directed inwards. More so on what she was about to say.

"Fine. I'll help you find Huy. Okay? Will that shut you up?"

Vinh gasped, as though getting the all-clear on some terrible disease. "Thank you, Acid. I swear you will not regret this. I will help you. Trust me."

"I'm only here for a few days, Vinh. Remember that. Once Spitfire's dead, I'm gone. Whether we've found Huy or—"

She trailed off as two motorbikes reappeared in the rear-view mirror. She'd noticed them a few miles back, but dismissed any worries as unfounded, the bats being overzealous. But now she wasn't so sure. She twisted around to watch them out the back window. The bikes were two car lengths away. Kawasakis. ZX10s, by the looks of it. Nice bikes. Except they remained a steady distance away despite the slow-moving traffic.

"Hey, Vinh, I think we might have—"

"Yes," he cut in. "They appeared right after we set off. I've been watching them too. I hoped I was mistaken, but they've matched our every turn."

Acid dragged the heavy bag onto her knees and was about to unzip it when Vinh put his arm across her.

"No. What are you doing?"

"What does it look like? I'm arming myself." She shrugged his arm away and unzipped the bag. Keeping her hands out of sight from the driver, she found one of the Berettas and screwed the thread protector cap from the end.

"Wait. You can't be shooting people in broad daylight," he whispered. "We'll get arrested. Or shot."

Acid hit him with her seasoned don't-piss-me-off stare. "Thanks, sweetie. I realise that. But if they are Cai Moi, then I want to be prepared." She gestured into the bag. "I'm attaching a silencer, see? Less attention."

Vinh looked over his shoulder. His face said they were still being followed. "Can we try something else first, please? How much money do you have with you?"

Acid went into her head, did the maths. "Around two million dong. Give or take."

"Can you spare it?"

"I suppose so. What're you thinking?"

Vinh leaned forward, pulling at his seat belt. He spoke to the driver in Vietnamese for a few seconds. The driver, a thin man in his late twenties, twisted around to look at Vinh. He said something in return but didn't sound happy. Acid watched the exchange, the two men barking at each other. They were clearly bartering over something.

She heard Vinh say, "Okay?"

But the driver went off again, pointing at the road ahead. Pointing out of the side windows.

Vinh held his nerve. "Okay?"

The driver made a loud tutting noise, but relented. "Okay," he said.

Vinh sat back and shot her an enormous grin. "Hang on," he told her. "I think it's about to get rocky."

Acid didn't have a chance to reply before the cab driver floored the accelerator. She grabbed the handle above the door, steadying herself as the car swerved into a hard left.

"Jesus. What did you say to him?" she yelled.

"I told him you were a famous English actress and if he lost those troublesome photographers on the motorbikes then we'd pay him two million dong."

She stuck out her lip and nodded. "Nice work. Woah. Shit." She gripped the handle tighter as the car swerved to the right and headed down a narrow back street. Through the windscreen they watched as people leapt out of the way of the speeding taxi. The driver kept his foot down all the way to the end of the lane then took another sharp left. Here the road opened up onto a three-lane carriageway. The driver straightened the car and turned around to Acid. He showed all his teeth as he grinned, looking her up and down.

"Hey, eyes on the road," she told him.

He said something in Vietnamese. It seemed positive enough, so she gave him the thumbs up and he turned back to the wheel before gliding across three lanes of traffic. He steered them down an exit lane off the main carriageway and circled around to join a minor road leading into an underpass. As they waited at traffic lights, Acid and Vinh glanced out the back window. No motorbikes in sight. But that didn't mean they were safe. Not yet.

"I told the driver to drop us a few streets away from my

house," Vinh said. "If the Cai Moi have been following you, then your hotel is compromised. You can't go back there."

She tensed. "My suitcase is there," she told him. "And my passport. And my jacket."

He shook his head. "We'll go later. When things have calmed down. For now, we need to get somewhere safe. Agreed?"

She didn't like it but she agreed, clutching the bag of weaponry to her as the lights turned green and the driver slammed his foot on the pedal. They sped off in a screech of tyres, the driver shouting, "Let's roll," in a bad American accent.

They left the underpass and the driver leaned on the pedal some more. A few minutes later the wide roads of downtown became the winding, narrow streets of the Old Quarter. Vinh leaned forward again and shouted something at the driver who, at the end of the next tree-lined street, slowed and turned into an alleyway wide enough for the car to pass through. At the far end they came to a stop and Vinh patted the driver on the shoulder.

"We'll get out here," he said to Acid. "My place is a few minutes away."

She nodded and went into her bag for the rest of the money. She handed it to Vinh, who slapped it firmly into the driver's waiting hand. The driver stared greedily at the pile of notes and stuffed them in his pocket without counting. Then he twisted around in his seat and said something to Acid.

"He wants a photo with you," Vinh told her.

She glared at him through her glasses. "Absolutely bloody not."

The driver unclipped his phone from the dashboard holder and held it up, smiling eagerly and nodding his head.

"It'll only take a second," Vinh said. "You'll make his day."

Acid seethed, but eventually gave in. They all got out the cab and she positioned herself next to the driver as Vinh took the phone and did the honours. The driver grinned excitedly, sticking both thumbs up to the camera. Beside him Acid folded her arms, sunglasses in place, dark red pout turned up to the max.

"I got a few good ones." Vinh handed the camera to the driver. "Now let's get out of here. Want me to carry that?" He pointed to the holdall at Acid's feet.

She gave him another hard stare over the top of her glasses. "I can manage. Thanks."

"Cool, cool you," the driver shouted. He waved at them as he climbed back into the bright green Toyota and held up his phone. The photo of him and Acid was already his wallpaper. "I see you, bye."

Acid and Vinh smiled politely and held their hands up in a wave as the driver revved his engine unnecessarily and pulled away. They watched as he got to the end of the alley and disappeared around the corner.

"You enjoyed that, didn't you?" she said. "Bloody famous English actress. I hate actresses. Nothing but hard work."

"You know, I heard the same about assassins. Apologies. *Ex*-assassins."

Acid flicked her hair one side, then the other. "You're not wrong."

Vinh smiled. "You made his day. And he helped us out. We all win."

She hauled the heavy bag onto her shoulder and was about to tell Vinh on this occasion she'd give her feminist pride a break and let him carry it, when she heard a noise behind her. A noise which sounded uncannily reminiscent of a motorbike engine.

Chapter Twenty-Six

Acid spun around to see her estimation was correct. One of the Kawasaki bikes waited ominously at the end of the alley. As she let the bag fall to the ground, she heard another engine and spun around to see the second bike at the far end. They had them trapped. The riders switched off their engines and kicked the bike stands down.

She glanced from one to the other as they dismounted. They wore matching leather bike-suits. Black gloves. Black boots. Black helmets too. If Acid wasn't so full of adrenaline and panic, she might have appreciated the effort. But as it was, all she could do was stand there with her mouth open as the riders crossed their arms over their chest and each drew two sharp tanto blades from behind their backs.

They edged closer, swords drawn, ready to spill blood. Acid glanced at the bag of weapons. No time to load up a clip or get one in the chamber. But she had the knives. She dropped to her knees and pulled out two blades and the push dagger too.

"Here, take this."

She held one of the knives up to Vinh. But he was no longer by her side. She raised her head up to see him running towards the rider at the far end of the alley.

What was he playing at?

The rider ran towards him, swords raised, ready to slice him in two. Acid grimaced. She didn't want to watch but couldn't take her eyes away. As Vinh got a metre or so away from the rider – just out of range from the sharp steel of the blades – he dived at him, feet first. His body became a human spear, going low and straight, smashing into the man's left knee with both feet. The impact forced his leg backwards and against itself with a sickening snap. Screaming in pain, the rider stumbled forward, dropping his swords and grasping desperately at his shattered knee cap. Vinh was on his feet in a second and dropped the rider with a sharp elbow below the helmet. The blow caught the man in the Adam's apple and knocked all the air out of him. For a finisher, Vinh yanked off the helmet and grabbed the rider's head in both hands, smashing it into the concrete. Over and over he went, lifting his bloody, broken head and pummelling it into the ground. A few more goes and his body went limp. Out cold. Possibly dead. Vinh glanced up at Acid with wide, frenzied eyes. "Look out!"

She scrambled to her feet, just dodging a blade as the second rider swung wildly at her. She side-stepped back on a diagonal trajectory, trying to escape the slashing blades as the rider came at her. With the push dagger in her raised fist, she jabbed impotently at the flailing whirlwind of steel and fury. The man was forcing her towards the side of the alley. A few more steps and she'd have her back against the wall, in more ways than one. She held the push dagger up, guarding her face. Above her she could see an old fire escape, one of those weighted ladders you could pull down to climb up. Or a better option – smash it down on your attacker's head. The ladder was old and rusty as hell, but it might work. The man swung at her again. A searing pain ripped through her forearm and she cried out, dropping the push dagger. She yanked her arm into her body. The laceration was long but not too deep. Except now she was unarmed. But now she was unarmed. Worse still, she felt the cold brick of the wall behind her. She glanced up, assessing the height of the ladder, the strength she'd need. In front of her the man crossed the blades over his shoulders, ready to slice her head off. She had one chance at this. Seconds to spare. She leaned back. Put all her weight on her quads…

But then…

Her attacker dropped to the ground as the reassuring sonic crack of a bullet leaving a barrel reverberated through the alley, hot gas hitting cooler air. The bullet had drilled a hole clean through the helmet like it was nothing. The man was dead. A few feet away stood Vinh, holding a pistol at arm's length.

Acid gasped.

Swallowed.

Found her voice.

"Jesus Christ. Thank you." She clocked the pistol. Not one of hers. "Where the hell did that come from?"

Vinh frowned. "We'll talk later." He stuffed the gun into his belt and let his shirt fall over it. "Let us go to my house, quickly."

She nodded. "Grab anything you can find from your guy. IDs. Wallets. Let's see who these pricks are."

Vinh ran back to the first man as she examined the dead rider at her feet. Blood was already seeping from under his helmet into a growing pool of sticky crimson. She unzipped his leather suit and located a wallet in an inside pocket. She flipped it open to reveal an ID card. Jackpot. She stuffed the wallet in her jacket and ran over to collect the holdall. In the distance she could hear the faint sound of a police siren over the dull hum of the city. Time to get out of here. Time for some answers.

Chapter Twenty-Seven

Vinh could sense Acid's intense gaze on him even though he had his back to her. Despite this, he kept his cool. Busied himself positioning, and then repositioning, the jug of coffee percolating on the stove top. Once that distraction became tiring he moved to the small cupboard above the counter and took down two white china cups. He padded over to the table and put one down in front of his guest and the other at the place opposite. He stepped back a moment, then leaned over and twisted his own cup around so the handle faced the opposite way. After which he returned to the stove.

"Come on, Vinh." Acid sighed. "Spill the beans."

He removed the now-whistling coffee jug and carried it over to the table. Picking up each cup in turn, Acid's and then his own, he poured out the coffee. All the while trying to ignore the palpable impatience and curiosity projected his way. He sat. Took a sip of coffee. It tasted good. Not as strong as he sometimes made, but welcome.

"What do you want to know?" he asked softly.

She leaned over to him. "You can start by telling me how an English teacher takes out a guy armed with a couple of Katana blades. That was bloody impressive."

Vinh fought a smile. "Tanto blades. Smaller."

"Semantics. Stop messing around."

He placed his cup down and moved his chair so he was nearer to her. Then he rolled up his shirt sleeve to show her the tattoo. A star in a circle, surrounded by a laurel wreath.

"You think you're the only one here with a past?" he told her. "I wasn't always a teacher." He traced his finger over the Vietnamese words under the main design. "These words say, 'Determined to win'. The motto of the People's Army of Vietnam."

"I bloody knew it when we shook hands yesterday," she said. "Teacher's hands aren't usually so rough. I figured some sort of handiwork at first."

"No, these are hands of war." Vinh brought them up inches from his face, staring into his palms. "I served with the army from the age of seventeen until I was forty-five. I was involved in many wars. Against China. Against Cambodia. You may have heard these wars referred to as conflicts. But they were not, they were wars. Many men died. My friends, but not me. I killed many. I have much blood on my hands but no regrets. So you see, Acid, we're not too different, you and me."

She raised one eyebrow. "So why leave the service? Why become a teacher?"

He took a deep breath, to be able to say what he rarely spoke of. "I was a good soldier. Loyal, brave. After serving for so long they allowed me a month's leave, to spend time with my family. I'd arranged for us to go on a day trip. To Ho Chi Minh City. District One. The area some still call 'Sai Gon'. My son was young, excitable. He saw something across the street and ran out without looking. The man driving the car had no chance. My son was killed instantly." A tear formed in the corner of his eye, but he made no move to wipe it. "My wife and I were devastated. We had been rowing when it happened and were not watching him. We could not deal with the guilt. The pain. She blamed me. I blamed her. Blamed myself too. We split up a few years later. Then I found out she'd killed herself. Overdose." The words stopped and the tear fell from his eye to roll down his cheek. He wet his lips to try again, tasting salt at the edge of his mouth. "I guess in this sense we're similar as well. Death drives us. Only I chose to use my pain to help others. I became a teacher. Tried to bury my grief in books."

He got up and went over to the old wooden chest unit in the corner of the room. Sliding open the top drawer, he slipped his hands under the scattered mess of papers and keys and bits of string. On reaching the back of the drawer, he traced along the rough wooden panel until he touched on what he was searching for. He removed the felt bag and opened it out on top of the unit. Then he pulled the gun from out of his belt and placed it onto the felt wrapping. His trusty service weapon. A K14-VN – a variant of the K-54 but with a longer barrel. Standard issue for the PAVN and manufactured locally at the Z111 Factory in Thanh Hoa. He was meant to hand it back when decommissioned from service. But somehow, amidst the melee of grief and confusion clouding those days, he'd hung onto it.

"Lucky you thought to bring the gun," Acid said behind him. "Didn't think to tell me though?"

Vinh stared down at the small handgun. It had saved his life on many occasions, but had remained in the back of the drawer for many years. It had felt good to hold it again. Like a part of himself he'd lost.

"I have put most of my past behind me," he said. "And have not spoken about it in so long. But when life became dangerous again, it felt right to bring it with me." He wrapped the felt cover around the pistol and shoved it under a pile of papers. Then he slid the drawer shut and turned around, forced a smile. "That's my story. Not a great one. Not a happy one. But as you can see now, I may be more useful to you than you first realised."

A frown twisted Acid Vanilla's face. "I don't get why you're doing this. I mean, sure, you're a nice guy, yadda, yadda. But you want to know what happened to this kid even if it means getting yourself killed?"

His turn to frown. "He was my student. Tam is my friend."

"Seems odd to me. Risking your life for someone else." She held her hand up. "But, hey, says more about me than it does you."

Vinh leaned back against the worktop and considered this strange woman sitting in his kitchen. She certainly had something about her. She was attractive, no question. With her dark complexion and full lips, not to mention those striking different-coloured eyes. But it wasn't only that. It was the way she held herself. Confidence, some might call it. But Vinh saw something more. A deeper, more intriguing element to her personality.

"Let me put the spotlight back on you," he said. "I understand these people killed your mother and you want revenge. But last night you also told me you wanted to get away from this life of killing. So which is it?"

She looked away, tracing her finger along a raised scar on her forearm, and immediately he regretted his words.

"I'm sorry," he said. "I shouldn't have asked."

"No. It's fine. And you're right. Cognitive dissonance and me – I could write a book." With the coffee mug poised near her mouth, she blew over the surface and took a sip. "Thing is, I've always had a lot going on in my head. Most of it pretty grim. Dark stuff. But I deal with it. Most of the time. What I mean is all this – wrestling with myself – it's all par for the course."

"I see," he said. And he did. It wasn't confidence he saw in her, it was cynicism. He understood that all too well. If you believed the world was against you, it prepared you for any eventuality. Nothing phased you. "Tell me about this Spitfire person."

"Spitfire Creosote." A deep frown crumpled her face, bringing with it an expression of sadness. But only for a second. "He's a prick. And a bastard."

"I see. That bad, huh?"

"That bad," she said and laughed. But he could tell it hurt.

"So, you do have a past, you and him?"

She wagged her finger at him. "You're good. I'll give you that." She sighed and sat upright. "But yeah, we have a past."

"Sorry, you don't have to tell me."

"He was one of my handlers. Trained me up when I first joined Annihilation Pest Control. Taught me how to shoot. How to fight." As she spoke she stared off into the middle distance, as though seeing her story play out in front of her. "Thing is, he wasn't even my type. Isn't my type. Him all tanned and chiselled and super-confident. But I don't know, there was something about him. My friend thinks it was a grooming exercise on their part, a way to keep me subservient, in line. But I'm not so sure. I was eighteen. Wily. Horny as hell. Plus I thought I was hard as nails.

And I was." She flipped her hand against her thigh. "Fuck. Who the hell knows?"

She glanced at him but he didn't respond. Experience had taught him when people were talking in this way it was best to give them space. In his own life he knew having a witness to his pain and suffering was a gift hard to repay.

"I liked him from the off, but pushed any thoughts about him away," she went on. "I was full of hate and anger and ready to show the world what I could do. Falling in love didn't fit with any of that."

"Love?" he repeated. "Ah."

"I think so. The only time. Never again." She laughed, but stopped herself. "Caesar sent us out on a job together. New York. My first time in the Big Apple. I loved it. The sights, the smells. All those places I'd read about. Sure, we were there to kill someone, but along the way something sparked between us." A loud sniff distorted her face, morphing it from whimsical reminiscence to bitterness. "And now I'm here to kill him."

"Do you think you can?" he asked.

She nodded emphatically. Her eyes flickered with purpose. "Absolutely. No question. He has to die, and he will. So yes – you help me find him, and in return we'll find out what happened to Huy."

"Thank you." He gave it a beat. Allowing the heavy atmosphere chance to clear. Then more breezily, he added, "What do you suggest we do?"

She pulled the motorbike rider's wallet from her pocket. "Sit. Let's see what we've got here."

Glad of something to do, Vinh grabbed the other wallet from the worktop and joined her at the table. They each rifled through the folds, pulling out credit cards, low-denomination notes.

"I've got an ID." He held up the card to show her.

"Me too. Let's see."

He handed her the card and she held it up next to the first one. "They're the same. Security ID. Door men at the Andromeda Club. You know it?"

He thought. "I think so. It's over in the Kim Ma district. Opened maybe two years ago. I've not been, but why would I? You think it's a front?"

She chewed her lip. "Not sure. But if our attackers worked there, it might be a good place to start."

"Good idea. But it won't open until later tonight. Ten at the earliest."

Acid sat back in her seat and raised her mug. "Gives us plenty of time for you to tell me all about your army days."

He looked down. "I don't know. Like I say, I've not talked about that part of my life for a long time. It feels like a million years ago now."

"Yeah, well," she told him, looking at the clock hanging on the wall above the table. "We've got six hours before we need to leave, so come on Mr Army Man. Most impressive kill. You go first."

Chapter Twenty-Eight

Five hours and plenty of gory tales later, Acid and Vinh left the modest apartment and headed for the Kim Ma district. It was a fair walk, but Acid had decided she needed the air. Four strong coffees had left her with a pounding headache she needed to clear. She was, however, pleased she'd won the kill-off. Not that she'd had any doubts she wouldn't. She hadn't met a person yet who could beat her well-told tale of the neck scarf and the high-heeled shoe. Although Vinh's tale of how he infil-trated a hostile's base and single-handedly took out four enemy soldiers, armed only with a piece of his dead friend's shin bone, was also impressive.

It was a few minutes after ten when they turned the corner and saw the lights of the Andromeda Club at the end of the road. It wasn't a particularly big or impressive-looking establishment – all they could see of it from here was a wide entrance, above which a neon sign quietly buzzed. More remarkable to Acid was the size of the bouncer leaning against the wall and staring blankly out in front of him. He had a few more inches on her and Vinh, and double their girth put together.

"Let me do the talking," Vinh whispered as they approached.

Acid rubbed at her bare arms, silently bemoaning the lack of a jacket as the hot day turned into a cool evening.

"No worries," she whispered back. She had every intention of letting Vinh do the talking, since her Vietnamese was embarrassingly non-existent. Spitfire and Davros had tried to get her to learn languages in the early days, but she'd resisted. It felt too much like school. She spoke some French and Spanish but that was all. The way she saw it, the only language she'd ever needed was that of the assassin.

At the nightclub door the bouncer slowly turned his head to acknowledge them. His eyes were bulbous and bloodshot, and he had the kinds of lips that were eternally moist. He eyeballed Vinh then moved onto her, his gaze lingering on her breasts. Instinctively she made a fist, but held her tongue. They'd come unarmed and the plan was to keep a low profile, find out anything they could and then get out of there.

Vinh addressed the man with a friendly tone, laughing and pointing first at her and then back to himself. The bouncer grunted, screwing up his face like he'd smelt something rotten. He drew his eyes her way for a few more seconds, then with a sneer waved them through.

"What did you say to laughing-boy?" she asked as they hurried down a short, dark corridor leading to a set of double doors.

"Same as before. Told him you were a famous English actress," Vinh replied. "Said you'd heard good things about the club and wanted to visit."

"I'm not sure he bought it."

"I just don't think he was too bothered."

"Clearly."

They got to the end of the corridor and took a door handle each, yanking on them in unison. A rush of hot air hit them in the face and the sound of loud electronic music filled their ears. They stepped through the doors and let them swing closed behind them. Once inside they waited for their eyes to grow accustomed to the gloom. Acid blinked. They were at the top of a long wide stairway that corkscrewed down to the basement club. The venue was much bigger than it looked from the outside. A thick cloud of dry ice hung over the central dancefloor, as more was pumped in from underneath the DJ booth, to the left of the large open-plan room. Opposite was the bar area, taking up the length of one wall. Red-fringed light shades hung from the ceiling over the counter, the only source of light apart from the cheesy lasers and occasional flurry of strobe lighting. Apart from the bar staff and DJ, they were the only two people in the club, but it was early doors for a Friday night. Acid looked at Vinh and shrugged. They made their way down the stairs and sat at a table at the far side of the room. Near the bar, but with sight lines all around the venue.

"Do you want a drink?" Vinh asked, shouting over the music. "I'm having a Coke."

She pulled a face. "Whisky, please. Unless they serve it in plastic. In which case I'll have a beer. Doesn't matter what, as long as it's cold."

Vinh bowed theatrically. "As you wish."

She sat and watched her companion as he sauntered over to the empty bar and held one finger up for the barman. He was growing on her. It didn't hurt that she found him attractive. He was older than her by a good fifteen years but didn't seem it. Not when he was in fight-mode, that was for sure. She had been mightily impressed by the skills on show earlier. Not that she'd ever admit it. Least of all to Vinh.

Her mind drifted to Spook once more, who'd been on at her before she left for Hanoi:

Be more open…

Let your guard down…

The kid meant well but she didn't understand. Her guard – her Acid Vanilla persona – it was there for a reason. Not to mention, if she let it drop away she was unsure what remained in its place.

Shit.

Spook. She still hadn't called her.

Acid pulled out her phone intending to drop her a text, let her know she was safe. But they were underground. No reception. She bit her lip and shoved the phone back in her pocket. First thing tomorrow, she'd call her.

Vinh appeared with drinks. "All plastic, I'm afraid," he said, placing a squat pint of beer on the table, followed by one for himself.

Acid picked up the pint and guided the flimsy container to her lips. "I thought you were having a Coke?"

"I changed my mind. Perhaps you are a destructive influence on me."

She winked at him over the top of her drink. "That's what they all say. They're probably correct."

The beer was weak but cold and went down well. She gulped down a few large mouthfuls and leaned back on her stool, scoping the place out.

Behind the bar a fresh-faced barman in a tight white shirt and black bow tie was being talked at by a shorter, older, rounder man wearing a black shirt and no tie. The older man was angry He shoved a stubby finger into the youngster's chest as he bellowed at him, before running his fingers through his thinning swept-back hair and storming off across the dancefloor. Acid narrowed her eyes as she watched him go. A glance back at Vinh told her he'd had the same idea.

"Manager?" she mused.

They watched the man unlock a door to the left of the DJ booth and disappear. Vinh turned to say something, but she was already on her feet. She drank the last half-pint in one gulp and placed the plastic beaker on the table. Then she was off, striding across the smoky dancefloor.

"Acid, wait," Vinh called out over the music, coming up alongside her. "What's our move here?"

She got to the door and turned to him. "We go ask some questions. Simple."

"But what if he's a part of it, one of The Cai Moi? It could get nasty."

"Let's hope so," she said, shooting him a manic grin before pulling the door open and stepping through. She waited until Vinh was clear before she let it swing shut. In front of them was a red painted stairway leading up to a small landing with a door on either side. Both closed. They made their way up the stairs and took a door each. Acid gently placed her hands against the one on the right and lowered her ear to the hollow wood. All she could hear was the throbbing bass emanating up from the dancefloor. She tried the handle and found it to be unlocked. Moving slowly, she eased open the door to reveal a small cupboard.

"Oh. Shit."

She opened it wider to show Vinh the mop and bucket, the two shelves stacked high with cleaning products. After closing the door, she joined Vinh at the other side.

"Can you hear anything?" she whispered.

"No. But this must be the office. Shall I knock? What's our story?"

Acid puffed her cheeks. She hadn't thought this far ahead. But she never did. Most of the time she preferred to think on her feet, let her instincts guide her. She closed her eyes, listening for the chiming chatter of the bats. They were always there, if she listened, right on the cusp of her consciousness. Like a gut feeling, but more cerebral. More creative. Right now, they said, *Go for it.*

Without consulting Vinh, she knocked loudly on the door. Waited. Knocked again. Still nothing.

"Screw it."

With the bats urging her on, she grabbed the handle and swung the door open. The man in the black shirt was waiting to greet her. He was standing in the middle of a small office, and in his hand was the unmistakable shape of a Glock 19 handgun.

He pointed it at her head.

"Who the fuck are you?" he yelled, the gun quivering in his grip. "You better talk. Fast."

Chapter Twenty-Nine

Acid raised her hands as the man shoved the gun in her face. Her gaze flitted around the room. The walls were bare. The room windowless. Behind the man was a large, cheaply put-together desk covered in chipped walnut laminate. A dusty laptop sat open on piles of papers and receipts. Over in the far corner was a beat-up metal filing cabinet that had seen better days.

"All right, mate. Keep calm."

She kept her hands raised, taking a deep breath in through her nasal canal, working on slowing her heart rate. Ironically enough, it had been Spitfire who had taught her how to do that. It was a biofeedback technique. In this case, controlled breathing. By focusing on long deep breaths you maintained oxygenation, which in turn helped clear your head and slow your pulse. That way you gained perspective on your next move. The only problem was, right now most of her perspective was taken up by the gun barrel inches from her face.

She felt Vinh's presence beside her. His hands were

raised. He remained still. Controlled. He spoke to the man in Vietnamese, but it was hard to judge the tone. She saw Vinh nodding, thought she caught some curse words in response. Despite's Vinh's composure, the man before them was clearly furious. But that was understandable. He turned his attention back to Acid.

"Who are you, why are you here? Did they send you?"

"Did who send us?"

The man gripped the gun tighter as a bead of sweat formed over his right eyebrow. Acid zoned in on his trigger finger. It was shaking. Tense. One false move and her head was a cloud of red mist. She took another deep breath and narrowed her eyes to slits, deleting as much peripheral vision as she could.

"We don't want any trouble," she told him. "We took a wrong turn, that's all, looking for the bathroom."

"That's what I told him already," Vinh said.

"See?" she said. "We're simply here for a good time. Now if you don't mind, I'm going to turn around and leave you to it. No harm done. We get it, you don't want people up here. But we aren't a threat to you."

She waited. Nothing happened. The tendons in the man's trigger finger relaxed a jot, enough that she'd risk it. With her hands still raised and keeping her eyes on him until the last moment, she turned around. As she passed Vinh she shot him a wink, hoping he'd know what it meant.

In one fluid motion, she dropped and swung her leg into the side of the man's shin sending him stumbling to one side. Vinh leapt forward and smashed the man's hand into the wall, enough that he dropped the gun. Acid grabbed it up along with a handful of the manager's lank hair and dragged him over to the desk. Once there she kicked the back of his knees out and shoved his head against the desktop.

"All right, sunshine," she said, pressing the muzzle of the Glock against his temple. "Now it's your turn to talk. Fast."

The man blubbered, trying to find the words. The whole turnaround had taken less than five seconds and he was in shock. He gasped something at her in Vietnamese. She ground the gun harder into his head.

"English."

"What the fuck?" the man wailed. "I did everything you told me. I promise. We are clean."

"We're not who you think we are," she told him. She reached into her back pocket and pulled out the two ID cards. "These men. They work for you, yes?"

The man twisted his head to view the IDs. Not easy in his current position. He closed his eyes in a grimace. "They did work for me. Not any longer. I was told to sack them."

She looked over at Vinh. He shrugged. Back to the man. "Who told you to sack them? Why?"

"The Cai Moi. The One," the man replied, through sobs. "They own this club now. They own me. Those men were my bouncers but I knew they sold drugs in the club. Confiscated them and then sold on. The One dislike drugs. They dislike anything they don't control."

"These men attacked us this afternoon," she said, closing her eyes. Every sinew in her body, every aspect of her psyche was screaming at her to pull the trigger. "Tell us why."

The manager had actual tears now. He tried to look up at her, over at Vinh. "I swear to you, I do not know. They were in here last night. Drinking. Dancing with my girls. Showing off with their money. Lots of it. Rubbing my face in it. They were with another. An English man, in an expensive suit."

She cast Vinh another look. Spitfire. He must have put them up to it. It meant he knew she was here.

"I don't understand," Vinh said, moving closer. "You said the Cai Moi want to clean up. What do you mean?"

"Please, let me up," the man wailed. "I cannot think with the gun in my face."

Acid paused a moment. Then dragged him up by the hair and shoved him towards the leather chair behind the desk.

"Sit," she ordered, the gun pointed at him.

The man did as he was told. He looked from her to Vinh and back again with an expression of resigned concern. "Where are they now?" he asked. "Tran and Le, the men who attacked you."

"Dead. Who are The One?"

The manager whimpered, but told her, "The One are the Cai Moi. The Cai Moi are The One. Same thing. Most of them are young. They like to play games with people's expectations. They came here a few months ago. Two of them. They told me they were taking control of my club and I had to accept it. They said the Andromeda was a bad element in the city. Drugs. Prostitution. But what can I say? It's a fucking nightclub!" He paused for breath and ran his hand over his damp hair, playing for time. Acid aimed the gun a centimetre below his nose, her arm rigid. He continued. "They told me they now owned my club. They take half my profits. Tell me who to hire. Their mission is to clean up the city. So they say. Yet they do this by killing people? Hurting people? I don't understand. But I hear stories. They are buying up lots of companies. Want a hand in all the industries in Hanoi. In

Vietnam too. I hear their goal is complete control of the culture."

"Where can we find them?" she asked.

The man leaned forward and put his head in his hands. Sweat poured from his forehead. "Are you kidding me? If I tell you, they'll kill me."

"Hey! Look at me!" she said. "If you don't tell me, I'll kill you." She closed one eye over the gun barrel. It was the first time in a while she'd felt like this. Blood lust, it was one hell of a rush.

"Fine. If I tell you what I know, you will leave?"

"Abso-bloody-lutely."

The manager shook his head. "I do not know of their main headquarters, I swear. But there is a factory across town. I can give you the address. I hear it has recently been taken over by the Cai Moi. They have people working there around the clock. No one goes in or out."

Vinh stirred beside her. "That's where Huy is. I know it."

She looked from Vinh back to the manager. "What are they making there?"

"I do not know," he replied. "The Cai Moi are secretive and their operations concealed. No one knows exactly what is going on. This is how they instil fear in the people." He scrabbled around on the desk and found a piece of scrap paper. He jotted something down and held it out to her. "Here. Please, do not tell anyone I gave you this."

She reached over with her free hand and took the note, passing it to Vinh without looking round.

"One more thing," Vinh said, moving alongside her and holding up the now battered photo of Huy. "Have you seen this man? The one on the left."

The manager leaned forward and squinted at the

picture. Then he looked to her, not Vinh, his eyes wide with fear and confusion as he said, "Why are you asking me this?"

"Well? Have you?" she asked. But this time the man shook his head.

"Never. I have never seen him before. I swear."

She exchanged a glance with Vinh as he shoved the photo back in his pocket.

"All right. Thanks," she told the manager, backing away. "I'll keep hold of this too," she said, holding up the gun. "If you don't mind."

"Take whatever you want. But leave me alone." He batted them away with a limp flick of his hand.

She didn't need telling twice. She turned and hurried back down the stairwell. At the bottom she halted and stuffed the Glock into the waistband of her jeans, covering it over with the hem of her vest top. Then as Vinh joined her at the door, they slipped out, moseyed across the dance-floor, and out of the club.

Chapter Thirty

Vinh waited until they'd got clear of the nightclub and out of sight around the next corner before he spoke.

"What do you think about this factory?" he asked.

Acid hit him with the same ironic half-shrug he'd experienced often since they'd met. It was annoying, but also kind of endearing.

"What else have we got to go on?" she said. "It can't hurt to have a look. If they are forcing people to work there, maybe Huy is one of them."

"It could be a trap."

"Everything's a trap."

He stopped walking and turned to face her. "What do you mean by that?"

Another shrug. "What I say. Love. Work. Life. It's all a trap."

He couldn't help but laugh. "You're a very cynical person, you know that?"

"So they tell me. Do you have the address?"

"We're going there now?"

"No time like the present."

"But don't we need some sort of strategy? Collect more weapons at least."

"I've got this." She patted her hip where she'd stuffed the Glock she'd taken from the nightclub owner. "It's got a full mag."

"Good for you. What about me?"

She sighed. "Look, we'll scope out the place and get inside as stealthily as we can. Once there, we'll find whoever's in charge and ask a few questions. Okay? There's your strategy. You don't need a weapon. I can handle it." He scowled, but she was having none of it. "Vinh, trust me. This is what I do. I'm a professional."

They carried on in silence for a few minutes. Vinh pulled out the folded yellow paper from his pocket and read the address the man had written. He knew the area. It was walkable from where they were. Thirty minutes.

"If this is a Cai Moi controlled factory, it'll have heavy security," he said, once they'd walked a mile or so. "What did your man say – 'Enough firepower to take down most of the Vietnamese army.' We need to be careful."

"Hey," Acid said, playing hurt. "I'm always careful."

Another silence. Vinh swallowed.

He was going to say it.

He needed to let the words out.

"You think Huy is dead. Don't you?"

She didn't respond. Which told him everything he needed to know. A shiver ran down his back. Though it wasn't like he hadn't thought the same. Did think the same. But saying it out loud? That was different.

"It doesn't matter what I think," she told him. "I've been wrong about a lot of things."

They crossed the street and headed down the side of a

long carriageway leading away from the centre. If his calculations were correct, the factory should be visible once they got to the end of this road.

"I don't know what I would do if he is dead," he spoke into the night sky. To himself as much as his companion. "After Danh died, my son, I was a broken man. I still am, I suppose. I have done a lot of bad in my life. I told myself it was payback. Maybe this is the same."

"Well, shit, Vinh," Acid exclaimed. "Sounds like me talking."

"Oh? Is that so?"

"Oh yes. I get it, my friend. Bad karma, it's a bitch."

"Either way," he continued, "searching for Huy – it has given me purpose again. Made me feel I am doing something good with my life. If he is alive, I must find him. If he is dead, then I need to know. At least then we can lay his memory to rest. Provide some peace for his mother."

"She seems cool," Acid said. "Tam, I mean."

He chuckled. "Yes. Tam is a wonderful woman. I have known her for many years. I served with her husband before he was killed in action. We were all good friends, my family and his. Then tragedy struck and everything fell apart." They got to the end of the carriageway. The factory was now in sight, next to a small patch of wasteland a few hundred metres away. He glanced at Acid. "So you feel this too, that you are to blame for your mother's death?"

"You could say that," she replied. Her voice was quiet. She didn't look at him. "Which is why I need to kill everyone involved. Bring some balance back to my life."

"Will it help?"

She sniffed. "Truth is, I'm not sure. But I've got no choice. If I don't kill them they'll only come for me and Spook one day."

"Spook? Your pet?"

"My friend."

"Ah, I see. Another codename?"

"A-ha." She wagged her finger at him. "You'd think, wouldn't you? But no, that's her actual name. Spook Horowitz. Her parents were hippies."

The factory was now veering up into the night sky in front of them. Vinh grabbed Acid by the arm and guided her into the shadows of the building opposite. "This is it. The Cai Moi factory. But please, Acid, if your man is here, don't start shooting up the place until we know about Huy. If he's a prisoner here, we need to step clever."

She grunted a response and it sounded like she was agreeing. But then she was off, striding over the road and heading for the factory yard where two trucks were parked in a huge loading bay. He followed on behind, running to catch up, then falling in beside her as they traced the side of the factory wall before coming to a stop behind one of the trucks.

"There," she whispered, pointing over to where the loading bay door was propped open. Beyond the doorway was a curtain made of clear plastic strips, each one a few inches wide. Beyond that, darkness. As they watched, a man appeared through the curtain. He was dressed in maroon overalls and carried a large box, which he placed in the back of the second truck before tracing his steps back into the factory.

"Come on," Acid said. "He's going for another load. We'll move nearer and slip inside when he comes back."

Silent, and keeping low, they edged down the side of the truck until they got to the rear doors. They stayed in the shadows, watching the plastic curtain for movement, ready to move. Minutes ticked by. No sound but their deep panting breaths falling in time with one another as they waited. Eventually the curtains peeled open and the same man reappeared carrying another box. They waited until he passed them, then scurried across the loading bay and up some stone steps into the factory. Once through the curtain they followed the corridor around until they got to a set of doors. Acid leaned against the wall and stretched out her arm to ease one of them open half an inch. She put her face against it.

"Clear," she said, then eased the door open some more and slipped through.

Vinh followed her into what looked to him like a canteen area, though it was unused and had been for many years. A layer of thick dust covered the wooden tables set up along one wall. Opposite the tables, two battered vending machines were empty of any goods.

They made their way across the room and out a door the other side. Beyond it was another sprawling corridor with windows along the left-hand side. Many years of dust and grime had rendered the windows opaque, but here and there Vinh noticed gaps in the dirt. He crept over and peered through to see a large room with six long tables lined up across its width. On each of the tables sat two rows of sewing machines – he counted sixteen on each table – with men and women feverishly working on them. He put his face closer to the glass. Every worker had the same type of material, a thick, maroon-coloured cotton. He recognised it as the same material as the overalls worn by the man loading the truck.

He lifted his head. "What do you think they're doing?" he asked.

Acid held her hand up to the glass and rested her forehead against it. "Looks like some kind of uniform." She squinted through the grime. "Do you see Huy anywhere?"

Vinh was already scanning the many faces of the workers. Men and women of all ages and sizes. The only likeness that connected them was how wretched and broken they appeared. As his attention moved from face to face he saw the same gaunt expression. Brows knotted with intense concentration. Eyes alert with fear. But no sign of Huy. He turned to Acid.

"No. I don't see him."

They continued along the corridor and through the door at the far end, which opened up into a larger room full of boxes similar to those being loaded into the truck. Before Vinh could stop her, Acid lifted one down and was knelt over it.

"Careful," he whispered. "We don't want to give ourselves away."

But she wasn't listening. She tore a long strip of packing tape from the box and lifted the cardboard wings either side. The box was full of clothes made of the same maroon material. Acid pulled out the top item and held it out at arm's length. A shirt. She held it by the shoulders, letting it fall so they could both see. The shirt had been made in a military style, with winged collars, two covered pockets, one on each side, and epaulets on the shoulders. But that wasn't all. On the left-hand side, above the pocket, was embroidered a small yellow circle, as though done in brushstroke. Underneath this, four symbols and Vietnamese words in the same yellow embroidery.

Acid held it close to him. "What does it say?" she asked.

He stared at the cloth. At the words written there.

"Cai Moi Liberation Army," he whispered. "What does that mean?"

Acid stuffed the shirt back in the box. "Means these guys aren't interested in organised crime, Vinh. They're forming a bloody militia."

Chapter Thirty-One

Acid returned to the box of uniforms and was pulling out a pair of stiff-cotton maroon trousers when she heard shuffling behind her and felt the cold metal of a gun muzzle prod her in the neck.

"Ah, shit."

She raised her arms in the air and looked up to see Vinh doing the same. Two guards. One behind each of them. Vinh's guy had a Type 56 rifle – the Chinese variant on the AK-47. Serious stuff. No doubt Sonny's merchandise.

She glanced at Vinh. "Keep cool," she told him. "We can handle this."

The guard behind her growled something in Vietnamese and prodded harder with the rifle barrel. He moved the muzzle into the small of her back as she slowly got to her feet. The unease coming from him was palpable. He was jumpy. Nervous. That could be useful. Or it could be extremely dangerous indeed.

She kept her arms raised as the bats screamed across her

synapses. The room shifted. Her awareness sharpened, from grey to technicolour. Relaxing into her peripheral vision she scanned the area. She still had the Glock in her waistband but that was a last resort. She'd never take out both guards without one of them killing her or Vinh. Even if, by some feat of superhuman ingenuity, she did manage to take them both out (it had happened before but when she was younger, more on form) the noise of the gunfire would alert more guards.

Enough firepower to take down most of the Vietnamese army.

It made sense now.

The two guards were shouting at each other, unsure what to do next. It was clear now they were new recruits, ordered to guard over the workers with no instruction on how to deal with intruders. The guard holding Vinh could only have been around eighteen. Acid thought of the street rats. That made sense now as well. Young, disillusioned men with no prospects were often ripe pickings for these sorts of organisations, easily moulded and manipulated to fit in with the leader's mad ideology. But it also meant they lacked experience. Their training the streets rather than the military. A few feet away she sensed Vinh's eyes on her, trying to get her attention. She followed his gaze over to where two thick ropes hung down from the ceiling, part of an old pulley system. She glanced back at him and gave one brisk nod. She understood. But he needed to get them over there.

Vinh turned his head and spoke in Vietnamese to the guards. He kept his voice soft, the rhythm of his words slow and easy. She held her nerve, glad he was here. More than anything, she knew now she could trust him. The low timbre of his voice was him creating an atmosphere of calm, letting the guards know he posed them no threat. It was textbook communication. How to act when confronted with stressed people holding assault rifles. A moment later she felt the prod of the rifle in her back, pushing her towards the door. Towards the ropes.

She shuffled forward. They had one chance at this. The ropes were a few steps away and perhaps a foot above their heads. It would be tight. She moved her attention inward, harnessing the old fight-or-flight hormones bubbling through her system as she ran through the next few minutes in her head. Mental rehearsals, so useful in these situations. Her hope was the amateurish guards would be too startled to react quickly enough. But it could easily go the other way. Young, disillusioned men with no prospects often had itchy trigger fingers.

Another shuffling step and they were underneath the ropes. From this angle they appeared higher than she had anticipated. But it was now or never. With a grunt, she leapt for the rope and got hold of it with both hands, swinging back so she was behind the guard. With her eyes fixed on his head she let go of the rope, hitting him with the full weight of her body. Her knees struck him in the shoulders and she rode him all the way to the ground, knocking the wind out of him and cracking his spine with her shin bone. To finish the job, she struck the nape of his neck with the heel of her palm and smashed his head into the wooden floor.

She looked up, panting, to see Vinh kneeling on the back of the second guard.

"Good work," she said. "What now?"

Vinh pulled the tattered photo from out his pocket and grabbed the guard by the hair. He yanked his head back and shoved the photo in front of his face.

Acid watched as the young guard regarded the photo with a stunned expression. Vinh yanked at his hair some more and the pain revived him. Vinh spoke at him fast, all the calm gone from his voice. He was asking him about Huy and the guard seemed to be talking. Then she heard the word *chet* and saw Vinh's shoulders drop. The guard was telling him what they both knew. Huy was dead. Vinh let the man's head drop to the ground and got to his feet.

"I'm sorry," she told him.

His eyes burned with a passion and a rage she hadn't seen before. His jaw was tense, his face hard. "We must find the Cai Moi," he said quietly. "They must pay for this."

"Now you're talking," she said. "What else did he say?"

"Not much we didn't already know. He was sent to guard the factory. He's a foot soldier for the Cai Moi. A new recruit. He says the leaders aren't here. They have a head-quarters in the city but he doesn't know where."

Acid shoved the Glock back into her belt and considered the assault rifles the men had dropped. Useful if they needed to fight their way out, but awkward too, noisy. She decided against it.

The second guard was beginning to stir, making low groaning noises. It was time to go. She didn't think they'd be stupid enough to risk sounding an alarm, but she wasn't going to wait to find out. She was heading for the door, back the way they'd come, when Vinh stopped and moved over to a pile of boxes by the door.

"Look, here," he said, picking up a piece of paper lying on the top box.

"What is it?"

He held it up, his eyes darting around the page. "A delivery note, by the looks of it. There's an address." He turned the paper around to show her, pointing at a series of symbols top-right. "I know the area. Over in the north. It's mainly derelict warehouses."

"You thinking that's where they've set up base?" she asked.

"Don't you?"

"It's worth a shot," she told him. "And my best chance of finding Spitfire. Let's go."

"Wait," Vinh said. "Don't you think we should rest first? I'm tired. My reactions are becoming sluggish."

She considered it. "Fine. We'll take a few hours and reconvene tomorrow. But we must wait until nightfall, that's an entire day wasted."

"Yes. But still plenty of opportunity to find your man and get your revenge." Vinh looked at his feet. "Acid, I am tired and weary. And now I know the truth, time doesn't seem so pressing."

Acid sighed. The bats were loud in her head and she hated to stop at this juncture. Especially as it gave her less time to find Spitfire. But she had to admit, she too was feeling the heavy weight of fatigue on her shoulders and legs.

"Fine," she said, and sighed. "We'll rest up. Visit the warehouse tomorrow night."

From the look on Vinh's face it was the right thing to say. He folded the delivery note into his pocket. "Thank you. Will you risk going back to your hotel?"

"I need my jacket and a few other items, but maybe I could crash at yours after? It'll be safer, like you say. And my weapons are there."

Vinh frowned. "Can't you do without your jacket?"

"Erm. No. Sorry." She was also planning on calling Spook. Although the call wouldn't be entirely an altruistic act.

"Okay. Fine," he told her. "As long as you don't make me drink again."

MATTHEW HATTERSLEY

"No," she said, sternly. "We need to be clear-headed for what comes next."

"Agreed."

"Maybe one won't hurt, though." She grinned. "Come on. Let's go get my jacket."

Chapter Thirty-Two

Spitfire Creosote sat upright in the bath, sending soap and water splashing over the side.

Bloody bastard shitting hell.

He'd been lying there trying to relax for the past forty-five minutes and had now become one with the steaming suds. He tilted his head in the direction of the next room, hoping he'd had water in his ears and misheard. But no, there it was again, his damned mobile phone going off. He reached over for his watch and let out a heavy sigh. 10 a.m. and already his zen mindset was in tatters.

The phone carried on ringing, announcing its shrill presence in the next room. Not only that, it was the specific ringtone he'd assigned to Beowulf Caesar. The big boss calling.

"Bloody hell!"

Spitfire had been ignoring Raaz's calls since getting the news about Acid. But he couldn't swerve Caesar. Not if he valued his balls. And his head.

He stood up in the bath, sending a torrent of coconut

and mango-scented soapy water gushing down his body. He stared at his reflection in the mirror over the marble sink unit opposite. Fifty-one years young. Still a fine figure of a man, if he said so himself. Godlike, he'd go so far as, even with the soapy residue lingering in his extensive chest hair, and less extensive (in fact neatly trimmed) pubic region. He stepped out onto the large Egyptian cotton towel he'd earlier placed on the marble floor and selected a second towel from the heated rack on the wall. With the mobile phone still resounding tiresomely, he wrapped the towel around himself and strode into the bedroom.

"All right, keep your hair on," he shouted, smiling to himself at the unintentional joke. Caesar had some hair when Spitfire first met him all those years ago, but it had soon fallen out. He said stress. Spitfire said weak genetics. Poor bastard.

He sat on the edge of the huge double king-size bed and picked up the phone. He selected speaker rather than handset and tapped Accept.

"Bloody bleeding Christ on a bicycle. I thought you weren't going to answer."

"Sorry, boss."

Spitfire coughed. His voice had sounded shrill. He cricked his neck and took a moment to ground himself. When he spoke again he was back in the deep velvet tonality he'd cultivated over the years.

"I meant to call sooner," he drawled. "But I was...otherwise engaged." The way he said it, as full-on innuendo, triggered a throaty laugh from the boss. Which was his intention.

"Dirty old fucker," Caesar growled. "You having fun over there?"

He sounded to be eating while he talked. The noise of

chewing and the squelching of spittle echoed out from the speaker. Spitfire placed the phone on his pillow. People eating on phone calls was one of his pet hates. He'd killed for less.

"Now then, my old mate," Caesar went on. "I hear your number one fan is in town. I'm hoping you are about to tell me she's been taken care of."

Spitfire counted down from five before he spoke. Another technique that had served him well over the years. Especially when dealing with men like Caesar. It paid to be the calm one, the sophisticate, that charming bastard with the devil in his smile. The person he had been before he met Caesar had been on the road to self-improvement – he worked out every morning, watched his posture, trained his voice, was a yearly subscriber to both GQ and Men's Health – but the day he became Spitfire Creosote that was all turned up to the max. Knowing he could now erase all the elements of his past he found distasteful, he transformed what was already a carefully orchestrated persona into something extraordinary. Some*one* extraordinary. Mr Sensational. The Flash Boy. Spitfire Creosote.

"She's proving somewhat – shall we say – tricky," Spitfire replied, archly. It was a textbook response. The delivery as well. Roger would have been proud.

"Stop being bloody cryptic," Caesar said. "Give me the pissing low down, will you?"

So Spitfire told him. How he'd hired two local thugs to take her out. How they'd let him down big time. "They told me they had it in hand. But I won't make the mistake again," he added. "Do we have any sightings?"

"No. We're pissing blind at the moment. The CCTV networks over there are virtually non-existent. Bloody Vietnamese. You'd think being so close to China they'd get their people in order."

Spitfire got to his feet and dried himself off. He placed a long, muscular leg up onto the bed and went to work on his thigh. The towel was soft and warm and felt good against his skin.

"Don't worry, I'll find her," he called over to the phone. "I've got a meeting with the Cai Moi later, to drop off the goods. I'll ask for some assistance in tracking her down. It is, after all, in everyone's interests to get shot of the pesky bitch."

He finished drying his leg and shoved the towel up between his arse cheeks, thankful he'd managed to fit in his monthly wax before the trip. Smooth as silk.

"You sure you can handle it?" Caesar enquired, sounding a little subdued.

"What the hell is that supposed to mean?"

"Calm down, Spitfire," his boss said. "You know what I bastard well mean. We both had a special place in our hearts for Acid Vanilla. Once upon a time. I'm only being assiduous. So, no issues then, as far as you're concerned?"

Spitfire fixed himself an icy stare in the mirror opposite the bed. "No issues at all."

"Excellent. Though to be honest, your − shall we say − entwined history might play out in your favour. I take it you heard what went down in Germany?"

"I heard something."

"The pathetic wretch couldn't kill me!" he bellowed through the phone speaker. "She had me cornered. Unarmed. All she had to do was pull the damn trigger. But no, she hesitated and I got away. Stupid bloody clown. She's lost it. So get it done. Nice and clean and quick. Although, do you know what? Messy as hell if you want, slow and painful. Bollocks to her. Whatever works for you. I'm sick to the back molars hearing about the bloody woman."

Spitfire took a deep breath and stuck out his sizeable chest. "Not a problem, chief."

"Fabulous. And the Cai Moi are accommodating? I've only had communication via our secure messaging system, but from what I've heard they're a riot."

"Oh yeah. They sure are," he replied, dryly. He placed his leg down on the thick carpet and moved the towel around to dry his back. He watched his reflection in the mirror as he went to work and couldn't help but enjoy how his penis – semi-engorged from the heat of the bath – danced around with the motion from the towel. Fifty-one years, and it was still his favourite thing in the entire world.

"Will they stick to the deal?" Caesar asked.

Spitfire stopped what he was doing and returned to sit on the bed. Serious voice. "I believe so. They're an unusual bunch, to say the least. But they're focused and they seem resolute in their mission. Reminded me of us, in our younger days."

"Piss off. You make us sound ancient and washed up."

"Not at all," he cut in. "All I mean is they're dedicated to their cause. The real deal. You ask me, getting this contract is a tremendous power move on our part. We get in there now whilst they're still finding their feet, we could clean up."

"Keep me posted then, old boy," Caesar growled. "And good luck with the meeting. I trust you've got everything you need?"

He glanced over at the pile of hard drives on the circular coffee table. "All set. As soon as I've made the exchange I'll give you a shout."

"Wonderful! I'll speak to you soon."

Caesar hung up and Spitfire went back into the bathroom to collect his watch. He wasn't due back at the Cai Moi warehouse until this evening. Briefly he considered getting back in the bath, but the moment had passed. He reached down and twisted the bath plug open. Then returned to the bedroom to package up the shipment.

Chapter Thirty-Three

Across town, it appeared that a deep introspection had fallen over Vinh Phan. Acid had sensed it the moment he'd shuffled into the front room a few minutes earlier and enquired, soft and morose as if he didn't have the energy to speak, if she was awake.

She was. She sat up from her makeshift bed on the couch and told him so, stopping before she divulged too deeply how incredibly well rested and ready for action she felt. It would only be salt in the wound. But the truth was, the night's sleep had done wonders for her mood. She was alert, powerful, full of vitality. She swung her legs onto the rough threadbare carpet and watched as Vinh lowered himself into a chair by the kitchen table. He looked broken, a brooding silence superseding the keen bloodlust and desire for vengeance that were so apparent back at the factory in the early hours of the morning.

"You don't have to come with me," she told him. "To the warehouse, I mean."

He glanced over at her. Looked through her. "Huh?"

"I'm serious," she told him. "I've been thinking about it. I don't see what you coming would achieve. I get you're angry. I get you want revenge. But if the place is swarming with militia, we can't start shooting up the place. I might have a death wish, but I'm not a fool."

Vinh frowned. "So what are you thinking?"

"Stealth. Like always. Once I know Spitfire is in there, I'll get him alone. Do it quick and silent, then slip away. It's the way I always worked best. Which why, maybe it's better I go alone."

He pulled at his finger and cracked a knuckle. "It's funny, I was thinking the same before you woke. I said to myself, 'Vinh Phan, you are not a young man anymore. And Huy is dead. Getting yourself killed won't bring him back.'"

It was good to hear Vinh talk like this. He was coming to terms with the truth, what Acid had suspected from the start, that Huy was dead. Probably had been for weeks. Months even. She'd only had run-ins with unsophisticated foot solders up to now, but you only had to see the abject terror in the eyes of the Andromeda Club manager to know the upper echelons of the Cai Moi were fearsome people. A small fish like Huy would have been wiped out without anyone missing a beat. The fact his body had never shown up proved that more than disproved it.

She shot Vinh a compassionate smile. Tried to, at least. "Well, if that's what you think."

"Yes. But then I realised something else," he continued. "That is what the old Vinh would have done. Put his head in the sand. Run away. Let despair take over. But no longer." He stretched his arms. "I want to come with you. I am under no delusion I can take down the Cai Moi or avenge Huy's death, but I have to see this through."

"I don't know, Vinh."

"I swear to you I will not jeopardise the mission. Let me help you find Spitfire. Please. It will give me purpose. An extra pair of eyes and hands never hurt, right?" He hit her with a knowing grin. "Besides, it's the school holidays. What else am I going to do?"

Acid rolled her shoulders back. "Well I guess an extra pair of eyes would be helpful." She peeled herself off the couch and carried her bag of weapons over to the table. She placed it down heavily on top. "But you follow my lead. And if we do see Spitfire, he's my mark. Understood?"

"Of course. Think of me as backup," he told her, and nodded at the bag. "Will we have enough firepower?"

"I don't know. We'll see, I guess."

"We'll see?" he repeated, chuckling to himself. "I thought you might say something like that. Would you like some tea?"

He got up and was already heading for the stove.

"Do you have anything stronger?" she asked, not looking up. "You look like you need it."

"My god, Acid. It is only a few minutes after eleven. We need to stay alert. Focused. You said those words."

Acid removed the guns and pieces of weaponry from the bag. "I say a lot of words, sweetie," she told him. "But we aren't heading anywhere until nightfall. A small one now will only help. Believe me."

Receiving no response, she glanced up. Vinh frowned and dropped his shoulders before lumbering over to a small cupboard under the sink. He lifted out a bottle of something yellow, then shuffled over to another cupboard next to his cooker where he picked out two small tumblers. Placing them on the worktop, he said, "A small one," and filled each one up to the brim.

Acid finished unloading the weaponry onto the table,

placed the empty bag down, and inspected each of the pieces. "Do you want to talk about it?" she asked, staring down the barrel of one of the Berettas.

"What is there to say?" he said. "My worst fear is true. I don't know how I will tell Tam." He returned to the table and placed the drinks down in front of him. "It's my fault. All of this. We had words, me and him, before he went missing. I said things I shouldn't have said."

"Oh?" She placed the Beretta down. "You had a fight?"

"I don't want to discuss it. But yes, we fought. Huy stormed away and I never saw him again. Now I never will." He raised the tumbler to his lips and drank its contents in one gulp. "I am to blame. For all of this. Like with my own son."

Acid paused before picking up the double shoulder holster and placing her left arm through the loop. Everything Vinh was saying sounded far too familiar.

"How do you do it?" he asked her.

"Do what?" She twisted her right arm around to find the second loop and hitched the leather straps onto her back.

"Kill people. As a job."

"I don't. Not anymore."

"You know what I mean. Does it not destroy your soul to know you are responsible for people's misery? Fathers. Mothers."

Acid fastened the clasp at the front of the leather harness and stretched her arms forward. She was pleased with her purchase. The leather was stiffer than she'd have liked, and it rubbed under her arm, but strangely it provided security. Like loving arms around her. Arms holding two 9mm pistols and four spare magazines. She looked at Vinh. He was waiting for an answer.

"I didn't think about it," she said. "The people I killed were evil people. Corrupt. Many of them murderers themselves."

"Even killers have parents."

She smiled. "That they do. Have you ever heard of pseudospeciation?"

"I don't think so." Vinh shook his head and picked up the next glass.

"It's how, as humans, we assign subhuman qualities to people we think are not like us. A mark. An enemy soldier. You'll have employed something similar in the army, no doubt. The concept can be harnessed into a mind game you play with yourself. You sit with the idea the person you need to kill is less than human and it frees you from any moral or philosophical pitfalls, things that might cause hesitation. Because we both know – you hesitate, you die."

"Does it work?"

"Sometimes. Other times the mark gives you such a runaround you can't wait to stick a needle of something grim in their neck." She threw up an eyebrow but he missed it, thought she was serious.

"Lethal injection?"

"Sometimes. Most often the client wanted an enforced accident, as we called them. To best swerve any homicide investigation."

She paused, realisation hitting her in the guts. Most of these words were Spitfire's. It was him who'd first explained the concept of pseudospeciation to her. Back when they were close. More than close. Their pillow-talk might have focused on weapons and killing techniques, but it was pillow-talk all the same. An image flew at her without warning. The two of them lying in bed in the New York loft apartment they'd rented, the first night they spent together.

She could still smell his scent. A fusion of musky pheromones and Tom Ford. She shook the memory away. It wasn't real, she told herself. None of it was.

"So anyway, it's a useful mindset to get into," she added. "Stops any indecision in the field."

Vinh raised his head. "I understand. But what happens when you go home. When you're alone with your thoughts in the darkness."

She grinned. "Well that's easy. You drink."

"Yeah. Not so easy though, is it?" He moved his eyes to look at her but not his head. "You drink a lot. You know that? Is it a problem for you?"

She opened up a box of ammo and inspected a couple of the rounds. "You know what they say: one girl's drinking problem is another's self-medication." She released the box magazines from each of the guns and lined them up next to the spares. She could feel Vinh's eyes on her. But he was deflecting, putting the attention on her so he didn't have to deal with his own turmoil. How could she blame him? She knew that game well.

"Don't worry about me, mate," she said, peering at him through her hair. "Seriously. I do what I need to survive. I have other issues, you see. A sort of mania, like bipolar, but more manageable. It can be rather useful for the situations I find myself in."

She had six magazines in total, two twenty-fours and the rest standard seventeens. A quick calculation gave her a hundred and sixteen rounds. Not as many as she'd like, but she'd make every one count.

As she stuffed the rounds into the magazines her mind drifted to the future. She pictured Spitfire on his knees, begging for mercy in front of her. Sweat dripped from his tanned brow, all his famous cocksure swagger melting away.

His perfect azure blue eyes, bloodshot and watery, wide open in fear and bewilderment. She saw her own hand as it raised a gun to his head. She saw her knuckles whitening on the grip. Her index finger was tense, trembling on the trigger. One squeeze was all it needed. She let out a long breath and held it at the other side. The bats screamed.

Do it!

Do it!

She opened her eyes to see Vinh had filled up the whisky glasses. He slid one over to her. She grabbed it and downed it in one.

"Cheers." She scanned the room. "Do you have everything you need?"

He lifted his shirt to reveal the K14-VN stuffed into his waistband.

Acid took one of the Cold Steel Recon 1 tactical knives and handed it to him. "Take this. Will come in handy." She stuffed the other down the side of her boot.

"Looking good," Vinh said. "I see it now. Deadly."

She shot him a wink. "I need to make a call. You good?"

"Sure. I'll put some coffee on."

Acid walked back into the small lounge beyond the open-plan kitchen. Moving over to the window she took out her phone. 11.48 a.m. She did the maths and winced. It was 4.48 a.m. in London. Damnit. She should have called last night. Should have done a lot of things different. But wasn't that always the way? She sighed. Nothing else for it, she needed to make this call, give Spook time to act. She scrolled through her missed calls. Winced again at how many she'd missed, read but ignored. She tapped Return Call and held the phone to her ear. Spook answered after the first ring.

"Acid? Fucking hell. Is it you? Are you okay?"

Acid moved the phone away from her ear. "Calm down, Spook. It's me. I'm fine. I'm alive. Were you not asleep?"

"Had the phone next to my head. Where are you? What are you doing? Did you find him?"

"Woah, kid, one question at a time. Yes, I've found him. Sort of. He's working with an underground militia called the Cai Moi. I'm not sure in what capacity yet, but we're planning to infiltrate their headquarters. With any luck the prick will be there."

"Geez, Acid. You can't start a one-woman war with a militia, you'll get yourself killed."

"It's not only me," she told her.

"Oh? What do you mean?"

"I have a friend here. An ex-soldier. Bit of a bad-ass, truth be told. So don't worry. He's got beef with the Cai Moi. Wants to right a few wrongs himself."

"What, two of you? How's that any better?"

"Hey! It's me you're talking to. We did okay, the two of *us*."

Spook grumbled. "I suppose."

"Anyway, Spook, the reason I'm calling is I need your help." Acid paused as Spook mumbled something under her breath. Ignored it. Carried on. "We've got an address we believe is the Cai Moi headquarters but some more intel would help. If I give you the details, you think you can look into it for me?"

"Well, yeah, but I don't know what you think I can find."

"Anything. Any CCTV you can get of the area, blueprints of the warehouses. Presently we've got nothing. I don't want to go in blind."

"Fine. What's the address?"

Acid gave it her and the phone went quiet. Then she heard the familiar tap-tap-tapping noise.

"When do you need it by?" Spook asked.

Acid glanced over at the clock standing on a small shelving unit in one corner. "This is why I rang so early." She closed one eye, working it out. "Could do with it by midday your time. Two at the latest."

"Shit, Acid. You don't ask for much, do you?"

"Come on, kid. You know you love me."

"Piss off."

"Thanks, Spook. I'm sorry I'm only now returning your call. All your calls. You're the best."

"Be careful, Acid. Please."

"Always."

She hung up and went back through to the kitchen to find Vinh had replaced his shot glass with a large mug of strong black coffee.

Chapter Thirty-Four

The day was fading to dusk as Acid and Vinh left his apartment and headed north. It had been another hot and sticky day in Hanoi and the onset of a cool evening breeze was welcome. Not that they had seen much of the day. After Acid had finished on her call, Vinh had made them a light lunch of mushroom and chicken broth, followed by fruit and a cold rice dessert, which was sickly but enjoyable all the same. The rest of the afternoon was taken up with talking and drinking coffee. It was relaxing. A calm before the storm. And what Vinh had needed. Acid might still have work to do on her outward displays of empathy and compassion, but she knew when someone was hurting. Her new companion had gotten a lot off his chest today, and while his shoulders still sagged from the twin burdens of guilt and shame, he appeared lighter than he had done first thing.

At the HD Bank they hailed a Grab Cab and had it drop them a half mile from the destination. Sticking to the back streets as much as possible, they travelled the remaining distance on foot. It took them ten minutes to get clear of the city and another five before the road ended. An expanse of concrete wasteland was now all that stood between them and a group of seven warehouses, the ancient buildings looking resplendent in the early evening light. Seven proud monoliths, symbols of a bygone age when industry ruled the world. Before the microchip came along and changed everything.

"The Cai Moi are in one of those buildings," Vinh said with certainty. "I can feel the electricity in the air. Like before a storm."

Acid looked up into the sky. "Could be an actual storm coming?"

"No." He screwed up his face. "This is more intense. A humming of evil. They're here all right."

The address on the delivery note hadn't listed a warehouse number so it was unclear which of the buildings it referred to. But from this distance they all looked the same. Not that Acid was expecting a big neon arrow stating, 'Bad guys here', but something at least. Her heightened senses and gut instincts were usually bang on the money. If Vinh was feeling their presence, why wasn't she? She cast her gaze from warehouse to warehouse but all she saw were dead shells, a broken landscape devoid of life. Had they made a mistake coming here? It was easily done. Sometimes you wanted something to be true so much you overlooked the obvious.

"Shall we move closer?" Vinh asked. "We may see some sign of life?"

"No," she said. "Chances are they'll have security cameras. Last thing we want is to announce our arrival before we know which building it is."

As if on cue, Acid felt the vibration of her phone in her

pocket. Spook. She dipped beneath the shrubs and took the call. "What have you got for me?" she asked, on answering.

"Oh? And hello to you too."

"Come off it, Spook. I haven't got time for this."

"Where are you?"

"Up in Tu Lien, in the north of the city," Acid replied. "Ho Tay Lake is on our left, the Red River over to the right. I'm looking at seven warehouses standing in a large area of wasteland. We think the Cai Moi might be in one of those buildings but we don't have a clue which."

"Then you're in the right spot," Spook said. "There are cameras present but the feeds have been scrambled. However, I did manage to hack into a private sector satellite and pull some images from the area of the last two days. I finished enhancing them a few minutes ago. The warehouse furthest north and nearest the lake has had the most activity. Trucks arriving. Cars."

Acid grinned at Vinh. "That's the one. Got to be. Can you tell me anything about exits and entrances?"

"Not much. A silver car has been parked out front several times – the side facing the lake, up by the far end of the building. I've also got images of a truck parked further along the same side. So my advice would be approach it from the river if you can."

Acid was already one step ahead of her. "Sure. Got it. Great work. Thanks, kid."

Spook sniffed it off, but it was clear she was pleased with herself. "Thank me by coming home safe and well."

Acid closed her eyes, letting the impulse dissipate before she spoke. "Of course. I'll see you soon."

She rolled her eyes at Vinh as she pocketed the phone. "She's young," she told him, by way of explanation. Then more serious, "Okay, it looks like the Cai Moi are in the far building on the right. We'll approach it in a wide arc and drop down on the side facing the river."

Vinh nodded. "Makes sense," he said. "So we're doing this?"

"Yes. But one step at a time. We'll only advance once we're certain we're clear of any cameras." She took in a deep lungful of air and smiled. "There's nothing like taking on an underground militia to get the blood pumping. Come on. Let's move."

Taking it slow and steady, they approached the warehouse from the west. Once they were a hundred metres away they circled around the lower warehouses and used these as cover. Keeping to the shadows, Acid pressed herself against the side of the building before hurrying over to the rear right corner of the Cai Moi warehouse. So far so good.

"What now?" Vinh whispered, as he joined her there.

She peered one eye around the side of the building. No one in sight. She looked over her shoulder at Vinh.

"Get in and find Spitfire. After that, not sure." She threw him a wink. "I always find it's best not to plan these outings too rigidly."

From Vinh's facial expression it clearly wasn't the reply he'd been hoping for. But it was all she had. All she could deal with. Her entire body fizzed with a strong desire for blood. She took another peek around the side.

"There's a back entrance around this corner," she whispered. "Half-way along. Maybe fifty metres. But there are cameras. One on each corner and one on the roof. They're all trained on the doorway in a decent-sized arc."

Vinh grimaced. "Can we get past undetected?"

"Doubtful. But there's an old fire escape on the corner looks to be clear of cameras. Only thing is, the bottom third has rusted away. So the first rung is about three metres high." She looked him up and down. "You reckon you can scale the wall, old-timer?"

"Hey!" He elbowed her in the upper arm. "I might have a few years on you, but I'm still fit."

"Calm down, I was only trying to lighten the mood."

"Lighten the mood? We're about to break into the headquarters of the most dangerous criminal organisation Hanoi has ever known. Armed with a couple of handguns and no plan."

Acid blew out a dramatic sigh. "Well, when you put it like that. Jesus." She cricked her neck. Shook off the playfulness. "Enough chat. Follow my lead and stay close."

She tensed her body and held the strain for a few seconds, then let her muscles relax completely. At the same time, she shifted her centre of gravity into her pelvis. Stealth-mode. Now her limbs were loose and her movements fluid, her breathing shallow and slow. Keeping her back against the wall, she slipped around the corner and was underneath the fire escape in four strides. From this angle the rusty metal ladder seemed higher than she'd first estimated. She could also see some of the brackets fixing it to the wall had rotted away. Not ideal. But it was their only option. As Vinh joined her beneath the ladder, she stepped back and linked her fingers together, ready to boost him up. He halted, perhaps struggling with some ingrained strand of machismo. She didn't have time for that. She glared at him.

Her face said, *Get a move on.*

It said, *Don't be a dick.*

A ledge stuck out a few feet above, and beyond this a couple of bricks jutted from the mortar far enough to get purchase. She had already tracked her own path. The key here was momentum – to let one movement drive the next.

She returned her attention to Vinh and shoved her clasped hands at him.

"Come on, Vinh. You can do this."

"Fine. I'll go first."

Bracing himself with a hand on her shoulder, he placed his foot in her hands. Then as she took his weight he straightened his leg and leapt for the ledge, grabbing it with both hands. From here he was able to reach the fire escape. Acid stepped back as he hauled himself up the metal structure. If she could take a run up she might reach the ledge, but the way the cameras were angled she didn't have much room. Vinh was already half-way up the fire escape, the ladder swaying and creaking uneasily as he went. She wasn't confident the remaining brackets would hold both their weights. But once Vinh was scissoring his leg over the top of the building, she took one more step back and went for it. Because of the camera positions, she had to approach the wall at an angle. She raised her foot and got some friction behind her. But as she grabbed for the ledge she only got three fingers to it. Desperately she clawed for purchase, feet scrabbling at the wall. It wasn't enough. She slid down the brickwork and landed on her feet.

Then she heard the dogs.

Only faint at first. A distant barking. But they were getting closer. She spun around and scanned the area. There were no streetlights around, but through the gloom she could pick out shapes. Six rabid eyes, glinting in the moonlight, three large beasts moving fast. Most likely these were Indochina dingoes. A native to the region, bred for hunting, and famous for being both wise and cruel.

She returned to her starting position, ready for another run-up. Above her she could make out Vinh, silhouetted against the blue-black sky. He leaned over the side, willing her on impotently. Behind her, Acid could hear the dogs approaching. A few seconds more and they'd be on her. She rocked back onto her heels and propelled herself forward. Half a metre from the wall, she leapt at it. This time she grabbed hold of a corner stone with her left hand, and with her right she found a loose brick with a gap down one side where the mortar had crumbled away. She dug her fingers in and held on, kicking her feet and searching for a foothold. Below her the dogs made their rancorous presence known, all snapping jaws and vicious barks.

With gritted teeth, Acid adjusted her grip. But she couldn't hold on much longer. She peered down at the mass of teeth and sticky strings of saliva. Six mad eyes filled with pure evil. They flung themselves at her as Acid readied herself to fall. But before she let go she pushed off, landing a short distance behind the dogs. The move surprised the hounds and gave her enough time to scramble to her feet. Before they turned, she was already running towards them. The bats screamed in her head. Time slowed down. The dog standing nearest the warehouse was the largest of the three, likely an older male. As she approached he locked eyes with her, gnashing his teeth and readying to pounce. But he wasn't fast enough. One more stride and she had her foot on his back. He was a sturdy beast and she could feel the thick layer of muscle beneath her boot. But still, with the full weight of an adult woman pushing off against him, the dog let out a pained yelp. She felt the mutt's back buckle, but with the extra height she could reach the ledge and scramble up her planned route. Her fingers grabbed onto the bottom rung of the ladder and she pulled herself to safety. Clear of the dogs' teeth, she hung there for a few seconds to catch her breath. Below her they were in a frenzy, the male dancing around chomping at the throats of his fellow beasts as though it had more to prove.

"Acid?" It was Vinh. He held his hand out to her. "Quick. Someone might hear them."

She pulled herself up to the first rung and clambered up the fire escape two rungs at a time to get to the top in a few seconds. Vinh grabbed her arm and helped her over the lip of the building.

"Good work," he whispered. "I thought you were in trouble at one point."

"Makes two of us." She brushed herself down, zipped open her leather jacket and pulled out one of the Berettas, checking the clip and putting one in the chamber. "We all set?"

Vinh gestured over the roof. "There's a door over the other side leads down into the building."

"Cool. After you."

They crept across the flat rooftop, taking small steps, up on their toes. They reached the doorway in a matter of seconds and Vinh tried the handle. Unlocked. He glanced at her. His eyes asked if it was safe – a trap? She scrunched up her nose. Either way it was their only option. She had one foot through the door when she heard a car engine. She moved to the edge of the roof to peer over.

Down below a silver car was pulling up. An Alfa Romeo by the looks of it. She watched as it came to a stop. The headlights went off, the interior lights went on. A few seconds after, the driver's door swung open and a man stepped out. He was wearing a well-fitted three-piece suit, made from a metallic petrol-blue material. It glimmered in the dull light coming from the lamp above the warehouse door. The man looked about him, then removed something from the inside of his jacket. A neat case which he flipped open to remove a cigarette. Acid recognised the case immediately. Custom-made, sterling silver, initials elaborately etched into its surface as if to remind him who he was.

"Here we go," she muttered, an awkward shiver running through her.

"Is that..."

"Sure is," she replied. "Spitfire Creosote."

Chapter Thirty-Five

Acid wiped the back of her hand across her forehead and gulped back a deep breath. Despite the breeze, the day's heat had subsided little and the sweat clung close to her skin. The air here was oppressive at the best of times. Made ten times worse by the sight of the only man you'd ever loved. Who you also hated. And whose beautiful, conceited, vile face you were seconds away from decimating with a carefully placed hollow point.

"Wait. Please," Vinh said. He placed his hand on the end of the gun and lowered her aim. Then he stepped around so he was face to face with her. Making eye contact, appealing to her better judgement. "If you kill him now, it blows our cover. We'll never get inside. I know I said I wouldn't jeopardise your mission but I need to see these people with my own eyes. See those who murdered Huy."

Her jaw was rigid. She stared at Vinh. "I can take him out, right now. Finish this."

"Finished for you, maybe. But what about me? Help me

get inside, that's all I ask. You can follow Spitfire when he leaves, take him then."

His eyes were as wide as she had seen them. He didn't blink. Not even when she asked, "Then what will you do?"

"I will take revenge."

"Was that your plan all along, Vinh? Because that's not cool—"

"No. I swear to you. But being here now, I know this is something I must do."

She tilted her head back. "This is a suicide mission, Vinh, you know that? What good can it do?"

He removed his service pistol from his belt. "Please, Acid," he said. "I've made my peace with this."

Acid seethed, but she couldn't argue with what she saw in his face. She peered over the side of the building. Spitfire had finished his cigarette. He flicked the spent stub into the darkness, watching it explode in a burst of fiery shards. Then he straightened his tie and cufflinks – the way she had seen him do so many times before – and strode over to the entranceway beneath her.

"Let's go," Vinh called softly. He was standing by the door.

Acid glanced down once more at Spitfire as he entered the building, then followed on behind Vinh. She let the door slam behind her as she stepped into the murky gloom, grimacing as he spun around to glare at her.

"Sorry. My head was elsewhere."

Vinh didn't answer. He gestured with the muzzle of his pistol, pointing down the stairwell. They descended the first flight of steps in silence and got to a small landing with another stairwell leading off it on the opposite side. At the bottom of these steps they found themselves at an open door. Beyond this was a narrow metal walkway which ran around the perimeter of the next room. In the centre of the room a large industrial machine rose up to the ceiling. It looked like a museum piece, unused for many years. They passed by it, the metal walkway clanging and vibrating under their quick feet. At the far end was another stairwell, and beside it a sign hanging on the wall with a plan of the building. Acid got there first and waited for Vinh to catch up.

"We can get down to ground level from here," she said, gesturing to the sign. "But listen to me – once we're there, let's be clever about this, okay? Don't go shooting the place up like a crazy person. If there's a chance we can both get what we want and walk away from this, let's go for that option. Agreed?"

"Agreed." Vinh held up his old service pistol. "Thank you, Acid. You have no idea how much you've helped me."

"Yeah, well. Don't thank me just yet," she told him. "You ready?"

His eyes shone in the dim light coming from the skylight at the top of the stairwell. There was an intensity in them she'd not seen before. "I'm ready," he said.

Walking sideways, Acid made her way down, tracing the steel handrail on the external wall with the small of her back. They got to the next level and paused. Across the landing, facing the stairwell, was a single door with a small windowpane at the top. Vinh got there first, but one look and he shook his head. Nothing. She had a look for herself. It was an old office space, now empty. A wall of windows looking down on the main warehouse space were clouded with dust and grime.

They continued, passing through the third floor and down onto the second. They stopped at each level, but like those above they were deserted. As they reached the first floor Acid turned to face Vinh.

"Listen," she whispered.

Voices, drifting up from the ground floor. Then music. Bass-heavy. It pulsed through the concrete chamber of the stairwell as they hurried down the last flight and arrived at ground level.

A set of double doors faced the bottom of the stairs and beyond these the main space of the warehouse. Where the doors met wasn't entirely flush and left a half-centimetre gap, wide enough for Acid to peer through. Though at what, she wasn't sure. The room was pitch black. Then, as the pulsing electronic music grew louder and the sub-rumble of the bass became heavier, a strobe light flickered on. At the same time, huge plumes of dry ice were being pumped into the room from all four corners.

As the strobe flickered its insane illumination, Acid could make out a white table standing on a raised platform in the centre of the room. In front of the table rested a large white cushion, and opposite were two white leather chairs. All empty. To her right, a few feet from the stairwell, were a pile of crates, similar to the ones in the factory. They were stacked two-high, three in places. High enough to conceal both her and Vinh. She closed one eye through the gap and assessed the distance. It was a few strides away at the most.

She leaned into Vinh. "Quick. Follow me," she yelled over the music. "We can hide. Something's about to happen."

Head down, she slipped through the doors and bolted across the room until she reached the crates.

"What the hell is going on here?" Vinh rasped as he shuffled to kneel beside her. "Looks like some sort of music concert."

"Sonny did say they were somewhat unconventional."

The music swelled, filling every millimetre of space in the room and scratching at their ear drums. It was unsettling. Acid positioned herself so she could peer, unseen, around the side of the crates. With her breath held in her throat, she watched as a lone male figure entered through a door a few feet away along the next wall. Walking slowly but with broad strides, he approached the centre of the room and stepped up onto the platform. From this angle Acid couldn't make out his face, but she didn't need to. She'd know that cocksure swagger anywhere.

Spitfire placed a shiny black briefcase down by his feet and stood tall, drawing his shoulders back and folding his hands over his crotch. Dry ice swirled around his head. Then as quickly as it had begun, the strobe lighting flickered off and the room was plunged into total darkness once more. Now the noise grew louder. And noise it was. Acid was done calling whatever this was music. It was so torturously loud, it messed with her thoughts. She grimaced, trying to hold on to her sanity. Though if it were ever there to begin with was another matter. Through the aural discomfort she forced herself to watch as two immense halogen spotlights flicked on to reveal hooded figures sitting on the opposite side of the table to Spitfire.

Finally, thankfully, the noise stopped. Or at least, the sound system ceased. She still had a shrill ringing in her ears.

"Welcome, friend." The hood's voice echoed around the vast space. He was speaking English with a strong Vietnamese accent, but the deep timbre was clearly an affectation. A put-on to further add to the mystery. "We implore you, please take a seat."

Spitfire didn't move. "I'd rather stand," he told them. "If it's all the same with you."

The hoods stiffened, but yielded. "Do you have the cargo?" one of them asked.

Spitfire picked up the briefcase. With considered poise he placed it on the table. Then he flicked open the clasps and raised the lid. Acid craned her neck to see what was inside, but the assassin's wide frame obscured her line of vision.

He spun the case around and slid it across the table. "Here we are, gentlemen. Seven hard drives. Enough information to take down the entire Vietnamese government. If that's what you want to do with it." He stepped away and placed his hands behind his back. "I mean, personally I'd use it for leverage. Blackmail enough corrupt politicians and the country is yours anyway."

"The country will be ours!" the hoods boomed in unison, and one of them added, "But we shall do this our way. The honourable way. This information will allow us to remove the cancer at the heart of the current administration. We will clean up our country from the inside out."

Acid glanced at Vinh. "Data? That's what this is about?"

Vinh shook his head but said nothing. She switched her focus back to Spitfire. He hadn't moved position but she noticed a slight quiver to his shoulders. Virtually undetectable, but it was there. When the bats were out, her senses were so heightened she could see what others couldn't. The fact that it was Spitfire meant something as well. And that quiver was dangerous.

"I take it our fee will now be released from your accounts?" he asked.

The hoods didn't answer. The one on the left leaned

under the table and brought back a small laptop. He placed it in front of him and eased it open before selecting a hard drive from the case and plugging it in. He leaned into the screen, his hood falling over his face as he typed. All eyes were on the enigmatic figure as he perused the screen. Then he nodded, tapped a few keys, and closed the laptop.

He turned to his partner. "The cargo is genuine." Then to Spitfire, "I have released the fee."

"Wonderful." Spitfire clapped his hands together. "Then I'm eager to begin our partnership. As is Caesar."

The hoods looked at each other, their faces still shrouded in shadow. "There will be no partnership," one of them replied. "Please thank your boss for us, but your offer is unnecessary."

Spitfire shifted his weight onto his right leg, jutting his hip out a way. Like before, it was almost unnoticeable. But Acid clocked it. A chink in his confidence. The hoods had fazed the old boy.

He scoffed. "Unnecessary? What we're offering you is priceless. Complete eradication of anyone who steps in your way. No links to your organisation. No fall out. No—"

"Enough!" the hoods bellowed together. "The One has spoken. We do not require further involvement with you or your organisation."

Spitfire's jaw jutted out the way of his hip. "I see. Well this is a novel occurrence. We considered the deal done."

"Well you were wrong to do that."

Spitfire was struggling to keep it together. Without making a sound, Acid raised the Beretta, ready for action. The atmosphere in the room was like a tinder box.

"Don't do this," Spitfire told the Cai Moi. He stepped forward and put both hands on the table. "I know you guys are passionate, but you're also new to this world. Organisations like ours, we work to a certain code. You break that code you risk pissing off a lot of dangerous people."

The final syllable hadn't left Spitfire's lips before both hoods were on their feet. The one on the right pointed a long finger at him.

"You dare enter our domain and threaten us?" The voice was less booming, less scary-movie-voice, but now with actual rage behind it. "After all we have paid you. How dare you come here and talk of codes and dishonour?"

"Apologies." Spitfire held up his hands. "But think about it, chaps. Can you actually progress without us? Sure, you've got your hired thugs and this army you're attempting to raise, but what about when you need to get your hands really dirty? Who's going to do that? You two? You're savvy people, you know what you want. But you aren't killers, are you?"

He finished speaking and waited. From her vantage point, Acid could now see Spitfire's profile. Could see the hint of a smirk throwing up the corner of his mouth. The room fell silent. The hoods bowed their heads as if deep in thought. Then the one on the left, the taller of the two, removed a handheld transceiver from under his robes. He barked into it, speaking in Vietnamese, and moments later a door opened and a man entered. He was short, but as wide as he was tall. He was wearing the now-familiar black jeans and black hooded sweatshirt combo with a SIG MPX submachine gun on a strap around his neck. Looking almost as deadly was his countenance, fixed in a perpetual snarl. He strutted towards the stage as the hood addressed him.

"Ho, collect the prisoners and bring them here. We have something we want to show our guest."

The man, Ho, bowed his head and left the room. Spitfire watched him leave, then turned back to the hoods. No one spoke. No one moved. The only sound was the faint hum coming from the halogen spotlights. Acid gripped the handle of her weapon.

Half a minute later the door opened and Ho stepped back into the room. He wore the same sour expression as before but was now dragging two more individuals in his wake. They were also wearing the Cai Moi uniform but with the added accessory of black sacks draped over their heads and tied with rope around their necks. They squirmed and whined and dragged their heels, but they were no match for Ho's strength. He brought them to the centre of the room and positioned them by the side of the platform.

The taller hood moved over to where Spitfire was standing. "So, you think we are weak, huh?" he intoned. "You think we are boys, who cannot do what is required for our cause?"

"I never said that," Spitfire replied. "Listen, I don't know what the hell is going on but—"

"Silence!" the hood yelled. He gestured at Ho, who untied the rope around the prisoners' necks. Next he removed the sacks covering their heads. Acid swallowed a gasp. The prisoners were young, teenagers even. But that wasn't what startled her. As the two men blinked into the light, she turned to Vinh.

"Aren't they…"

"Yes," he whispered back. "The street rats from Tam's place."

"You talk of codes and honour, Mr Spitfire," the hood began. "These men have broken the code of the Cai Moi." He turned to the street rats. "Your thuggish actions have brought shame on our cause. You are not The One. You are not part of the Cai Moi. Now, do you have anything to say for yourselves?"

The teenagers glanced at each other, then back to the hood now looming over them from the edge of the platform. One of the street rats opened his mouth to speak, but before any words left his mouth the hood pulled a gun from under his robe and shot him in the face. At that close range the blast took out all his features and most of the back of his skull. As his flaccid body drooped to the ground, his friend let out a terrible scream, cut short a second later as the hood put a bullet through his temple and blew his brains out the other side.

"Fuck," Acid whispered.

"Fuck!" Spitfire shouted. He stepped back, inspecting his shoes. "Careful there, friend."

"This is our honour," the hood roared. "This is our code. So tell your boss, tell the world – we are ready and able to kill for our cause. To kill those who wrong us. We are the Cai Moi. We are The One."

Spitfire raised his finger as if about to speak, but thought better of it. Instead he shook his head and let out a soft chuckle.

"Fair play, gents," he purred. "I suppose I'll be off, then." He brushed down the arm of his suit jacket and straightened his tie. "Drastic, though, if you ask me. I mean, you made your point, but you've made a real mess of—"

"Enough of your insolence," the taller hood cried, pointing the pistol at Spitfire. "You have your money. Now leave. We are done."

Spitfire looked at the gun in his face and ran his tongue along his teeth. The man standing in front of him was the tallest of the two hoods, but Spitfire still had a foot on him. He placed one huge hand on the man's shoulder.

"Listen, friend," he said. "Let's be civil about this, shall we? No need to fall out—"

"We are not friends," the hood said. "We will never be friends."

Grabbing Spitfire's hand, he flung it away and made to turn his back, but the action had stirred something in Spitfire. Acid tensed. She'd been expecting this. In fact she'd been willing it to happen. She knew his temper, knew laying a hand on him was a grave insult. In a sharp movement that sent the platform rocking, he sprang forward and shoved the hood into the table.

Then all hell broke loose.

The bats screamed. Acid's hand tightened on the Beretta. She was already on her feet as Ho grabbed up his SIG MPX and raised it at Spitfire. Without a second thought she squeezed a heavy torrent of metal furies into Ho's torso, opening up his chest in a blooming eruption of claret and bone and cartilage. He fell backwards, firing a hail of bullets into the ceiling as he hit the deck.

Those on the platform dived for cover, uncertain where the bullets were coming from. Acid's first thought was to do the same, duck back behind the crates, but she remained where she was. It was already too late, her cover was blown. Instead she doubled down, pulling out the second Beretta and taking a step forward.

"Fucking hell!" Spitfire cried, spotting her across the room. He scrambled to his feet and, taking advantage of the situation, grabbed hold of the armed hood and twisted his arm up his back, yanking the gun from him.

Then he shoved him away and aimed the pistol in her direction.

"Oh, classy," she said, returning the gesture by pointing both Berettas at him.

Spitfire shrugged. "Well, what can ya do?"

The hoods got to their feet, though those titles were now inapt. In the commotion the cowls had fallen from their faces, revealing them to be young men in their early twenties. The taller of the two, the one who'd been doing most of the talking up to this point, glared at her. He had a thin pale face, but it was his eyes that got her. They were big, intense, with an intelligence to them. Kind too. She squinted at him. He looked familiar.

"Who the hell are you?" he shouted, the deep voice now sharp with tension. "You will pay for this—"

He stopped abruptly. His eyes bulged.

Acid held her ground, aiming one of her guns at him. But he wasn't looking at her. She glanced at Spitfire, then followed the man's gaze to a few feet away where Vinh was standing, arms hanging loosely by his side.

"Vinh," she whispered. "What the hell are you doing?"

But he didn't answer. He was too busy staring, open-mouthed, at the man on the platform.

"Huy," he murmured. "You're alive."

Chapter Thirty-Six

A malignant sneer distorted the man's exposed face, now recognisable as the boy from Vinh's photo.

"What is going on?" Vinh asked. "We thought... Your mother thought... I was told... I don't understand."

"Who the hell is this bastard peasant?" Spitfire yelled.

"Everyone put your guns down," the second hood ordered, drawing his own gun and pointing it at Spitfire.

No one moved, faces white with panic and rage and confusion. Acid held her nerve and the Berettas at arm's length. One aimed at Spitfire, the other dancing between Huy and his friend.

"What's your play here, Acid?" Spitfire asked. "You got one? Or letting your crazy whims guide you as usual? The bats."

Her finger flexed on the trigger. "Put the guns down," she said. "All of you."

He sneered at her. "I'm not sure you're in any position to be telling anyone what to do."

She sniffed. The gun aimed at Spitfire trembled as the

bat chorus permeated her psyche. From this distance it was an easy shot to take. Over in a blink of an eye. But the same was true for him. She took a deep breath and settled into her peripheral vision, snapping her awareness from one person to the next. The second hood was shitting it. That was clear from his stance and the rigidness of his gun arm. Not a threat. That left her and Spitfire.

"Why, Huy?" Vinh said. "I don't understand."

"You don't understand because you're old," Huy told him. "You're part of the old order." He walked around the table and reached underneath, coming back up with another pistol in his hand, a Bersa .38 he pointed at Vinh. "You know, I heard you were looking for me. That you thought I had been killed or taken by The One. Well now you know. I *am* The One. We are all The One. All of us who demand a better future."

Vinh stepped forward with his hands up. "But your mother, she is so worried about you. She has not been well."

"My mother is no concern of yours," he replied, waving his hand the way of the fallen street rats. "Did you not see the fate of these insolent pigs who tried to take from her, who beat her? I will look after my mother, and I will reveal my truth to her when the time is right."

"What does that mean?"

Huy considered the question, and an enormous grin cracked his face. "With the information Mr Spitfire here has provided us we can now begin our next phase. Building an army and taking down the Vietnamese government. After this we move our own ruling system into power. First in Hanoi. Then the entire country."

"You want to overthrow the government?" Vinh yelled. "And who will lead, then? You?"

"Why not? But not in terms you would understand," he

replied. "The One believe such terms are outdated and piti-ful. We believe in complete control by the people we serve. We are all The One."

Acid sighed. "Yes, you said that already."

"Who the hell are you?" the second hood asked.

"She's nobody," Spitfire replied. "She's here for me. But she's fucked everything up for herself. Haven't you, darling?"

The words hit less than Acid thought they might. But that didn't mean much. Her body was tingling with so much manic energy it was hard to know what she felt about anything. She remained still. Out of the corner of one eye she saw the second hood point his gun at her. Meant her growing desire to risk a shot at Spitfire was off the table. She might have got him before he fired, but with the two other guns on her she couldn't risk it. She flexed her grip on the Berettas as a bead of sweat tricked down the side of her face. Three guns aimed at her. It had got a lot hotter in here the last few minutes, and her options a lot slimmer.

"Vinh?" she asked, keeping her voice as stable as possi-ble. "Get your pistol out, will you? Point it at James Bland for me."

Vinh did as instructed.

Spitfire sneered spitefully at her. "The Dullahan already made that *hilarious* joke, you pathetic cow. And I used to think you had a wicked sense of humour. Then again, I used to think a lot of things."

Acid kept the Berettas high. She wasn't taking him on. He was trying to mess with her. Throw her focus.

"So what next, chaps?" she asked the room. "I enjoy a game of musical statues as much as the next girl but we can't stay like this forever."

"Quiet," Huy shouted. "We are not here to play games.

We are not here to waste time with pettiness. You have issues with each other that do not concern us. Leave. All of you."

"Tell him to lower his weapon," Acid called over.

The request elicited another cruel laugh from Spitfire. "Sure I will. Once I've put you in the ground." He tilted his head to one side. "It's over, Acid. Awful that it has to be this way. But you should have left things alone. I don't understand why you're doing this. You've got money, you could have disappeared forever."

"You killed my mother."

"Oh, do shut up. We did you a favour."

Her finger quivered on the trigger. That one hurt.

"Stop it!" Vinh yelled. "No one has to shoot anyone. Let us talk. Huy, help me understand. Please. You gave no indication you were interested in politics."

"You have no idea who I am," Huy replied. "You never did. You're too full of lies and bullshit to hear anything else." His voice broke as he ranted. Flecks of spittle illuminated in the halogen glare like tiny fireflies. "The One understand the importance of self-control, of taking full responsibility for one's actions. Only then can we grow as a nation. Only then can we become untouchable. You are a weak man and you mean nothing to me. As far as I'm concerned, you're dead. You are not my father. And you never were."

"Father? What the..." Acid glanced at Vinh.

Confusion swirled her attention.

Only for a split second.

But it was all Spitfire needed.

She felt a rush of air then came a sonic crack as a bullet flew past her ear at 500mph. A centimetre to the left and she'd never have heard it. She flung herself behind the crates, firing off a couple of wild rounds in retaliation as she went. The bullets went wide but drove Spitfire back. As she steadied herself around the side of the crate, he turned and ran for the exit.

"Stop, you bastard."

She was back on her feet and running for him, firing off more rounds as she went. But she was shooting blind and Spitfire could easily zig-zag around them before disappearing through the door. She kept on his tail. Once he was out in the open she'd have a clearer shot of him. But she was a few feet from the exit when four men dressed in black burst through it and blocked her path. A second later another four ran in from another door on the far side. She screeched to a halt. Her eyes fixed on the eight submachine guns pointed at her.

"Ah, shitting hell." She held her hands in the air and turned to address Huy. "Come on, Huy. This isn't your beef. You said yourself you're done with him. Let me go."

She glanced over her shoulder at the exit, at the armed guards. "Look, I have zero interest in what you're doing here. We don't have to even bother with each other. I get that you and Vinh have a lot to talk about but let me go after Spitfire." She was speaking fast. Babbling. She glanced back at the door. Another minute and she'd have no chance of catching him. "I need that man dead. I heard him threaten you. He could be a real nuisance. Or worse. Let me go so I can kill him. Do us all a favour."

Huy thought a moment, before waving his hand dismissively. "Let her go," he told his men. Then gesturing to Vinh, standing motionless with a bleak expression wilting his features. "But you take this old fool with you. And don't let me see either of you anywhere near me again. You understand? We are not the same. We never will be. Nothing will stop The One. We are—"

"Understood. Thank you," she butted in. She ran over to Vinh and grabbed his shirt sleeve. "Come on. We need to get out of here. Before he changes his mind."

"But, I—"

"Now, Vinh!" Dragging him along behind her, Acid pushed through the line of men blocking the door and through into a long corridor. "We'll talk about this later. Right now I need to put that flash bastard in the ground, once and for all."

Chapter Thirty-Seven

Vinh's head was still spinning with what he now knew as he followed Acid down the corridor. All the time spent searching. All those sleepless nights. Huy hadn't been murdered by the Cai Moi. He *was* the Cai Moi. The concept just about broke Vinh's mind. His heart too. Huy had been such a good student, so conscientious. He could have done anything he wanted with his life. So why this? Why put them through this? His mother especially. Nothing made sense to Vinh as they barged through the double doors leading outside. Once there however his pondering stopped abruptly as two car headlights on high-beam blinded his vision and the muzzle flash of a high-calibre handgun brought him crashing back into the present.

"*Xuong*," he yelled, forgetting himself. "Get down."

Acid was firing blindly into the lights. An open target. Vinh found his footing and flung himself towards her. He grabbed her and scrambled them clear behind a large metal dumpster, bullets blasting the crumbling brickwork of the old warehouse behind them.

"What the hell are you doing?" she yelled, shrugging him off.

"Saving your life," he replied. "You can't avenge anyone if you're dead."

She glared at him as more shots thumped into the dumpster. Vinh held his trusty service piece to his chest. His heart beat fast and heavy. He was in this up to his eyeballs, he knew that. He had to see it through. Even if he couldn't get the thought out of his head, paraphrasing himself:

You can't make things right with Huy if you're dead.

Acid got to her feet but crouched, shoving past him and moving to the edge of the dumpster to fire off a few shots before ducking back for cover. They waited. No return fire. She went for it again, a few more shots. Still nothing. She moved into the light. A clear target once more.

Insane woman. What was she thinking?

Vinh braced himself. Time stopped. Then before he could blink she was running from the building at speed. He scrambled to his feet and chased after her.

"Acid! Wait!"

He caught up with her fifty metres down the side of the next warehouse but she didn't slow down.

"Keep up," she panted. "See, up ahead. He's heading for the city."

In front Vinh could make out the silhouette of Spitfire Creosote as he sprinted away with long leaping strides.

"You know... I thought you were saying it to be cool..." Vinh got the words out between gasps of air. "But you actually do have a death wish. Don't you?"

Acid kept her eyes ahead, on Spitfire. "It's a long story," she replied. "I'll tell you about it once this is all over."

"If," Vinh said. "If this is all over."

"It'll definitely be over," she wheezed. "One way or another."

She hit him with such a perfect smile he couldn't help but smile back. This despite the fact his head and heart were twisted up in fierce turmoil. He had so many questions. So much he needed to know. And how was he going to tell Tam? He'd found her son – their son – only for him to be the head of the most notorious criminal organisation in the country.

He gasped for more air. One thing was certain, he wasn't cut out for this. He hadn't run in five years. Until yesterday he hadn't killed anyone in nearly ten. He glanced over at Acid Vanilla. She would likely get them both killed. But he wanted to be near her. To help her. If only to experience what she might do next. Because quite frankly, after what he'd already seen, he couldn't guess. She was a perplexing enigma wrapped up in a whole lot of trouble. But those eyes. That smile.

"Over to the left," she yelled, breaking the spell. "Down the side of the hotel."

They'd reached the north of the city and could see the banks of the Red River over to the west. Spitfire was still two hundred metres in front of them, but they were sticking with him. Vinh gritted his teeth and kept pace as best he could, ignoring the fact his heart felt like it might burst any second. They got to the corner of the hotel and turned down a narrow street leading to an overground car park with a tall metal fence running around it.

"He definitely came this way," Acid whispered, as they ducked under the barrier. She put her hand on his shoulder. "We can flush him out. You go left, I'll go right. Move around the perimeter and we'll meet at the far end. Keep your weapon up, and if you see anything move – anything at all – shoot it. You hear me? I know I wanted to be the one to do it, but we've gone beyond that. He needs taking down."

He nodded, still catching his breath.

Another smile softened her hard expression. "You can do this, Soldier Man. And once Spitfire's dead you can tell me all about why the hell Huy is calling you father."

"I *am* his father."

The smile drifted from warm to something more sarcastic. "Yeah, I got that," she whispered. "Why didn't you tell me?"

The muscles in the back of his jaw tightened. "I'm not sure. Shame, perhaps. I didn't want it to muddy the waters."

It was hard to tell if she was convinced. "We'll talk more later," she said. "For now, I need you to focus. Are you ready?"

"Ready as all hell."

From warm to sarcastic, and now bemused? "Okay then. See you at the other side."

Feeling both embarrassed and foolish (but no less determined to show Acid Vanilla who he was, what he could do), he broke away and edged down the side of the car park. Despite the hour, most of the spaces were taken up. Cars mainly. A few trucks. Plus a campervan, which Vinh made a beeline for. Once alongside it, he pressed his body against the cream fiberglass exterior and moved under the back window. Raising his head he peered into the campervan and out through a side window on the other side. More parked cars. And beyond those, the empty space of the rest of the car park, not a soul in sight.

Vinh moved around the campervan and towards a beat-up Mitsubishi. He stopped. Over the far side of the lot he'd noticed movement. He threw himself behind the car, gave it a moment, then peered over the bonnet. He straightened the arm holding the pistol, his finger tight on the trigger. The figure moved into a beam of light bleeding through the gaps in the cars. He tensed.

"*Ten de tien.*"

Releasing the breath he didn't realise he'd been holding, he got to his feet. It was Acid. She saw him and gave a blunt salute, gesturing she was going in deeper. Vinh responded in kind and sloped down the side of the Mitsubishi, leaning into the metal fence as he passed behind a Transit van. Once clear, he stopped, scanned the area. Still nothing. He was close to the rear of the car park and no sign of Spitfire. Had he given them the slip?

He kept low as he edged along. Up in front he could see Acid creeping alongside an old minibus, both Berettas out in front, aiming between each vehicle she passed. But nothing to shoot at, no target in sight. A few more strides and they'd joined each other at the rendezvous spot.

"I don't understand," Vinh whispered. "There's nowhere to go. He can't have disappeared."

The fence around the car park was more than six foot high. It was possible he'd been able to scale it, but four bright spotlights were positioned around the lot to deter would-be car thieves – they'd have seen him.

Acid wrinkled her nose up. "I had him. I bloody well had him and—"

"Acid! No!"

A figure stepped out from behind the minibus. Vinh saw him at once. He grabbed the collar of Acid's leather jacket. Pulled her towards him. In the same movement he twisted around her, putting himself between her and the figure. Acid yelled something as Vinh pushed her away, but it was a muffled noise. Nothing Vinh could pick out as words. Something was wrong. His ear canal felt like it had collapsed. His senses were in haywire. He could see Acid in front of him. Could see her mouth, distorted in a punishing scream. But still no sounds. She reached out as he stumbled forward. An immense pressure invaded his chest. Like someone had hit him with a baseball bat.

He tried to speak.

Couldn't.

Tried to breathe.

Same.

Acid caught him as he fell. But he couldn't feel her touch. His body was numb. His mind too. She laid him down with his back to the cold concrete and got to her feet. He watched her raise her arms. Watched her fire off a flurry of bullets that kicked her shoulders back and screwed up her face in venomous concentration. Saw the muzzle flash of both pistols lighting up the dark skies above.

He pushed against the ground with his elbows. He had to help her. But he couldn't get any further. He was too weak. And felt hot. Hot and wet. He looked down at his body. That's when he saw the hole in his chest. To the right of his sternum. Saw the blood bubbling out of the hole. He'd been shot. The bullet had gone right through.

Despair descended like a shroud. Hope left him. Not even panic came through the numbness, but on his next breath the pain arrived. Searing hot, it ripped through his chest and left his entire torso itching with a burning ache.

Then cold.

Shivering cold.

Uncontrollable shaking.

And everything fading.

Chapter Thirty-Eight

"Bastard, bastard, bastard!" Acid screamed as she emptied both magazines, firing until the action locked back on her. It was a futile gesture. A way to assuage her own blind fury. Spitfire had already disappeared behind the length of cars on the opposite side of the parking lot.

She holstered the guns and knelt beside Vinh. Him on his back, staring at the sky, staring at nothing. She placed her fingers on his neck. He was still alive. His pulse racing and erratic. As she leaned over him, he whispered in her ear, "Help me."

The bullet had gone straight through. The exit wound was on his right side and had missed his heart by less than an inch. Maybe Vinh would think he got lucky, but she knew better. A wound like this was intentional from Spitfire. If he'd killed Vinh outright – with a headshot, for instance – she would be on the assassin's tail right now instead of here, caring for her friend as he bled out in front of her.

"Don't try and move." She took off her leather jacket and unfastened the shoulder holster. Then she pulled her vest top over her head and bundled it up, pressing it onto the bubbling wound in an attempt to stem the bleeding. Not much use. Within a minute the thin material was saturated and sticky.

The psychogeography in her head had the nearest hospital three miles away at least. Vinh couldn't walk there himself and she couldn't drag him there. But if he didn't get medical attention soon he would die. Acid pulled out her phone. It was a long shot. But it was the only move she had.

———

"WHAT DID I bloody well tell you?" Sonny scoffed, as he brought his van to a stop a few feet away from them. "A girl and a teacher against that mob! Although, you look like more like a prozzie in this evening's get-up!"

Acid looked down at herself. In only her bra with her jacket open. She yanked the zip up to her throat.

"Less of that talk," she said, breathless after dragging Vinh the length of the parking lot. "It's been a tough few hours."

Sonny shoved the van in neutral and kept the engine running as he climbed out. He grabbed Vinh under the arms and helped her manoeuvre him into the middle seat of the cab. "You're lucky I like ya," he wheezed. "Lucky The Dullahan and I go way back."

"Lucky you were nearby too, huh?" she said, lifting Vinh's arm off her shoulder and taking her own seat by the passenger window. "Thing is, I don't feel so lucky presently. But thank you, I appreciate this. I'll pay. Make it worth your while."

"I'm not a bloody taxi," he said, before breaking out

into a wheezing laugh which ended in a phlegmy cough. "Nah, you keep your dong to yourself."

"I think that's a rule we could all live by," she replied, casting Sonny a quick up and down.

"Fair," he replied. "Righto, let's get this one to the hospital before he makes any more mess on my bloody upholstery."

He shoved the stick in gear and pulled the van away. Vinh groaned and leaned into her as they moved across three lanes of traffic towards the centre of the carriageway.

"Stay with me," she told him. "We're getting you help." Vinh's whole torso was covered in sticky crimson and his skin was clammy. Not good. Not good at all. "How much further?" she asked Sonny.

"There are a few hozzies nearby. I reckon St Paul's is your best bet. Five minutes at this time of night." He looked at her, then at Vinh. "So go on then, what happened?"

"My ex-colleague," she said. "The one I'm here to kill."

"I see. Not going too well for you then, this one-woman revenge mission?"

She turned to the window. "Just drive, please."

Out the window, the business district flew past, the bright lights of the city reflecting off glass-fronted office blocks. A glance at Vinh. His eyes were closed. She nudged him softly on the arm, held his icy hand in hers.

"Vinh? We're almost there," she told him. "Now listen to me. I can't stay with you. I'm sorry. I'll take you as far as I can, but I can't risk being detained. Do you understand?"

On the other side of her, Sonny snickered to himself. She ignored him, leaning closer to Vinh as he tried to speak. "Kill Spitfire," he said. "But please... not Huy. He is a good man... he is just..."

Acid slapped at his face as his head lolled forward.

"Come on, Vinh. We're nearly at the hospital." She looked over at Sonny who nodded out the window.

"We're here," he said. "I'll drop you down the side. No cameras there. I'll help you get him out but after that you're on your own."

She understood. "No worries. I appreciate the lift."

"I know you do, love. Tell you what, think of me in the future. If you survive this, I mean. I'm not always in Vietnam, you see. Am what you might call an *international* arms dealer. I prefer jetsetter. But either way, you need any more equipment, let me be your man."

"Good to know," she said.

He brought the van to a stop in a dark side street running alongside the hospital. Vinh was falling in and out of consciousness and was like a dead weight, but they managed to get him out the driver's door and onto the pavement.

"You'll have to drag him to the foyer," Sonny said, climbing back into the front of the van. "You'll be all right. S'only fifty metres or so."

He slammed the door and gave her a cheap salute before checking his mirrors and speeding away into the night.

Acid watched the van as it got to the end of the street and disappeared. Then she turned back to Vinh. Avoiding the bullet wound as best she could, she slid her arms under his armpits and linked her fingers together across his upper chest. Using all the strength she had left, she dragged him to the main entrance and laid him down in the stark light spilling out from the foyer.

"Vinh? Can you hear me?"

The man's eyelids flickered and what looked like a half-smile turned the corners of his mouth. "Yes," he wheezed.

"Okay. I have to go. I'm so sorry. But you'll be in excellent hands now. Tell them you were mugged and fought back. Tell them they shot you and you dragged yourself here. You understand what I'm saying?" Another half-smile. An attempt at a nod. "Good man," she said.

She got to her feet. And as a hospital porter appeared at the other side of the glass doors, she ran off into the night.

Chapter Thirty-Nine

Tam Quan stirred under her thin cotton sheet. This again. She rolled over and reached for her watch on the night-stand. One a.m. She sat up and plumped her pillow before slumping down once more on the bed, already accepting it would be one of those nights. Tam hadn't slept well in over six months, ever since Huy had disappeared. Or maybe before that, back when she'd first started noticing the signs, her suspicions growing. She'd tried various types of pills, drinking a strong night cap before turning in, Vinh had even bought her a music player with some meditation tapes already loaded onto it. But nothing had helped. Now, with the start of the hot season, it was only going to get worse. She closed her eyes and felt the soft pillow beneath her cheek. She'd give it one more try then switch the light on, read some of her book, watch TV. Anything to keep her focus away from the nagging thoughts in her head.

Tam was close to her only child. She had brought him up alone, a single parent, and they'd only had each other. But she had noticed a change in him over the last few years. She never commented, never made a fuss. But it was a worry. Even more so leading up to his disappearance. His choice of reading material, the online documentaries he watched, the internet search history he didn't think she knew how to view, they all pointed in a certain direction. For a long time Tam had brushed it off as youthful exuberance. It was important, she told herself, for a young man finding himself to rail against the system. She herself had defied her parents and teachers' expectations by moving to Australia when she was eighteen to train as a nurse. In 1979 Vietnam, so soon after the American War, it was unheard of for a young woman to do such a thing. So she got it. The rebelliousness. The desire for something new.

She sat up in bed. It was no use. She leaned over and was about to click on the bedside light when she heard something. A dull banging noise. She froze. Listening into the darkness. The noise went again. Louder now, more rhythmic. It sounded like someone banging on the door of the bistro.

Tam swung her legs onto the cool lino and tiptoed over to her window. Rather than open the net curtains, she leaned her face into the material, pressing it against the cool glass to peer unseen through the gap in the bottom. But if anyone was down there she couldn't see them.

The banging went again. Whoever it was, they weren't giving up. Tam scurried back over to the bed and pulled her dressing gown off the bed post, wrapped it around her. Then she slipped her feet into a battered pair of honeycomb sandals and headed for the stairs. She didn't turn the light on as she reached the main restaurant, but slid around the counter and leaned around the side of the kitchen door. Her hand found the wooden handle of her favourite knife and she pulled it to her, holding the handle against her chest with the blade pointed out at a right angle.

Through the front window she could see a silhouette. About her height. A woman from the looks of it. The hair was long and had a slight wave to it. Thick, too. Western hair. She risked a few more steps towards the entrance. Then she heard the voice.

"Tam, please. Can you open up? It's me, Sid. From the other day. We've found your son. We've found Huy. He's alive. But Vinh's hurt. I need your help."

"You've seen Huy?" Tam was at the door in a second. She slid the bolts out, top and bottom, and twisted open the latch.

The woman slipped inside. "Shut it and lock it. Quick," she told her.

Tam did as instructed. Turning around she found Sid pacing up and down. She had on the same black jeans as she'd worn when she was first in here, but they were a mess now. Filthy, in fact. Like she'd been rolling around in the dirt. Her hair was lank and stuck to her face in places, and her skin was moist with sweat and grime and what looked like blood. It was on her neck. Down her shirt. Lots of it. Tam shook her head, trying to make sense of everything.

"Are you hurt?" she asked.

"Not me. I'm sorry for waking you, I couldn't go back to my hotel, I didn't know what else to do." She was speaking fast. Too fast for Tam to keep up. Her eyes were wild and unblinking. "My name isn't Sid, by the way, it's Acid, Acid Vanilla. Yes, I know it's a weird name and I'll explain later but right now I need to gather my thoughts together, figure out what I'm going to do and... Bastard. Bloody bastard shit."

Tam stared. The girl, Acid now apparently (was that her

real name?), hadn't stopped pacing the whole time. She was like a wild animal, prowling around in search of prey.

"Please. Sit down," she tried. "I'm not sure I understand. Vinh is hurt?"

The woman yanked a chair out from underneath one of the central tables and slung herself down on it. Still unblinking, she gestured for Tam to sit with her.

"It's my fault," she said. "Like always. People get hurt. They die. Sorry, let me start over. Vinh and me, we've been helping each other. He's been looking for your son as you know, who is alive by the way – just so you know – though don't get too excited yet. Anyway Vinh was helping me find someone and we found him. Same place as your boy. We chased him into the city but he ambushed us. He shot Vinh in the chest." She stopped and gulped back a mouthful of air.

"Is he going to be okay?" Tam asked. "Where is he?"

"Hospital. St-something-or-other. He's in a bad way. But I had to leave him. Couldn't risk being questioned."

"All right," Tam said. "I'm going to make us a pot of tea. Why don't you try to calm yourself, and then you can give me the full story?"

Acid swallowed but nodded her agreement. "Thank you," she said. "I'll do that. But believe me, it'll be a lot to deal with. Maybe grab a bottle of something stronger if you've got it."

The pain in her eyes. The desperation. Tam saw it all. She touched her on the arm and smiled. "Just tea, I think," she said softly. "I won't be long."

Chapter Forty

It took Acid less than five minutes to relay to Tam all that had happened in the last forty-eight hours. Once done she sat back and sipped at the mug of green tea.

Yep. Still tasted like cat piss.

She put the cup down and pondered Tam as she sat opposite her. Acid had been expecting more, to be honest. A few minutes ago she'd found out her only son was the criminal mastermind behind an organisation planning on overthrowing the government. Perhaps she'd not heard her correctly. Acid knew she herself had a wonderful speaking voice. It was clipped, clear, precise, years of practice had made it so. But when the bats took over – when her manic sensibilities shoved reason and decorum out of the driving seat – she did tend to blurt. She sniffed, ready to explain further, when Tam let out a deep sigh, as though releasing something heavy she'd held in for too long.

"This man who shot Vinh, he works for Huy?"

"Sort of."

"And you know him?"

"Sort of. I knew him once. In my past. Not anymore. But I was the one chasing him, I put Vinh in harm's way." She bowed her head. "It's my fault he got shot."

"He will not die." Tam said, with conviction. "He is strong."

"I hope you're right." Acid looked up at her. "But you don't seem surprised. About Huy."

"I knew he wasn't dead. I don't know how. I just felt it. Everyone told me to expect the worst. But I knew."

"And the fact he's building an army to overthrow the government?"

She sighed, becoming visibly more relaxed as she did so. "He was always a deep thinker, my son. Clever. Passionate. I remember when he was only nine years old he told me he was going to make the world a better place for us. Somewhere we could be truly happy."

"You think that's what he's doing with the Cai Moi − making the world a better place?"

"I believe he thinks so." Another beatific smile. "To me he's still the same boy he always was. Passionate. Intelligent. Even if his methods are − perhaps − severe. I know he cares strongly about people. About his country."

Acid pondered her words. It was heartening to hear a mother stand by her child so vehemently. Would her own mother have done the same if she knew the full story?

"Do you think I'm crazy?" Tam asked. "Or as bad as him?"

Acid paused. Truth was, she couldn't decide whether what she was hearing was the most ridiculous thing she'd ever heard, or the most beautiful.

"Listen, Tam, I am in no position to give anyone advice or offer moral judgement, believe me. If it works for you, go for it." She crossed her arms on the table in front of her.

"One thing I can't understand, however. Why let Vinh run around on a wild goose chase, putting himself in danger, if you knew Huy was alive?"

Tam turned away. "I didn't know for certain. And I was scared. I didn't think Vinh would go to the authorities but I couldn't be certain. He blamed himself for Huy's disappearance. He wanted to do this. Vinh has had a lot of tragedy in his life."

Acid sat back in her seat. "His son?"

"He told you?"

"Yes. I know everything." Tam stared. Getting a read on her. Acid nodded her head. "Yes. Everything."

"I see," she said softly. She gazed into her tea. Didn't look up when she spoke. "It was only one time. We were never together. I was mourning my husband's death and Vinh was a good friend to me. One night our friendship went too far. I was sorry for what it led to – the repercussions. But without that night I wouldn't have my son."

"Repercussions?"

"Vinh's young son. His marriage. We were friends, his wife and I. I told him not to tell her, but the guilt ate at him. For some reason he chose to tell her while they were on holiday. They fought in the street. No one was watching Danh. He ran out in front of a car." She stopped, her voice breaking. "Vinh blamed himself. Still does."

Acid forced down a mouthful of tea. "How come you never told Huy that Vinh was his father?"

A sadness fell over Tam's face. "I should have. But Vinh was married, and then later heartbroken. It never seemed the right time. As far as everyone knew I was carrying my dead husband's child. That's what Huy was told as well. Until he discovered the truth."

"I take it he didn't relish the discovery?"

Tam finished her tea and held the empty cup in the palm of her hand. "He was angry. More than angry. We fought. That was the last time I saw him. But he has a good heart. He will see me when he is ready."

Acid cricked her neck. "Wow," she said. "I think that's incredible."

"What do you mean?"

"That you still give him the benefit of the doubt – still love him – despite everything I've told you." She held her hand up. "Don't get me wrong, I think it shows real strength."

"You do not have this?" Tam asked. "Where is your mother?"

Acid snorted loudly but didn't look up. She ran her fingers around the rim of her cup. "My mother's dead. Same reason Vinh is in hospital. Because of me."

"Oh? What did you do?"

"You don't want to know."

"Try me," Tam told her. "We are awake now, yes? It will be morning in a few hours. Then I shall call the hospital. Find out about Vinh."

Through her hair, Acid saw Tam's slim hand reach out to touch her on the wrist and give it a squeeze. "It might help," she told her. "Something tells me you have a lot of stories weighing you down, Acid Vanilla."

"Oh Tam," she sneered. "You really have no idea."

Chapter Forty-One

It may have been because her mind was still racing, taking longer than normal to come down from its manic high - or there may even have been something in the green tea that she didn't know about - but over the next hour, Acid told Tam everything. Or at least, told her as much as she could without compromising herself or totally freaking the old woman out. She stuck to the story of young Alice Vandella, explaining how she'd killed her mother's abusive lover before being sent to a home for dangerous girls. Despite the anger and confusion knotting her stomach, despite the bats screaming at her to shut up, Acid spoke candidly and with vigour. She did, however, brush over any mention of her previous career less she get carried away with the oversharing. That she'd fallen in with some bad sorts (the man who shot Vinh being one of them) and regretted many of her life choices was as far as she went - adding that she was here in Hanoi looking for justice and closure. As she got to the part about her mother's illness her voice began to waver and she paused for a sip of tea.

"You poor thing," Tam said, patting her hand. "This is a great burden for you, I can tell."

"They killed her because of me, because of my mistakes. How can do I even deal with that?"

Tam left her hand on hers. "You do it one day at a time. She would not want you to suffer."

Acid shook her head as a bitter laugh crept out of her throat. "You really don't know the half of it. Even trying to put it right I'm still messing everything up, putting myself and others in danger." She sighed. "Vinh got it right. I do have a death wish."

She glanced at Tam, the gentle woman with the kind smile and sad eyes. She didn't look shocked, or afraid, or anything at all but composed.

"Do you want to know the worst thing?" Acid asked, finding her rhythm. "A part of me is glad she's dead. I'm angry as hell, sure, but I'm also relieved. How can I think that when it's my fault?"

"You did not kill her."

"They killed her to get at me." She gripped her knee, digging her fingernails into the flesh. "I'm bad news. Vinh's lying in hospital because of me."

"Don't be too hard on yourself." Tam replied. "These people you speak of sound like a lot of people I have known - nasty, evil, bullies. Weak too, but not like Vinh. He is a survivor. Like me. Like you. Like your mother too, from what you tell me."

Acid sneered away a shudder of emotion. "You think?"

"Don't underestimate the love a mother has for her child," Tam said. "Despite who he is, what he has done, I will always love Huy. I'm sure your own mother was the same. It doesn't matter who you were or who you are now. She will always love you." Acid opened her mouth to speak but Tam raised her hand and fixed her dead in the eyes. Her voice dropped an octave. "But this is not over for you. You have to pull yourself up and do what you need to do?"

"And what do I need to do?"

"Find this man from your past, who has this hold over you." Acid opened her mouth to speak but Tam held up her hand. "You don't have to explain. I see it in your face. In your body. He brings you great pain. So find him and face him. Kill him, if that's your destiny. This is how you find peace."

"Woah, there, Tam. You're a dark horse."

"I am a fighter!" she yelled. "Also like you. We kill the demons inside of us by facing them head on. It sounds like you are on a mission to rid the world of bad people. Like my son, in his own way. Keep sight of that. But also, beware of allowing hate to guide you. This is a destructive energy. One that clouds our judgement."

"You're a wise woman Tam," Acid told her. "And a better one than me."

"I'm not so sure about that. And you are not a bad person. Just troubled. You love your mother and want justice for her. She would have been proud of you, I think."

Acid rubbed the back of her hand over her eyes. "She was proud of me. I know she was. When I was in Crest Hill she was there every visiting day. A four-hour round trip."

Tam let out a long sigh. Nothing else to be said.

Acid sat back in her seat, glad her instincts had brought her here. Tam was right. She had to finish this. To get justice for her mother, and Vinh, and herself too. It was the only way she was going to move forward. The only way she could live a life approaching normality. She stretched her arms wide, feeling the muscles in her neck pop.

The clock on the wall read 4 a.m. It was clear Spitfire's time in Hanoi was done. He'd be on the next plane out of here. Which meant she didn't have long. Hours, if she was lucky. But she was ready. She knew where she had to go next. She knew what she had to do.

Chapter Forty-Two

Spitfire Creosote was seething with a rage that was uncomfortable. After giving Acid Vanilla's little boyfriend a new blow-hole, the thought had crossed his mind to trek back to the Cai Moi warehouse to retrieve his car. But he'd decided against it. He'd set up the hire using a cloned card, so it was no bother to him and, besides, the walk back to the hotel would do him good. Clear his head. The plan now was to get his things and get a flight back to Blighty.

As he got to the edge of the French District, and the Hoan Kiem Lake, he slowed his pace. Gave himself time to reflect on the last few hours. To better focus on the bile twisting up his guts.

The fact Acid was here in Hanoi trying to kill him wasn't giving much cause for consternation. Yes, she was angry. Out for blood. And yes, she might have killed Davros Ratpack, but Davros had been getting slow these last few years. Spitfire would have never said it to anyone, but he suspected the man's heart wasn't in the game the way it once had been. But no one could say the same for *him*. Spitfire Creosote was still a force to be reckoned with. A deadly killer. The same Mr Sensational he'd always been. Acid Vanilla was no threat to him. But that didn't mean she hadn't pissed him off royally.

As if to make matters worse his phone was now vibrating against his chest. He took it out and stared at the caller ID as he steadied himself internally. Caesar calling. He waited another few seconds, then, when he was suitably grounded, he answered.

"Good evening, boss."

"Don't you good-evening-boss me. I've just pissing well heard. Where are you?"

"News travels fast."

"That it does, Spitfire. Raaz found a backdoor into their comms channel. We've been monitoring them for the last twenty-four hours."

Spitfire was impressed. Over twenty years with Annihilation and they were becoming the multi-media network Caesar had always promised.

"So you heard the meeting?"

"I heard they're not taking us on long term. I heard they took the bastard data files and told us to piss off!"

Spitfire clenched his fist, a white-knuckled ball of hate, but his voice remained calm. "I tried my best, C. You know me, I can sell ice to Innuits. But they weren't interested. Bunch of freaks. Didn't help matters when Acid turned up, of course."

Caesar grumbled over the line. The words were indecipherable as the line crackled. Then his voice came back, serious-tone to the max. "Listen to me. Acid Vanilla is always going to be a pain in the arse, until she's put in the ground. But right now, we've got a bigger problem. Those Vietnamese shits have fucked us. If the data we've sold them

– at a bloody reasonable price, I might add – is used the way they say, they could well become an exceedingly powerful force in the Far East in the next year or two. We needed that contract, Spitfire. Not so much the money, but the foothold it would give us in the region. Them backing out makes us seem weak. Makes us seem like amateurs. I will not have that, you hear me?"

Spitfire was a block away from his hotel. Best to finish this conversation in the open air. He chose a bench opposite the Ly Thai To Garden and sat.

"I totally agree," he told Caesar. "So what do you want me to do?"

"Where are you now?"

Spitfire glanced down the street. Over a small copse of trees, he could see the large bronze head of the Ly Thai To statue. Beyond that, the Tonkin Palace and the impressive white facade of his hotel. The Sofitel Legend Metropole Hanoi. One of the most expensive hotels in the city, but still a steal at five and a half million dong per night.

"To be honest, I was going to pack my case, get a drink and then get the hell out of here," he told him. "But I'm thinking now you might have another job for me."

"You thought correctly, my friend."

"I see," said Spitfire. "So what's the call?"

"You know what," Caesar told him. "Go to Plan B."

Spitfire got up from the bench and smiled. Good. Spitfire liked Plan B.

"No problem, boss," he said. "Consider it done."

Chapter Forty-Three

The fluttering pressure of a million bat wings filled Acid's soul as she approached the Cai Moi warehouse. She was alert, focused. Every muscle hard. Twitching with readiness. As she neared the main entrance, she crossed her arms over her chest and grabbed a Beretta in each hand. Each pistol held a new magazine. Seventeen rounds per gun, plus one in each chamber. She stroked her index finger along the smooth metal triggers and pressed on.

There had been a passing thought, as she had travelled here from Tam's place, that she might enter via the roof, as before. But she'd quickly dismissed the idea. The time for stealth and strategic movement was over. Somewhere between Vinh getting his sternum blasted open and the walk over here, she'd shifted from reasoned tactician to manic killer. Her body and mind ached for vengeance. Desperate to squeeze hot lead into any bastard who deserved it.

As she entered the yard an image flashed across her mind's eye. A time many years ago, when she first met Spitfire Creosote. They were standing in the main room at Honeysuckle House, Caesar's covert assassin training academy in the country. They were both sweating and breathless, after a particularly gruelling sparring session.

"You know, darling, you're becoming a real good fighter," Spitfire had purred in that deep voice of his. "But technique alone won't make you a world-class killer."

Acid had been in awe of him back then. She'd asked him to explain, and hung on his every word.

"Mindset is as important as action," he'd continued. "It's imperative you cultivate a killer's mentality – a way of channelling your awareness. That way you free yourself of fear, and anger, and apprehension."

Over those first few months Spitfire had been so helpful. Caring too, as he'd explained eloquently about the 'Characteristics of The Killer', as he called them. Fifteen mindsets Acid would have to hone and harmoniously integrate into her persona. Only then, Spitfire told her, would she have a true killer instinct.

He was bang on the money too. Honing those killer characteristics had made Acid Vanilla into who she was. The world's deadliest female assassin. And now, despite her doubts over the last few years, she had to step back into that persona again. She had to utilise every one of those characteristics. Tunnel vision was an important one. Heightened situational awareness as well. But Acid knew the major player in this situation was the one she'd always found trickiest to control. Lack of emotion.

She reached the building and pressed her back against the cold brick, edging her way towards the door. Tam had made Acid promise she wouldn't kill Huy. But as far as she was concerned she had leeway if she needed to apply pressure. She was here for answers and she was running out of time.

Acid got up to the door and stopped. Over in the distance the faint yelp of the dogs mixed in with the hum of the city traffic drifting up from the south. But coming from inside, nothing. No sound at all. She nudged against the door, opening it an inch and peering inside. A pink neon glow bathed the walls of the long corridor but there was no one in sight. She slipped inside, letting the door suck shut behind her, and crept down the long corridor as it zig-zagged around to reveal a doorway at the far end. Despite the gloom and minimal lighting, she could see the door hanging open. Beyond that she couldn't see much further, but no guards were present.

She reached the end of the corridor and squinted into the next room. It was a small holding pen leading into the main space of the warehouse, but the way the room was set out, in an L-shape, she could only see the wall in front of her. A large splatter of bright red blood ran from one corner. It was still wet. With every muscle tense, and unsure what she was going to find, Acid stepped further into the room.

"Ah, shit."

The bodies of two men were slumped in the corner by the far door. They'd fallen one on top of the other. On the ground a few feet away lay their UZI 9mms and a scattering of empty cases. So they'd fought back. Or tried to at least. Acid got her boot under the chest of the body on top and rolled him over. He was only a young man. His face was a tragic tableau of fear and fury – frozen that way the moment someone put a bullet between his eyes.

A noise came from the next room and Acid sprang to her feet. Gripping the guns tight, she moved over to the door. Listening. It was a dull wailing sound, like some sort of animal. She kicked the door open and strode into the space with guns at arm's length. She didn't blink. The room was dark, but she caught sight of something moving over by the wall. Before she could get a proper look, a hooded guard appeared from behind a pile of crates. Acid saw the muzzle flash of the UZI before she heard it and leapt backwards through the door as a hail of bullets chiselled at the stone surround.

She gave it a beat, waiting until the initial flurry of shots subsided. Then before she had a chance to consider the danger she moved back into the room. The guard was standing in the same spot, waiting for her. His eyes were wide and crazed. He gnashed his teeth and yelled something in Vietnamese as he aimed the UZI her way. But Acid was too quick for him. She aimed at his waist and opened fire, zippering a burst of shots in a rising string directly up the centreline of his body. She didn't wait around to watch the man fall. Aiming the guns in a wide arc to cover the entire space, she moved along the side of the room with her back against the wall. As she reached the nearside corner of the room, she noticed four bodies lying on the raised plat-form area. More of the Cai Moi guards. All dead. Along with the two in the corridor, and the man she'd killed a few moments ago, that made seven. She'd counted eight guards the last time she was here.

There it was again. The muffled wails of a dying animal. She cast her attention around the room. There, behind the platform. The last guard. She hurried over, moving in a semi-circular path, an eye on all doorways. The man was lying in a pool of his own blood. He'd taken a couple in the chest and one in each leg for good measure. As she got closer, he reached out, said something she didn't understand. His face was clammy with sweat and his skin glowed white in the subdued light from the moon.

Not long for this world.

The phrase came into her head as if from nowhere. It was one of Caesar's ironic witticisms. If you could call them that. But the thought of her old boss stirred up renewed vigour in Acid. She put a mercy bullet between the guard's eyes. The least she could do.

A few feet away was another body. This one laid out on his back with his arms spread wide. The hooded cowl of a long ceremonial cloak covered his face.

"Ah, Huy. No." Acid knelt beside the body and rolled it over. "Bloody hell."

The surge of relief surprised her. It was the smaller hood. Not Huy. She scanned the man's body and took in a sharp breath. It confirmed what she'd already suspected. Spitfire had done this. She recognised the go-to shot pattern. Two in the chest followed by a shot to the throat, straight through the spinal cord. Then the coup de grâce: a bullet through each of the eye sockets. Him showing off.

She got to her feet as she heard a noise drifting across the warehouse. Sounded like a stiff door being forced open. Guns raised, she moved swiftly over to a door at the opposite side of the room. Nudging it open with her hip she was met with a rush of cold air to the face. It was welcome. Focused her attention. A narrow corridor lay in front of her, which opened out into a room at the end.

Acid moved stealthily down to the end the corridor and flattened herself against the wall. From this position she could see into the next room, but only the nearside wall. She listened. No sound. She side-stepped inside, leading with the FSs. The room's low ceiling felt oppressive after the expansive height of the main warehouse. She moved her aim around the room. Tense and ready. A wooden sink unit stood along the short wall to her left, and in front of her two tables pushed together to form a square, with small wooden chairs placed around. Beyond this, in the far corner, a fire exit door was hanging open.

In the centre of the table a laptop lay open. The same one Huy had been using earlier. Draped across it was another ceremonial cloak, the sort the hoods had worn. Acid lifted the cloak and held it up in the moonlight. A bullet had ripped through the left shoulder, below the neck. She stuck her finger inside. The shot had only gone through the first layer of material. No exit wound. Not a good sign for whoever was wearing this when they got shot. Something told her that the someone was Huy. She flung the cloak on the ground and shuffled around the table to get a better look at the laptop. A cool breeze blew in from the open fire exit as she tapped the space bar impatiently. The screen immediately lit up to reveal a professional file-shredding application. She clicked on a few more keys, ran the track pad over the main finder-window. Nothing there. No files. No programs. The entire hard drive had been obliterated.

Acid closed the laptop and moved over to the fire exit. Remaining cautious, still with the FSs high and ready for action, she stepped out into a barren courtyard. Moss and weeds covered the ground, poking up through the cracked concrete. Opposite, she could see a short alleyway leading to the main road beyond. But Huy, Spitfire, they were nowhere in sight. She shoved the Berettas back in the holster and ran from the building. With the Cai Moi dead, Spitfire would have more impetus to get out of the city. She needed to find him. And fast. But first she needed answers. From the only person who would know where he was.

Chapter Forty-Four

"Where is he?" Acid asked, as Tam inched opened the bistro door twenty minutes later.

"I don't know what—"

"Don't you bloody say it," Acid said, shoving a finger in the old woman's face. She stepped inside and looked about the room as Tam shut and bolted the door behind her. "The rest of his crew are dead. He's been shot. There's only one place he could have gone. So where is he?"

Tam looked at her hands. "Please, don't hurt him."

Acid grabbed her by the shoulders, dipped her head to look her in the eyes. "I'm not going to hurt him. But I need to speak with him. I need to know where Spitfire is. Now."

Tam sighed and looked up. Her eyes were red and watery. "He isn't a bad man," she said.

Acid straightened, softened her voice. "I don't care about that. But he's been shot. So let me help him."

She heard rustling behind her and turned to see Huy standing in the doorway. He was wearing a dirty white t-shirt and grey sweatpants, as though he'd been doing nothing but lounge upstairs on his Xbox all evening. It was only his face gave it away. His skin was pale and drawn. His eyelids were heavy but eyes super alert, like they'd seen far too much. He spoke to Tam in Vietnamese, then to Acid.

"What do you want to know?"

"You need patching up?" she asked.

Huy pulled down the collar of his shirt to expose a large purple bruise. "I was wearing a vest," he told her. "We were beginning to mix with some heavy people. I felt it was a savvy move."

Acid arched an eyebrow. "Indeed." She nodded at Tam. "She says you're a genius. That right?"

Huy smiled. Tried to hide it. "My mother has always been my biggest fan."

"Yeah. Mums. Gotta love 'em," Acid replied. "All right, Huy. Sit down, I need answers."

Standing here now in his mother's domain, Huy looked younger than ever. He twisted his mouth to one side. "Fine," he relented. "But let us talk upstairs. It is safer there." He gestured to the large window at the front of the café and the blackness of the still-early morning beyond.

"Fair enough."

The three of them trudged upstairs to the flat above the bistro. It was a small space. Three rooms – two bedrooms and a kitchen-come-diner-come-lounge. A tiny bathroom cubicle led off from the main living space, but even the most creative and cunning of estate agents wouldn't have dared call it a room.

A small wooden table had been placed underneath a square window at the top of the stairs, and a squat candle sat in the centre, the only source of light. Acid sat, followed by Huy. Tam fussed around for a few moments asking if anyone wanted drink, and then joined them.

"Have you apologised to your mum for all you've put her through?" Acid asked.

The slight hint of a sneer twisted Huy's mouth. He shrugged. "I was doing this for her. She knows that."

"Does she?"

"Don't you, Mum?"

Tam smiled, simpering at her boy. It was kind of heart-warming, Acid thought. But she didn't have time for gooey reunions. "I need to know where Spitfire Creosote is," she said.

Huy shook his head. "He killed my friends and then shot me too. I was lucky. He was standing over me as I feigned death. I told myself it was over for me. He was preparing for a more decisive shot. But then he heard the gunshots coming from the main room."

Acid pursed her lips. "That was me. So what happened next?"

"He ran. I waited thirty seconds, as long as I dare, and then I ran as well. All the way here."

"What was on the laptop?"

"Everything." He placed his hands on the table as an air of despondency fell over him. "I had dumped any incriminating files. It was part of our exit strategy, if we were ever discovered by the authorities. My friends, they thought Spitfire had returned to up the offer, but I was wary. Then he began shooting people. Killing my friends."

"You don't want to get on the shitty side of Beowulf Caesar." Acid sighed. "I should know."

He frowned. "Who are you exactly?"

She glanced at Tam. "I'm an old friend of Spitfire's. And I need to know where he is, where he's staying. I want to kill him. That's all. I don't care about the Cai Moi, or you, or anything else.' She hammered her finger on the table, emphasising each word. "All I want is Spitfire Creosote dead."

Huy's wan features looked more miserable in the candlelight. He glanced from her to his mother and back again. "I'm sorry, I cannot. That man is dangerous. If he discovers I have given him away, he'll come looking for me. Kill my mother too."

Acid leaned across the table at him. "Well that won't happen. Because he'll be dead. I'll have killed him."

This time Huy did little to hide his sneer. "Forgive me, but if the mighty Cai Moi were no match for him, I don't think you'll be able to—"

Before he had a chance to finish she was on her feet with both Beretta barrels in his face.

"You were saying, sunshine?" She pushed one of the guns into the thin flesh of his cheek as beside her Tam began to wail softly in Vietnamese. A prayer, perhaps. Acid ignored her. "Look, I get it. You want to protect your mother. But maybe you should have thought about that before running off to join the circus. Are you aware your men were knocking her around before I stepped in?"

There was a slight shift in his expression, a hardening of his eyes. "I was not happy with what happened," he mumbled. "I did not want the others to know she was my mother, so I let them continue collecting from the bistro. But when I heard they had become rough, I was enraged. As you saw, those men regretted their actions."

"Yes, I did see that," she answered, nostrils flaring. "So the Cai Moi was your idea?"

Huy slowly raised his hands, to try to move the guns from his face. She held her ground for a second longer, then lowered her aim, raising her eyebrows at Huy to continue.

"Not at first. I was selling drugs, to get more money.

Some Cai Moi soldiers found me on their turf and I was brought in front of the leader." He looked at Tam as he spoke, but she didn't meet his gaze. "I was terrified. I'd heard of the Cai Moi. We all had. Even then, in their infancy, they instilled fear in people. But it transpired the main man behind the scenes was my old friend, Le Ho."

In that second everything fell into place. The man Acid recognised at the warehouse, the second hood. The one Spitfire had used as target practice. He was the other boy from Vinh's photograph. Le Ho.

"We had lost touch. But back when we were close we'd talk often of revolution. Of creating a better city for ourselves. A better future. Le Ho was a passionate man, but he was driven by anger. He only wanted to destroy. But slowly, as we rekindled our friendship, I convinced him the Cai Moi could be so much more. He asked me to join him in his mission. So I did. I took over operations and we wrote a manifesto. It was me who had the idea to weaponise the data."

"But isn't Vietnam a relatively decent and peaceful nation these days?" Acid asked. "What is there to rebel against?"

"Everything!" Huy cried. "We are a proud nation. But since the relaxing of communist policies, we see western influence everywhere. KFC, McDonalds, fucking Burger King. We need to take our country back. And no politician is decent. You must know this. You have to understand, our plan was to move the Cai Moi away from violence and crime. We dreamed of transforming the organisation into an underground resistance group. Multi-media activism on a large scale, to bring about real change for our people."

Acid returned to her seat. "All admirable, I suppose. But *you've* got to understand, Huy, that when you build allegiances with people who like violence, it's rather hard to stop them being violent." She rubbed at her eye, at the burning tiredness there. "One thing I don't understand. Why did the Cai Moi guards at the factory tell us you were dead?"

"This is our way," he replied. "When you join the Cai Moi, you cut all ties with your past. Become known as The One. The person you were is gone. So, in truth, Huy Quan is dead."

Acid sighed. She knew how that went down all too well. "Well it's a real bloody mess we've found ourselves in, isn't it? If it wasn't for you – Mr Weaponised Data – Spitfire wouldn't be in Hanoi. And neither would I. And Vinh, your old man, he wouldn't be lying in hospital."

Huy looked at Tam, then away. He mumbled something under his breath.

"It's time to start talking, Huy." Acid leaned over the table. Enunciated each word. "Tell me where I can find Spitfire Creosote."

Tam stirred in her seat. She whispered to her son and the two of them spoke in Vietnamese. Acid held her nerve throughout. But time was running out. Another few hours, maybe less, and Spitfire would be on a plane out of here. After that he was in the wind and she was on her own. She could kiss goodbye to any further assistance from The Dullahan if she messed this up.

Huy fixed her with a stern look. "If I tell you, please do not say it was me."

She bit her tongue. "I told you," she said, her voice staccato-like. "I'm going to kill him. He isn't going to hurt you. Or anyone."

Huy nodded. "Fine. He has been staying at the Sofitel Legend Metropole."

"You sure?"

"I booked the room. But he has no more business here. He may have left already."

Acid got to her feet. "Which is why I'm going there right now."

She grabbed her jacket and pulled it on as she raced down the stairs and headed for the door.

Through the café window she could see the day's first light rising over the roof of the building opposite, casting the new dawn sky in a wash of rich oranges and deep fuchsias. It was set to be another beautiful day in Hanoi. And it was time to finish this.

Chapter Forty-Five

Spitfire leaned against the wet tiles of the shower cubicle and watched the pink water as it spiralled down the plughole at his feet. Once it ran clear, he straightened himself and turned his back to the powerful streams, enjoying the piping hot sting against his taut skin. Satisfied, he turned off the shower and stepped out onto a carefully placed bathmat to dry himself. He could feel his heart beating fast as he rubbed the warm towel down his torso. That was unusual for him but not entirely unexpected. He wasn't getting any younger and the last hour had been spent rather strenuously. He paused from drying himself to rub the towel across the steamed-up mirror above the sink. Despite his wet hair, and his skin, puffy from the heat, he was pleased with what looked back at him.

Whatever it was, he still had it.

There were few fifty-one-year-olds who could single-handedly wipe out an entire criminal organisation. He ran his fingers through his hair and smiled at himself. His work here was done.

And yes, his trip hadn't gone entirely to plan. He hadn't been able to secure the contract. But Annihilation Pest Control's reputation was intact. They were still the deadliest and most un-fuckable-with criminal network in the world. So, good job, old chap. It was time to pack up his kitbag and return to dear old Blighty.

Though as Spitfire was thinking this a sickening twinge twisted at his stomach. He had hoped as he'd heard the gunshots coming from the main warehouse that somehow they wouldn't register in his psyche. That he could get gone and not have to think about what they meant.

Because of course it was her. And he could have stayed, taken her out, put an end to this pathetic vendetta once and for all.

So, why the hell hadn't he?

He wrapped the towel around himself and moved through into the main space of the hotel suite. His vintage Rolex in brushed gold sat on the bureau, along with his ruby-encrusted signet ring. He strapped on the watch and slipped the ring onto his right hand. The ring had belonged to his father and was one of those items you wore so often it became a part of you. Now, looking on it with fresh eyes, he remembered a time long ago. Acid lying beside him in the bed, her head on his on his chest, running a tender finger over his stomach. She'd been comparing their hand sizes, laughing at how small hers were compared to his. She'd tried to remove the ring but couldn't pull it over his knuckle (he was a tad heavier back then – all muscle, of course). She'd asked him who'd given it to him and despite his train- ing, despite the strict Annihilation code, he'd told her every- thing. He remembered it feeling like a weight off his shoulders, being able to talk to her about it. After that, they talked lots. Sharing secrets. Sharing everything. Until they didn't anymore. But that was for the best, Spitfire knew. You didn't get into this life for happy endings in suburbia.

He walked over to the mini bar and yanked it open, dismayed to see it was empty.

"Bollocks."

He needed a drink. A scotch or three. Enough to dilute these troubling thoughts so he'd sleep well on the plane home. He finished drying himself off, and had slipped on his underwear and a crisp white shirt when his phone vibrated on the nightstand.

"Bollocks," he said again, louder this time.

He snatched it up and put it on speaker, threw it on the bed.

"Is it done?" Caesar's voice crackled over the line.

Spitfire walked back to the wardrobe and selected a pair of pale blue trousers. "Affirmative," he called over, stepping into the trousers and sliding them over his muscular thighs. "The Cai Moi is no more."

"Good work," Caesar told him. "What about other chapters? I heard they were spreading out into different cities. Will that be an issue?"

"Doesn't seem to have got that far," he replied, fastening the metal clasp on his trousers and zipping them up. Then he returned to the wardrobe and selected a teal suit jacket and tan leather belt. He lay the jacket on the bed and threaded the belt through the eyelets of his trousers. "You ask me, they put far too much focus on their branding. Yes, they had good ideas, but no real implementation. Bunch of amateurs. They've a whole factory devoted to making uniforms for an army that doesn't exist yet. And don't get me started on the bloody magic show. Kids today. It's all style over substance. Not like the old days."

Caesar chuckled. "And what about the pest?"

Spitfire froze mid-way through fastening his gold Walther PPK-shaped cufflinks.

"I've not seen or heard from her," he said, keeping his tone in check. "All I can think is she's bottled it. Gone dark."

"Mmm." Caesar made a low grumbling noise down the line. He didn't sound convinced.

"I've got a flight out of here in four hours," he went on, changing the subject before the boss could respond. "I'm heading back to London first, then I'll take the job in Zurich if Magpie hasn't already. The atomic scientist. That good for you?"

Caesar cleared his throat. "Fine. Speak to Raaz when you get back. I'm going to be otherwise engaged for the next two months. Kenya, then Beirut." He let out a laugh. Happier now. "It's all bloody go, isn't it? Talk about getting what you wish for. Okay, my friend, we'll connect soon. Safe journey. Oh – and Spitfire?"

"Yes, Caesar?"

"Just so we're clear. If you had run into our mutual friend – you wouldn't have had any problem disposing of her, would you?" His voice dropped, sounding more sinister than usual. "Because dark or not, I still want the crazy bitch eradicated. In the most despicable way possible. Is that understood?"

Spitfire finished with his shirt cuffs and buttoned up the front. "Of course, boss. Goes without saying. After I take care of the job in Zurich, how about I arrange a meet-up with Magpie and Raaz? Plan our move?"

Caesar sniffed back loudly. "Yes. I like it. And when you find her, make sure she suffers."

He raised his chin and did up his top button. "Got it."

"Good man. Bye for now."

The phone went dead. Spitfire slipped on the suit jacket and snatched his phone from the bed and wallet from the bureau. He gave himself a quick once over in the mirror and checked his watch: 6.30 a.m. A wonky smile cracked his face. He'd had several good reasons to insist on this particular hotel, and the twenty-four-hour bar was up there. With an hour to kill before the airport, and an intense desire not to be alone with his thoughts, it was essential. He brushed a piece of lint from his shoulder and headed for the door.

As the assassin rode the lift down to the hotel bar, he made a pact with himself. One drink. Maybe two. But that was all. Enough to centre himself. A sandwich too would be good. He'd swallowed a couple of Modafinil and some B12 pills along with a protein shake a few hours earlier, but some actual sustenance would do wonders. As the elevator pinged its arrival at ground level, and the doors opened to reveal the open-plan foyer, he was feeling good about himself. A few drinks, a bite to eat, and then a long sleep on the plane. By the time he touched down in Blighty he'd be refreshed and rested, able to put this whole trip behind him.

Despite his size, despite his age, and despite his carefully managed persona, Spitfire had a spring in his step as he strutted into Le Club and headed for the marble-topped bar. So what if he'd had a slight wobble? It was only natural for him to be unsettled, considering their past. He wasn't a psychopath. Far from it. He'd done the test, many times. So screw her and screw his stupid feelings. He'd gotten the job done. He was still an elite killer. Still the best of the best. Still—

Shit!

He stopped in his tracks.

Sat on a high leather-backed stool, and leaning seductively against the bar top, was Acid Vanilla. In front of her was a large gin martini. Two olives.

What the fuck else.

She saw him at the same time he saw her – reflected in the mirror behind the bar. A look of bemused recognition spread across her striking features and she turned to better acknowledge him.

"Fancy seeing you here," she purred. "Can I buy you a drink?"

Chapter Forty-Six

The Le Club Bar of the Sofitel Legend Metropole was a vision of beauty. It looked expensive and smelt it too – the mahogany wood and dark leather conjuring up an atmosphere of aristocratic smoking rooms or a 1920s speakeasy. Beyond the bar was a row of perfectly set tables, complete with crisp white tablecloths and polished silverware. Beyond those, French doors hung open, overlooking the glorious hotel garden courtyard. Despite the early hour, the sun was already making its presence felt, warming the greenery and pitching rich floral scents into the room. The fact Acid was perched at the bar sipping at an ice-cold and perfectly made martini while other guests would soon be arriving for breakfast bothered her none.

Acid turned her full attention back to Spitfire. She wouldn't have put him in those pale blue trousers, but other than that he looked good. Sharp. Not that she'd expect anything else from Mr Sensational. Once again, she was reminded of how odd it was she'd fallen for this man. With his neat hair and obsessive attention to detail, he was so unlike what she'd thought her ideal man to be. Acid had a punk-rock heart. She liked men with messy hair and scruffy clothes. Or so she thought.

Spitfire was still standing there, gawping.

"Are you not going to join me?" she asked, patting the stool next to her. "One drink. No harm is there."

She turned to the stoic barman, doing a sterling job of ignoring the palpable tension in the air. "Can my friend here have an Old Fashioned, please? Made with a single malt. The most expensive you have." She glanced back at Spitfire. "That's right, isn't it?"

He let out a low growl as he swung one leg over the stool and sat. He faced forward, not looking at her. "That's right. Two chunks of ice. Lemon peel, not orange. Unwaxed, if you have it."

The barman bowed his approval and scurried off to prepare the drink. Spitfire turned to her. Arched an eyebrow. "So, here we are. Like old times."

"Wonderful, isn't it?"

He narrowed his eyes at her. The small wrinkles at the corner of his eyes were more pronounced. But if anything they made him more handsome. *The bastard.*

"How do you see this going?" he asked, laying his forearm elegantly on the padded surround of the bar top.

"Haven't got a bloody clue. But after the last few days I needed a proper drink." She put her hand on his thigh and opened her eyes wide, giving it the full bit. "What a lovely hotel you've chosen, by the way. Mine is nowhere near this fancy. But to be honest, I've hardly been there the whole trip. You know how it is."

She took another long drink. It was going down too well. With no sleep and the manic bat energy at fever pitch, a few drinks could send her over the edge.

So, how *did* she see this going?

What if they said, screw it? Ran away together. It could be easily done. They could live abroad. South America, say. Somewhere hot. Where nobody knew them. Where they could be together...

Well, shit.

She'd been spiralling again. It happened.

She barked out a cough, an attempt to bring herself back to the present. As her awareness snapped together, she clocked Spitfire's expression and he looked away, shaking his head.

"What the bloody hell happened to you?" he mumbled.

"How do you mean?"

"You had it all. Riches. Purpose. Prestige. You were the best female assassin there's ever been. Some said."

She sniffed back. "Drop the female."

"Excuse me?"

"Drop the female. The best assassin there's ever been. No caveat."

He laughed, but it wasn't his usual laugh. More bitter. Nastier. But then, Acid knew, perception was everything.

He tilted his head her way and whispered, "Four hundred and seventy-three."

"Kills? Bullshit."

He nodded proudly. "No. That's a fact. What you on?"

"Never kept count."

"No. You never did, did you? But numbers don't lie, Acid. Facts don't lie."

She hit him with a side-eye. "I hope you're not counting the Moscow job in that number."

"Why wouldn't I?"

She swivelled on her seat so she was facing him. "Come off it. We've been through this. It was me who took them down. A perfect head shot to Lebedev and then a classic zipper up Smirnov as he ran away."

"Smirnov?" Spitfire frowned. "He was called Ivanov, I'm sure of it."

"Whatever. My kills."

"You've drunk too much Smirnov, if you believe that."

"Wow. That was lame, even for you." She shot him a sarcastic smile and took a gulp of her martini. "But if it means so much to you. Jesus. You take them."

"I bloody well will!"

Acid leaned forward as their eyes met. In that instant, the years fell away. She was back in his arms. Back in his big brass bed in his old flat in Whitechapel. She breathed him in. Same scent as always.

Shit.

"All in the past. Isn't it?" She sat up. Moved away. "No point going back over the numbers. Four hundred and seventy-three, four hundred and seventy-one – still impressive either way. What a clever boy you are. So scary too. And manly with it!"

Spitfire let out a laborious breath. Him letting her know he was staying calm, rising above her teasing.

"You still haven't told me," he said. "Why throw it all away?"

The barman sauntered over and made a show of presenting Spitfire his drink - placing down the heavy-bottomed glass and twisting it around so the lemon peel twist sat at two o'clock. When he left once more, Spitfire took a long drink before pulling a face. Meaning it was a good cocktail - though not the best he'd ever had. He put the glass down and considered her once more, waiting for an answer.

"I ask myself the same question," she told him. "I don't

feel like my feet have touched the ground since I killed Barabbas Stamp.."

"Barabbas, Hargreaves, Banjo," Spitfire mused. "And now Davros too. Bloody hell, Acid, when you say it out loud, does sound kind of crazy. Surely you can appreciate Caesar's stance."

Acid tensed. "He killed my mother. She wasn't a part of this."

Spitfire sucked air through his teeth. "Yes, but he had to send a message. You know he did." He went quiet. His head bowed. Then without looking at her, he added, "You know I wasn't there that night, don't you?"

The words hit her in the chest and sent her heart racing. She'd wondered every day since it happened. Spitfire didn't have any reason to lie about it.

She drank the rest of her martini. "Doesn't change anything," she said. Her voice was quiet. The quivering nervous energy spurring her on a few minutes earlier had dropped like a lead weight into her stomach. "Everyone has to die."

He nodded along. But asked, "Why?"

"If I don't kill you, you'll kill me."

"Who says?"

"Caesar says. You know he does, you silly sod."

Spitfire baulked. She turned away.

Bloody hell. Silly sod?

The playful words hung in the air, taking them back to a time when it was normal for her – only a few months into her twenty-second year and much less jaded - to try to rile her handler with spirited banter.

Spitfire cleared his throat. He'd sensed it as well. He gulped down the rest of his drink and chomped an ice cube between his back teeth.

"Walk away," he told her. "Now."

"I can't. I'm sorry." She turned to him and their eyes met. "I'll make it quick."

"Is that so?"

He pointedly raised his hand and peeled open his suit jacket, revealing a SIG Sauer strapped under his arm.

Acid stuck out her bottom lip and opened her jacket to reveal the two Berettas. She pushed her tits out too – no harm in reminding the flash bastard what he'd given up. In turn he hit her with a crooked smile. The one he knew sent her wild.

"It seems we've both come prepared."

"Appears that way," she said. "But not here."

"God no. How gauche." He tilted his head and rested it on his hand. Another rich smile cracked his perfect face. "You ever wonder what life would have been like if we weren't who we were? If we didn't do what we do?"

She shrugged, chewed her lip. Of course she'd wondered. There hadn't been a month gone by in the last twelve years where she hadn't wondered.

"No point thinking like that," she told him.

"Such a shame though."

"You dumped me."

He frowned. "Not how I remember it."

"Yeah, well you remember it wrong."

"I did love you."

A hot shiver shot up her spine and down each of her arms. The sensation wasn't unpleasant, but it wasn't welcome either. "Fuck you," she whispered.

He sneered. "Not right now. I've got somewhere to be."

"Haven't we all, sweetie?"

"Why are you here, Acid?" he asked, leaning into her. "What do you hope to achieve?"

"I told you, I wanted a decent drink." She watched the barman as he lifted a tall champagne flute from the sink under the bar and examined it closely. He'd been listening to their conversation, she knew it. But so what? "And I guess I wanted to see you again, Spit. Face to face. One last time. To make sure."

"Make sure of what?"

"That I was ready to kill you." She glanced at the barman. He didn't flinch. "That I'll be able to do it when the time comes."

"I see. Well don't spoil it for me. I'd rather not know." He shot her a cheesy grin, revealing two rows of perfect white teeth. "But if I had to bet on it? Hmm. Tricky one. I mean, you're clearly pissed off. And you are... *were* rather tasty when you wanted to be. But then there's what happened in Germany."

"A mistake," she said. "A blip. Believe me, it won't happen again."

Spitfire pouted his lips. "Can you confidently say that about yours truly, though?" He leaned in further, his voice low and deep. "Think about it, Acid. All those nights. We shared so much."

"Screw you," she said. "People change. Seeing you now, I feel nothing. Davros was harder to kill than you will be."

He chuckled joylessly to himself. "You always were a real flirt. But don't worry, I know what you really think."

He lifted his hand to her face and held her chin in his palm. His thumb traced down the side of her face. Then before she knew what was happening, he was kissing her. His lips lingered on hers. Soft, but firm. The right amount of moisture. Like she remembered. She closed her eyes and let out a deep sigh as he moved his mouth into the curve of her neck. His warm breath tickled at the fine hairs on her cheek as his lips caressed a path to her ear.

"I don't want to hurt you," he whispered, each consonant popping in her ear canal, sending shivers through her body. "So, Acid. Darling. Let this be a fucking warning."

Something hard dug into her stomach. Below the ribs. And as Spitfire slid from his stool, an intense vibration overtook her from head to toe. As though the Incredible Hulk had grabbed her by the shoulders and was shaking the life out of her. The pain was excruciating. She thought she was going to piss herself. She couldn't move. Couldn't scream. All she could do was ride it, as every muscle in her body went into seizure.

Then as quickly as it had started, it stopped.

She slumped on the bar, gasping for air as the world swam back into focus. She was on her feet in an instant, her hand straight inside her jacket, reaching to draw.

Shit.

Apart from the barman – who was now cutting up lemons with his back to her and oblivious to the attack – the room was empty. Spitfire was gone.

"Shit. Shit. Shitting shit."

Cursing herself for being so stupid, Acid picked up the martini glass and flung the olives into her mouth. She chomped the salty orbs down in one bite then pulled out her phone.

"Are you near a computer?" she asked, before Spook had a chance to say hello.

"Umm, yeah, I'm sat at my desk. Why? What's up?"

Acid hurried towards the exit as the barman shouted something after her. She hadn't paid. No time. She ran through into the main foyer of the hotel, barking instructions down the phone as she went, giving Spook the name of the hotel, the street they were on. She pushed through the revolving door and exited into the warm Hanoi day. The street was long, with main thoroughfares intersecting at both ends. She glanced left and right. No sign of him.

"Can you find a feed? Anything?" she asked.

"Maybe, Acid. But it's going to take me a few hours at least."

She gasped. "Spook, I need this now."

"I got lucky last time," she whined. "But what you're asking takes time. It's not like in a movie where I bang in some code and get straight into a secure network."

"Fine." Acid got to the roadside and scanned the area. In front of her was a large roundabout where five roads met. In the middle of the circular plinth arising from the long grass was a 3D advert for Vietcombank. Big enough to climb on and tall enough to provide a decent view. "Listen, Spook, it's fine," she rasped down the phone. "I can take it from here."

She hung up before Spook could answer and skipped over the road, dodging through a bustle of bicycles and mopeds as she went. Her legs were shaky after the Taser attack, but she reached the roundabout unscathed and clambered up the side of the structure.

"Come on, you bastard, where are you?"

She squinted into the against the dust thrown up by the heat of the morning sun, casting her eye down each street, searching for a shock of dark-blond hair amongst the blacks and browns of the locals. The streets were already full of people, but it didn't take long for her to spot him. When you were a good six inches taller than everyone else around, you did kind of stick out. He was two hundred metres or so along the street in front of her, moving in the manner of someone trying to run away without drawing attention to themselves. He ran some more, then slowed his pace, then ran again, shoving past those who got in his way. She watched as he crossed the street and disappeared behind the International Centre.

"Got you," she sneered.

She clambered down off the structure and gave chase. He wasn't getting away from her this time. Up ahead was the sprawling construction of the Plaza shopping centre. She crossed over the street to get a better view. He was still in sight, his suit jacket flapping dramatically in his wake. Another hundred yards and he passed the Cartier show-room before disappearing down the side of the mall. She was closing in. A minute behind him now. She had no plan what to do when she caught up with him, other than an untainted desire to remove him from existence. If it had to be here, on the side of the street, so be it. She'd take her chances with the authorities. Right now her only focus was on catching him. Spitfire Creosote. Mr Sensational. The flash boy who broke her heart twelve years ago. She had him in her sights. She was ready.

Chapter Forty-Seven

Despite the fact it was Sunday and the large office buildings and shopping malls in this part of the city closed for business, the streets were already swarming with people. Locals mainly. Spitfire growled at them as he rushed past. Shouting for them to move, to get out of his damn way. Some did. Most stood their ground. Looked at him like he was crazy. Maybe he was, but those people got an elbow to the ribs or a palm to the face as he shoved past them.

On the corner by the Vietnam Cuba Hospital, two young women in floaty summer dresses blocked his path. He danced around behind them a moment before barging through the middle, sending them flying off in each direction. Screw it. Spitfire had never had any qualms about hurting people. Men and women alike, he didn't care. He was what he liked to call an 'equal opportunities killer'. It didn't matter who you were, what sex, gender or age, how good-looking you were or how much money you had in the bank. If you had a target on you, he was coming. And he wasn't going to stop.

"Move! Move out of the bloody way!"

He took a left down the side of the hospital and then the next right, which took him past a new hotel complex that had been one of his accommodation choices. The Hotel Melia. It had a pool, he remembered, though he wouldn't have had much cause to use it. Maybe next time. Because, of course, there would be a next time. Acid Vanilla might be on his tail, but she wasn't going to take him down. Not a chance. He was the one who'd trained her up, for Christ's sake. Taught her to shoot. Taught her about the psychology of a killer. He let out a sneer as he left the hotel behind. Taught her to fuck, as well.

"Get out of my bloody way."

These stupid people with their petty little lives. Didn't they know he had a loaded gun in his jacket and he was so close to using it? He felt the reassuring weight of the SIG Sauer against his chest. A P32 X. Not his usual choice, but the P365 – although lighter and easier to conceal – was becoming so passé these days. And so far so good, it was one of the best striker-fire pistols he'd ever handled, and had made short shrift of those Cai Moi fools. Now he looked forward to getting home and revelling in the applause no doubt coming his way from his colleagues. He couldn't help but think of Magpie Stiletto. She'd been flirty with him recently, he'd noticed. Maybe he'd have a crack at her when he was settled back in London. She was perhaps older than his recent playthings, but no less attractive. And it paid to be with one's own now and again. Made life so much easier.

Though as Spitfire reached the corner of the street and glanced back to see a streak of black appear at the far end, he realised how ridiculous that statement was.

"Keep up, darling." he muttered to himself. "Just a few more feet."

He crossed over the street and took a right past the supreme court. It was a pointless detour but intentional. He was a fit man, ran 10K every morning, plus at least an hour in the gym, plus meditation, plus breathing exercises. Not to mention a healthy bedroom workout most evenings. Acid, on the other hand, looked tired and wired and like she hadn't had a decent meal in weeks. He already had the upper hand, but putting the knackered-out bitch through her paces was only going to help his plan.

He ran to the top of the next street and stopped. There it was, half-way down on the right-hand side and painted yellow to match the morning sun. Hao Lo Prison Monument. Once a notorious prison for POWs during the Vietnam War, it was now a museum. Perfect for Spitfire's needs. It was dark, confusing, twisted. The same as his and Acid's relationship.

Spitfire slowed his pace. A minute more and he'd be outside. But she had to see him enter, that was the point. He marvelled at the oddly painted building – once a place of torture and despair, it now had a large blue 'Welcome' sign hanging outside. He walked straight past the main entrance and around the corner to the staff entrance, visible from the road down which Acid would come. Once at the door he paused and closed his eyes. Time to focus. Time to get his head in the game. Acid Vanilla might be a messed-up, washed-up has-been and half the killer she once was, but she was still a killer. She'd taken down half of Annihilation Pest Control single-handedly. He wasn't taking any chances.

He slowed his breathing, seeing her in front of him in his mind. Her dark hair hung down over her shoulders, bounced as she walked. And of course she was wearing that bloody black leather jacket, the one she always wore. He couldn't even shake the dirty old thing from his own damned visualisation. He had tried to get her to chuck it out on many occasions. For starters, it stank. And it certainly wasn't the sartorial elegance she should be favouring as an elite assassin. He'd even had a word with Caesar about it. But the jacket remained. If anything, she had dug her heels in more, started wearing old band t-shirts and ripped jeans. But that was Acid Vanilla for you. Obstinate. Pig-headed.

Back in the visualisation, she turned to look at him, her face melting into an expression of pure fear. Those big eyes of hers – one petrol blue, one chocolate brown – startled now as he towered over her. She appeared so vulnerable. Her mouth hung open, expectant. He raised his gun. He'd make it quick, he told himself. None of his usual showboating. He was a gentleman, after all. One in the heart. One in the head. She'd be dead before she hit the ground.

He paused, checking in with his emotions. It was important to deal with any issues before the event. Hesitation was not an option. Hesitation got you killed.

But he had nothing to worry about. Any feelings he'd once had for Acid Vanilla were gone. Like dust in the wind. He opened his eyes and took out his lock-kit. An old lock like this took him only seconds to get open. He checked his watch: 7.10 a.m. Being as it was Sunday, the museum didn't open until the afternoon.

Spitfire stepped inside and left the door open. Acid was only a few hundred feet behind him. Now the fun began.

Chapter Forty-Eight

Spitfire was entering the Hao Lo Prison museum as Acid rounded the corner at the top of the street. She slowed to a stop. Best to compose herself. Find her breath. The way he'd shot her a look before he entered the building – he wanted her to follow him. Cautiously she approached, drawing both guns before she got to the door. This was a trap. She was certain of it. But surely Spitfire knew she wouldn't fall for something so obvious. He was messing with her head, the double-bluffing spiralling in on itself until she couldn't think straight.

"Screw it."

People got too caught up in 'whys' and 'hows' and 'maybes.' You could overthink everything. Most of the time, Acid knew, instinct ruled.

Listen to the bats.

Not that she needed reminding. The needle on her manic energy metre was well into the red as she crept inside the museum. The old prison windows had been covered over but the lights were on, illuminating a long room

flanked on both sides by glass display cases of prison memo-
rabilia – earthenware pots and bowls, ragged sandals, rusty
old leg shackles. Open doorways faced each other at both
ends of the room, but the lights were dim in the other
rooms beyond. Acid picked the doorway on the right (if in
doubt, pick right), but as she sidled towards it the entire
museum was plunged into pitch blackness. She couldn't see
the guns in front of her face.

Tense but prepared for anything, she continued on her
path, putting her back against the glass display case and
following it until its end. She side-walked the rest of the way
to the open doorway and shuffled through into the next
room.

"Jesus."

She flinched as the lights went on to reveal two men a
few feet away. She fired a double-tap at each. A chest shot
followed by a head shot. She watched as their hard bodies
splintered, sending particle clouds of dusty fibreglass into
the room. Display models. Prisoners. In what was once a
real cell.

Acid sighed. They weren't even lifelike. Their plastic
hair was blue, and their bright orange skin shone in the
stark lighting.

"Very good," she called out. "You had me there. Real
Man-With-The-Golden-Gun shit."

Spitfire would get the reference. Scaramanga's house of
mirrors. He'd always played down the James Bond connec-
tion, brushed it off as something others noticed, not
anything he ever refined or involved himself with. But Acid
knew. Most English men of a certain age had a Bond fetish.
Couldn't help themselves. It was one reason she suspected
Spitfire had joined Caesar's merry band of hired killers in
the first place. With his petty-crime background he would

never have made it into MI5. Working for Caesar was the closest he'd ever get to an international man of mystery life-style and a licence to kill.

The thought brought with it a strange wave of emotion. But for once, when considering Spitfire, it wasn't dread or dismay or sadness. This was pity she was feeling. Scorn too. She'd stepped away from the troubling quagmire of jaded nostalgia. And that was a good thing.

The realisation spurred her on into the next room, a narrow passageway with black cast-iron doors either side of her – old cell blocks preserved for posterity. The walls were high and made from raw concrete, crumbling now in places and adding to the sinister atmosphere. Further along, the iron doors became iron bars, standing floor to ceiling and exposing the cramped cells beyond. With her breath held in her throat, Acid skulked through the room, desperately trying to hold her nerves together as she encountered more dioramas of despair. Bony plastic hands clasped around cell bars, the prisoners' faces twisted in anguish, their ribs like plastic xylophones.

A noise from the next room sent her alert systems into overdrive. She moved quickly and pressed herself against the side of the doorway.

"Enough games, Spitfire," she called out. "Why not do this like adults? If you're so certain you can take me, let's do it. Face to face."

She waited. No response.

"Coward."

The word hadn't left her lips when the museum was plunged into darkness once more. She dropped to a crouch, her back against the wall. A few seconds and her eyes became accustomed to the gloom. Staying low, moving silently, she crept into the next room where a window covered in thick hessian provided some light. But not much.

She could make out human shapes on either side of her. More fibreglass inmates. Around twenty of them. They were sitting in two rows, facing each other across the room. Their rigid plastic legs were in real iron shackles, their bodies designed to be thin and bony to best highlight the terrible conditions imposed by the old regime.

Acid eased off her haunches and got upright, twisting her body from side to side in a wide semi-circle as she went, covering all areas. In the middle of the room she stopped as something caught her attention. One of the inmates had a dark-teal suit jacket draped over his shoulders.

Spitfire's jacket.

As the penny dropped she spun around, in time to duck under the swing of a large knife as it swished through the air.

"Go to hell," Acid roared. She kicked out and her boot connected with his thigh. At the same time, she shot wildly in front of her, the muzzle flash of the Berettas illuminating the room like a strobe light. But the angle was too narrow. Spitfire rushed between the blasts and grabbed her around the waist, slamming her whole body into the display. She cried out. Felt something break. Next she was on her back, dazed and winded. The head of one of the prisoners lay on her stomach. She shook it off and got to her feet. But before she could ground herself, Spitfire was on her again. He grabbed her right arm and smashed it against the wall, making her drop one of the Berettas. With his muscular torso pressing against her she was unable to get a clear shot with the other. Struggling to breathe, she leaned forward and clamped her teeth into his shoulder. He cried out and released his hold. Enough for her to reach for the push dagger in her belt. Flipping it into position, she speared him with a flurry of punches, slashing at his side with the short blade.

That got her a heavy elbow to the face.

She stumbled and went down but was able to fire off a few shots. She saw blood. Saw Spitfire recoil as his shoulder exploded and he fell backwards into the display. He recovered enough to draw his own piece and fire. The bullet tore through her jacket and grazed her trapezius muscle, but that was all. As the bats screamed across her synapses, she pulled herself together and flew at him. She had the push dagger in one hand, a Beretta in the other, rage in her heart and one simple thought in her head.

Kill him.

But he wasn't going to let it happen so easy. As she closed in, he flipped himself over. From a crouching position he grabbed her leg and swept her feet from under her. She stumbled into the back wall, dropping the gun and twisting her ankle, giving him time to get back on his feet, the tables turned. She scurried backwards on all fours. Nowhere to go. The room was closing in. As was Spitfire.

He held his side, blood seeping over his fingers. "Here she is, folks," he sneered, looming over her. "The world's deadliest assassin. What a fucking mess."

Acid licked at her lips. Blood was gushing from her nose. She watched him, her eyes wide, her body tense. As he stepped closer, she raised the push dagger at him in a final display of nerve. But it was an impotent gesture. They both knew it.

"I did say I didn't want to hurt you, didn't I?" Spitfire knelt beside her and picked up his gun. "Got to say, I'm annoyed at myself now, truth be told. But a gentleman keeps his word. So let's make this quick. You won't feel a thing." He raised the gun to her forehead.

"Fuck you," she spat. "You're not a gentleman. You're a nasty little boy who never grew up."

It prompted a chuckle from him. "Well you seemed to get off on it."

"I was inexperienced. A kid. Not anymore. I see you." It hurt to talk. The pain was kicking in, a reminder she wasn't invincible. But she kept on all the same. Talk was all she had while staring down the bullet that would end her. "You can pretend you're James Bond all you like, but deep down you'll always be that lowlife thug from Tower Hamlets. You can't escape your past, *Stephen*."

"Don't you dare."

"What's wrong, Stephen? Don't you like being reminded of who you are?"

"Do you, Alice?"

"Maybe I don't mind so much these days. Maybe I'm realising who I was isn't the problem."

"Jesus Christ," he yelled. "Give me a second while I get out my fucking violin."

"Just get on with it," she sneered. "I'm ready."

He waved his gun at her. "You know, I do feel kind of cheated," he said, gesturing around the room. "You haven't seen the best bit yet. There's a bloody great big guillotine in the next room. Still works too, so I'm told. We could have had so much fun. But no. You had to spoil it by being so pathetic." He spat the last word at her, his jovial tone shifting, his true colours showing.

"What can I say," she rasped. "I'm a real killjoy." She still had the dagger raised, but her arm was shaking.

"That you are," he replied. "What a shame. I suppose there's nothing left for us to talk about."

There was something in the darkness. She'd seen it as he talked. "Guess not," she told him, buying for time. "I only hope you can live with yourself after this."

"Oh, I think I'll be fine." All the emotion drained from his face. "Goodbye, my sweet." He reaffirmed his grip on the gun and closed one eye.

She braced herself.

Time stopped.

His finger trembled on the trigger.

He couldn't do it.

Sheer torment played across his classic features. He was angry at himself. Angry at her. He closed his other eye. Readied himself. But before he could take the shot a hooded figure emerged from behind him and smashed a fire extinguisher around the back of his head. The blow knocked Spitfire to the ground. Knocked all the life out of him. Then the figure stepped forward and held out a hand to her.

"Quickly," Huy whispered. "Let's get out of here."

Chapter Forty-Nine

Huy helped Acid up and steadied her as she reached for the gun at her feet. Her head was spinning but remarkably the pain was receding. This despite her plummeting hormone levels.

"I thought I was a goner," she said. "Where did you come from?"

"I followed you from the hotel," Huy replied. "My mother, she made me see I had to help you. I have to make amends for what I have done."

Acid took the hem of her t-shirt and wiped some of the blood from her face. She looked at Huy. "You want my advice, try to swerve that desire in future. Making amends can be a real drag." She nodded towards the body. "Is he dead?"

Huy peered over. "I think so."

"Yeah." Acid glanced at Spitfire's prone form. Blood seeped from a large gash in the back of his head. She closed her eyes. She wanted this over, but at the same time seeing him finished off this way, it felt wrong. Huy stepped over to the fallen assassin and made to lean over to check his pulse. But his hand halted mid-air.

"Wait. Acid." They both saw it at the same time. A slight twitch of the hand. "I don't think he's—"

"Huy, move," Acid yelled, raising her gun.

He did, spinning around just as a loud bang reverberated around the room. Blood splattered up the wall. It hit her in the face as Huy lurched forward, staring wide-eyed at her. He followed her gaze down his torso, to the large exit wound which had blown half his stomach out. He looked back at her, made a strange gurgling sound and fell to the ground.

Behind him Spitfire scrambled to his feet, gun in hand. He fired a few shots her way but she leapt for cover, concealing herself behind a display. She gripped the handle of her remaining Beretta, readying herself for a reprisal, but Spitfire was unrelenting. Shot after shot pummelled the model prisoners providing cover. A large piece of fibreglass splintered off and sliced her cheek as a prisoner's head exploded. She reached around the side of the display and returned fire, shooting blindly in Spitfire's direction. But it was no use. She couldn't get a clear shot. Dropping onto her stomach, she crawled around the other side of the display, but before she had a chance to retaliate Spitfire was up and stumbling out the door.

She scrambled to her feet and made to run after him. But moving to the door, she saw Huy stirring. Poor bastard, he wasn't dead. She knelt beside him and assessed the damage. Spitfire's hollow point round had bloomed like a chrysanthemum in the kid's belly, shredding his guts like they were Playdough. He was in shock. Bleeding out. He had minutes, if that.

"Tell my mother I am sorry," he groaned. "Tell her, I was trying to create something wonderful."

Acid forced a smile. "She knows. She loves you."

"Thank you," he whispered, closing his eyes. "And make sure you kill that bastard."

She didn't need telling twice. She got to her feet, watching Huy as the last breath left him and his body went limp. Then she gripped the handle of the Beretta and took off after Spitfire.

The new day's sun was filtering through the cracks in the old prison walls. Acid moved into the next room and saw Spitfire heading for the side entrance. She fired off a salvo of rounds, forcing him away from the door and into the belly of the prison. He returned fire for a second, but his gait was clumsy and his aim off. Moving swiftly but cautiously she trailed him as he staggered into the next room. Then an arm appeared, firing a flurry of shots in her direction. She dived for cover below the ticket office desk and returned fire.

"You're done, old man," she yelled. "Give it up."

The shooting stopped. She waited. She got up and edged over to the doorway, peering around the side. A trail of blood spatter led down a long passageway which opened out into a bright room at the far end. It wasn't part of the museum. Some sort of office space. With her body taut and senses alight, she stalked along the corridor until she got to the end. In the office a wooden desk faced the door with a dusty old computer sitting on top, and a row of metal filing cabinets spanned the adjacent wall. Scanning the perimeter of the room, Acid's eyes fell on the emergency exit in the corner. She side-stepped over to it and bumped the central release bar with her hip. No joy. She tried again with her elbow. Same story. The door was locked.

Where the hell was he?

Breathless and confused she strode across the room, stopping in front of the desk. She narrowed her eyes, noticing droplets of blood on the surface of the table, on the computer keyboard too. It was wet. She snapped her head up to see a trapdoor in the ceiling with a thin leather thong hanging down. Holstering her gun, she climbed onto the desk. She had to jump for it, but on the second attempt she got her fingers to the strap and yanked the door open. Now, using the computer monitor as a stepping stone, she was able to get a hand either side of the hatch.

Taking a deep breath, she braced herself for the very real possibility of a bullet in the head and scrambled up into the cavernous roof space. She steadied herself and sat on the edge of the hatch to catch her breath. No bullet in the head. No sign of Spitfire. Although it was hard to see even a few feet in front of her.

The roof above sloped down on both sides but no floor to speak of, just thick wooden beams spanning the width of the building, wide enough to walk across. She squinted into the gloom. Fifty metres down on the left she could see a crack of daylight. A window of some sort. Getting to her feet she strode quickly from beam to beam and was over there in a few seconds. The light came from the surround of a small wooden shutter leading out onto the pitched roof. She eased it open, wincing into the bright sunshine.

The second she felt the hot sun on her face a bullet ricocheted off the slate tiles by her feet. She let go of the shutter frame and slid down the roof until her feet hit the level gangway running around the side of the building. As she righted herself she saw Spitfire's head disappearing down the far side of the building. With the pulse in her neck throbbing, she ran over to the edge where she found a rusty ladder descending to the flat roof covering the lower levels of the museum. Spitfire was already at the bottom. He saw her and fired a few shots but the bullets whizzed over her head. As he staggered away, Acid noticed the red, sticky hand gripping the back of his head, the knife wounds in his side. He was stumbling all over. Seeing this once great man like this wasn't easy. But it didn't stop her closing one over the barrel of her gun and putting an expertly placed bullet through his right knee. The way he had taught her.

The broken assassin cried out as his leg buckled. But he kept going, dragging his shattered limb behind him. A second bullet took care of his left knee. This time he went down fast and heavy. She clambered down the ladder and watched him as he raised himself onto his elbows and tried to shuffle away. He fired a few more rounds her way but she didn't flinch. He was done. The bullets went wide. She stalked him for a few more yards before she raised the Beretta and shot the SIG Sauer out of his hand. She didn't mean to blow off his thumb and index finger as well, but he wasn't going to need them. His killing days were over.

As she got closer, she could see how bad a shape he was in. But fair play to the man, he'd given it his best – the blunt head trauma would have finished off most people. He curled his lip at her. Grunted through the pain. Still playing the big man. He brought his bloody hand to his chest as she stepped over him.

"Do you remember you told me once I was your worst nightmare?" she asked.

Spitfire grimaced. Didn't look at her. "Sounds like something I'd say."

"Hearing that hurt me at the time," she told him. "But you were correct. I am."

Spitfire had shuffled himself to the edge of the building.

He peered over his shoulder. It was a ten-foot drop to ground level. But where was he going to go? He had no knees and no weapon. Couldn't fire it if he had one. He turned back to her.

"You can't kill me. Not after everything we've been through. But what if I help you? I know where they all are. I can give you Caesar." He spluttered the words out as she closed in, held his hand up. "We can do it together. Like old times. Me and you. We could start our own organisation."

She curled her lip. "Nah. I'm done with organisations."

"I loved you, Acid," he cried. "I still do. I know you feel the same. What if—"

A sonic crack echoed through the morning air as she shot him through the heart. He stared up at her, his expression morphing from confusion to disbelief, to abject fear. His eyes bulged. His mouth sagged. Then all the air left him.

What if?

What if?

Acid bowed her head. Then she shoved the Beretta back into its holster, and walked away.

Chapter Fifty

Tam was at Vinh's bedside when Acid poked her head around the curtain two days later. Most of that time had been spent resting. Now, clean and fed – and with her injuries patched up thanks to some QuikClot gauze and duct tape – she was ready to say farewell. She'd already stayed too long.

"How's he doing?" she whispered, moving further into the room.

Tam raised her head to greet her. Her eyes were red and her skin pale, but she smiled regardless.

"The doctors say he'll be able to come home soon."

"That's good. He was lucky." Acid perched on the end of a small wooden seat in the corner of the room. "And how are you?"

Another cheerless smile. "My heart is broken."

"I understand." Acid looked at her hands. "I'm sorry for my part in what happened."

"You are not to blame," Tam said. "Huy was a good man. But he made bad choices."

"I know all about those," Acid said, and sighed. "I think he got blinded by his own vision. Didn't see what he was doing until it was too late. He was doing it for you. For a better life."

"I know this," Tam replied. "I hope it will help. But not now. It is too raw. I am too sad."

Acid tucked her hands into her jacket pockets. "You're a strong woman, Tam."

"How else can I be? A part of me has died." She gripped Vinh's hand in hers. "But I will try and carry on. One day at a time."

"All you can do," Acid said. "It does get easier. If you want it to."

Tam frowned but didn't reply. She turned her attention back to Vinh. "He is distraught," she said. "He never got a chance to be Huy's father."

Acid hadn't wanted to leave without saying goodbye but being here now felt wrong.

"Huy knew you both loved him," she tried. "Hold onto that. And he did the right thing in the end."

She had called Spook once she got back to the hotel, had her hack into local and national police networks. All reports pointed to the Cai Moi being finished. Monday morning the museum caretaker had discovered the bodies of Spitfire and Huy and, helped along by an anonymous tip-off from Spook, the police had connected the deaths to the warehouse massacre. A rival organisation, the report said, although unofficial sources were already claiming it as the result of a covert government undertaking. Either way, Acid was in the clear.

"I wanted to say goodbye before I left," she told Tam, getting to her feet. "But I'm due at the airport. Do you need anything before I go?"

Vinh stirred and opened his eyes. "Acid?"

"Hey, there." She moved over to the bed. "How are you, soldier?"

"Tired. Broken. But alive."

She gave him her most compassionate smile. It felt clunky. But sometimes clunky was all she had. "You saved my life," she told him.

"I'm not sure about that. I was standing in the wrong place." He let out a low wheezing laugh. It looked to pain him. "You got your man?"

"Yes. Thank you." She glanced at Tam. "I'm so sorry for the toll it's taken on everyone."

Vinh closed his eyes. "These are sad times. But it's not your fault."

"I have to get going," she said. "Thank you both, for everything, and I hope you find peace. Eventually."

Tam gripped Vinh's hand tighter. "We shall see," she told her. "You have a safe journey."

Once Acid had left the hospital, she pulled out her phone and scrolled through her contacts. She had another call to make before she put this particular episode behind her.

The phone rang three times before The Dullahan picked up. "Bleeding hell. Acid Vanilla. I thought I was never going to hear from ya!"

Acid sighed. "Been busy. You know how it is."

"You got the fecker, then."

"You heard?"

"News travels fast in our world. You know that. Suffice to say the fat eejit is beside himself."

Acid couldn't help but smile. "I guess that puts a bigger target on my back."

"You knew that'd be the case already. But don't worry, if I get wind of anything important I'll let you know."

"I appreciate it, Dullahan," she told him. "I owe you one."

"Well that you do. And it's Jimmy, remember."

"Sorry." She was never going to get used to calling him Jimmy. In the same way he wasn't going to forget she owed him.

"What's the plan now, lassie?"

"Got a flight back to London in two hours. After that I guess it's back to my search for Caesar."

"Good girl. I'll let you know if I hear anything."

Acid hung up and walked the short distance back to her hotel to collect her luggage. It was true. The long-term plan was to find Caesar. Him and the remaining members of Annihilation Pest Control. But her short-term plan? That was much simpler. And it involved at least three decent glasses of something strong and tasty, and a long sleep on the plane home.

———

BACK AT THE house a week later, Acid felt well enough to open up the tall wardrobe by the window. She stood in silence a few minutes, considering the seven bullets in front of her. And one in particular. She reached in and picked up the one with 'Spitfire' engraved down the side, rolled it in her palm. Standing here today, with her moods and hormone levels stable, it was hard to believe he was dead. That she'd killed him. Spitfire Creosote was no more.

A part of Acid Vanilla had died that day as well. But that was a good thing. We have to kill parts of ourselves for true growth to occur. She placed the bullet back on the shelf, laying it on its side

"Goodbye, Stephen," she whispered.

She reached into her bag and pulled out the photo frame she'd had made that morning. She held it up, captivated by the happy faces of the people staring back at her. A young Alice Vandella and her mother, Louisa. She placed the frame on the shelf, alongside the bullets, and closed the wardrobe door.

Tam was right. Hate was too destructive an energy. It ate away at you if you let it. As Acid had come to terms with this realisation over the last few days, she'd noticed a shift in her motivation. She felt lighter. More in control. She didn't know how long it would last, but for now she was enjoying the feeling. The knowledge that for once her path was a righteous one, even if it was destined to be dark and dangerous and incredibly bloody. Because whilst she'd learned to let go of hate, it didn't mean she was any less determined. If anything, her conviction had grown stronger. Beowulf Caesar was going to die. If it was the last thing she ever did, Acid Vanilla would make sure of it.

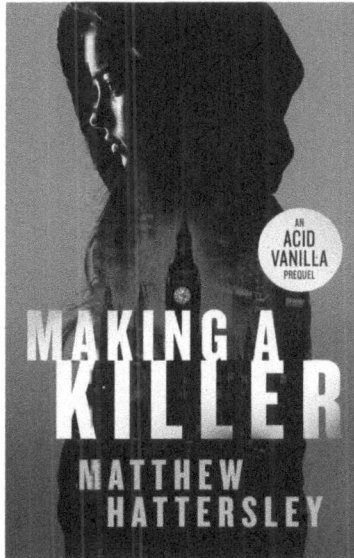

About the Author

Over the last twenty years Matthew Hattersley has toured Europe in rock n roll bands, trained as a professional actor and founded a theatre and media company. He's also had a lot of dead end jobs ..

Now he writes Neo-Noir Thrillers and Crime Fiction. He has also had his writing featured in The New York Observer & Huffington Post.

He lives with his wife and young daughter in Manchester, UK and doesn't feel that comfortable writing about himself in the third person.